# Definitely Memorable

written by:
Cara Roman

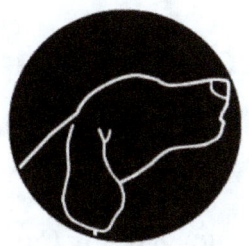

Baying Hound's Dark Side

USA

Disclaimers and Copyright

This is a work of fiction. Names, characters, places, and incidents either are products of the author's imagination or are used fictitiously. Any resemblance to actual persons, living or dead, events or locations are entirely coincidental.

No part of this book may be reproduced, stored in a retrieval system or transmitted in any form or by any means without the prior written consent of the author or publisher.

# Definitely Memorable

Published by Baying Hound's Dark Side

*For cousins that are more like sisters.*
*Thank you for giving me the courage to keep*
*spreading my wings, and the air to keep me flying*
*when I had my doubts.*
*You are a complete bad ass, and I love you!*

# Chapter One

The suitcases were all stacked and waiting by the door, and just seeing them brought a gigantic smile to Caitlyn's face. A lifetime of dreaming was somehow zipped inside those sturdy, reliable bags. She was finally doing it, and there wasn't a happy dance long enough to truly demonstrate how that made her feel. Purchasing those tickets a month ago had felt like the best birthday and Christmas present rolled up into one. Going to Ireland had always been Caitlyn's idea of a dream vacation. Back when she was young, ready to set the world on fire, and full of plans she never doubted she would make it to the magical island that called a siren song to her soul. Somewhere along the way though, that dream got shoved into the back of a closet, behind the flotsam of life. Not that she was complaining, life always worked out the way it was supposed to. She had accepted that she just probably wasn't meant to be going to Ireland until now. Pinching her arm just a little to make sure it was really real this time though, Caitlyn walked out of her tidy bedroom and called out to her sons.

"Boys! Are you ready to go to your Dad's? He is

going to be here to pick you up any minute." Seeing her oldest son Wyatt with his blonde head shoved inside the refrigerator looking for yet another snack, as if she hadn't fed him dinner less than an hour ago. She walked over and handed him an apple, wondering if he was already growing again. Keeping him in clothes that fit was becoming a full-time job in itself. When he looked dubiously at the fruit in his hand, she reminded him, "It is portable, and won't make a mess in the car if you're still eating it when Dad shows up." That seemed to make sense, so he walked away munching and crunching with abandon as only a teenage boy could.

Mason, her lanky youngest son laying on the couch, the ever-present cell phone clutched in his hand. The sound of crashes, thumps, and grunts told her he was battling it out with some of his friends on a game. "Mase, do you have everything packed?" He nodded his head without even looking up at her. "Honey, I'm going to be an entire ocean away, I can't just stop by and drop off whatever you forgot." Which knowing her son, and she did, would be half of what he actually needed.

"Mom, Wy and I both got keys to the house... Dad can drive us over to grab anything we don't have. Besides, we spend half of our time there anyway, lots of my stuff is already there," Mason replied, this time looking up at her. The comment about dividing the boys time stung, though she knew Mason didn't mean anything by it. Divorce just manages to leave scars that jump up and surprise you with little jabs of pain, even after you think that you are well and over it all. Nodding her head, Caitlyn took a deep breath waiting for the flicker of pain to pass when she heard a car pull in the driveway.

"Guys, your Dad is here!" Not adding in the petty *and on time too* that had floated through her head. Does dealing with one's ex-husband ever get easier? I mean, this is the man you had planned on spending the rest of your life with, before everything crashed and burned. Wyatt jogged in from the other room, apple already finished, and opened the door. At fifteen he was as tall as his Dad now, the flash of memory of him at five years old flew through her head. Her first-born baby was as tall as his Dad now, when exactly did that happen? Shaking the mushiness away Caitlyn walked over to her ex-husband.

"Hey, Bryan. They're all ready for you, hopefully they have everything, and as Mason just reminded me, if not they've got keys to the house." Caitlyn smiled, doing her best to be friendly.

Bryan nodded his head, seeming just as uncomfortable with her as she was with him. Seeing him shifting his weight from foot to foot, unsure of what to say, reminded her that he had lost something too. "Yeah, no big. Who's taking you to the airport in the morning?"

"My Dad'll be here at four, I have a seven AM flight, and so I figure on getting there by at least five," Caitlyn answered. That would leave her enough time to get through security without any additional stress. He nodded his head at her answer, careful with his words now.

"Well, I'm sure you will have a great time. The boys and I have some plans, so don't worry about it. Will your cell phone work overseas, ya think?" he asked as the kids shuffled in and out of the house carrying their overnight bags to his waiting truck.

"Not for calls and texts, I guess. I really don't want to have to pay the astronomical roaming charges. But I will be checking my email regularly. I have the itinerary already set, and rooms booked. I made sure everywhere I'm going to stay has free Wi-Fi for their guests. I'll send you the list of hotels with phone numbers so you will be able to get ahold of me that way too."

"Makes sense, they're thirteen and fifteen now Cait, we can handle you being busy for two weeks." Bryan laughed.

"Yeah, Mom. We aren't babies. Have fun and bring us back something cool. You know you're gonna end up emailing us dozens of pictures anyway." Wyatt slung his arm around her.

Leaning her head on his shoulder a moment

she reached up and patted the hand resting on her arm. "I know honey. I'll just miss my boys, that's all."

"You deserve this Mom, when was the last actual vacation, not work trip, you took that didn't involve us tagging along?" Mason asked looking at her. "Never. You haven't ever had a break. Besides, it's not like you're going to be drinking tequila on a tropical beach and making out with pool boys. It's Ireland, doesn't it rain there literally every day? You're going to look at old ruins, and boring stuff, like being in history class." Mason gave a mock shudder and shook his head, his thick ginger hair, so much like her own swaying with the movement. The look on his face left no doubts about how much fun he thought she was actually going to have.

"Umm, seriously can we not talk about Mom getting drunk and hooking up? Love you and all Mom, but that's just gross." Wyatt punched his brother in the arm looking a little green at the thought. "I don't need that visual Mase, ever."

"What your Mother does on vacation, or in her personal life is none of our business anyway, until she decides to make it our business." Bryan jumped to her defense, but the look on his face clearly said that he didn't want to think too much on that particular subject either. Who could blame him? Nobody wanted to picture their ex wound around someone else.

"Good lord guys, if I was actually in the market

for a man, I'm sure there are plenty available in this country. I am not spending hours on a plane to search for someone to have an affair with. I've always wanted to see Ireland. You guys know that. She is a lovely land, and I want to soak up all her culture."

"Whatcha wanna bet all she soaks up is gallons of rain, and butt-loads of mud?" Mason said laughing hysterically at himself, looking at his brother Wyatt who had a big goofy grin on his face too.

"Alright guys, maybe I'm not actually going to miss you as much as I thought I would," Caitlyn said with a wink. Her boys both knew better than to believe her, and they laughed even harder. Turning to Bryan she added, "I'll let you know when I land. See ya'll in two weeks."

She breathed the scent of each son deep into her lungs as she hugged them goodbye one at a time. Storing it to memory for later, in case missing them got to be too much for her. This was the part she dreaded. It had her going back and forth with her decision for weeks before she said, '*To hell with it, I deserve this,*' and booked the flight. She walked them out to the truck and waved while they pulled out. She stood there watching until the truck drove down the road and out of sight. Sniffling back the tears she absolutely refused to shed she walked back into her house.

Telling herself not to be such a damn baby

about this she walked around the house picking up all the debris two teen sons constantly left in their wake. Grabbing her cell phone off the counter she put her music on shuffle and turned it up nice and loud. Letting the music work its usual magic, sanding down the sharp edges of her sadness until all that was left was the previous excitement again. Dancing like a fool around the kitchen Caitlyn unloaded the dishwasher. Putting the plates up in the cupboard, and the silverware in the drawer. It was mundane everyday stuff, but she didn't want to leave it for when she came home exhausted from all of her wonderful adventures. Besides, the thought of a dirty house waiting for her would most likely mess with her happy vibes all vacation.

After that was done, she double checked everything was ready for the morning. It was only seven PM, and she wasn't tired even though she knew how early she needed to get up in the morning. So she walked into her bathroom and turned on the faucet in the big bathtub. Flying always dried her skin out, and the nearly ten-hour flight to Ireland would definitely have plenty of time for it. Considering this she poured in a healthy dose of scented oil into the running water. It didn't froth up deliciously like her favored bubble bath did, but it would make her skin feel silky smooth, and fingers crossed, keep it from getting parched when her flight deposited her in Dublin tomorrow.

Slipping gently into the steaming water, just this side of scalding hot, Caitlyn closed her eyes. The subtle soothing scents of aloe with olive oil relaxed her while her music still played somewhere in the background and she let her mind roam wherever it wanted to. She pictured bustling streets filled with people, their wonderful melodic accents washing over her, and rolling hills so green they all but burned your eyes with their verdant beauty. All the tips and tricks for traveling to Ireland she had read zoomed past the back of her eyelids, but she didn't try very hard to hold on to those. Soaking in the tub was just not the place for rational thoughts. There would be plenty of time to worry over all that tomorrow on the lengthy flight. After a little while the water started to cool, so she popped the plunger with her big toe, letting the water drain around her in a whoosh. When the tub was down to only a quarter full, she stood up very carefully so as not to slip in the oiled water, and stepped out. Walking the few feet across the room into the enclosed shower she turned the water on. Caitlyn moved mechanically through washing and rinsing out her long hair. There was no way she was going to attempt to wash it at the crack of dawn. Stepping out and wrapping a towel around her body she ran her usual frizz control cream through the ends of her hair before wrapping it up turban style in a second towel. Opening the jar of face cream sitting on the counter she scooped out some and gently patted it all over her face and neck. Glancing around one last time to make sure there was nothing she needed in the bathroom and forgotten to pack Caitlyn swiped her phone off the counter and turned off the light.

Pulling on a blue tank top, and a pair of white cotton boyshorts she plugged her phone into the charger, checking, then double checking to make sure the alarm was on. Turning the television across the room on she pulled back the covers and crawled into bed. There was a cheesy, completely predictable, romantic movie playing, the perfect thing to watch, but not think too much about. Figuring nerves and excitement would have her tossing and turning all night, but less than ten minutes later she was deeply asleep.

The insistent buzzing of her alarm cut through the lovely dream she was having. She was reaching out to hit the snooze button, intending on getting more sleep, when her eyes suddenly flew open and she remembered what today was. Turning the alarm off and sitting up with a big stretch Caitlyn felt the towel she forgot to take off trying valiantly to stay on her head. So much for having decent hair on the flight over. Walking into the bathroom to pee she dared a glance in the mirror. As she suspected her hair was a huge jumble of wild auburn curls. Thanking her lucky stars she remembered to at least put some product in it before bed she gave it a shake and gave up. Her hair had always had a mind of its own, and she learned a long time ago stressing out about it wasn't worth her time. The more she messed with it, the less she ended up liking it. So most days she put a little something in it, and let it do whatever the hell it wanted.

Splashing some cold water on her face she picked up the tube of her daily moisturizer with sunscreen and put that on. The sun protection probably wasn't needed right now, but it was the one she always used. It didn't irritate her sensitive skin, or make her face feel greasy and oily at the end of the day. Why bother switching it? Besides, on the off chance she encountered some sun today she would probably be grateful for that SPF30. Not wanting to clog her face up with layers of product for the flight she swiped on a coat of mascara, and her favorite lip balm. It smelled like lemon frosting, and gave her lips the slightest pink tint. Adding some deodorant, and a spritz of perfume to finish it off. Nodding at her reflection in the mirror she tossed all the products back into the travel bag, zipped it up, and walked back into her bedroom.

Thinking comfort was key for this flight Caitlyn pulled on a pair of jeggings, a white t-shirt, and a light weight heathered gray cardigan. Bending over she folded up the ankles of the pants once and slipped on tiny socks. Feet tucked into the well-worn pair of gray shoreline Converse, she brought the largest of her luggage out into the living room. Snagging a water bottle from the refrigerator on her way back into the bedroom to grab the carry on, and her purse. Caitlyn checked the time, it was quarter to four, she put the cellphone in her back pocket and walked to the front window to watch for her Dad to pull in the driveway.

He was exactly two minutes early. Caitlyn already had the door locked and was walking out with her bags when he opened the driver's side door to help her.

"Morning darling. Got everything you need?" He leaned in and kissed her cheek. His question was so similar to the one she asked her boys the night before it had her smiling.

"Morning Dad, yeah, I've got it all, double and triple checked. Tickets are in my purse, we are good to go!" They walked back to the trunk of his car. Knowing her Dad, she left him to heft the suitcase up into the trunk, even though she could have. She would be hauling it all over on her own later today anyway. Once the bags were safely inside her Dad slammed the trunk shut, and they each walked to their sides of the car, climbing in.

"Did the boys get off to Bryan's alright last night?" he asked as they turned out of her neighborhood heading south towards Grand Rapids. It was a good thirty-minute drive to the airport, but thankfully there wouldn't be much traffic to contend with at this time of day.

"Yeah, they basically live at both of our houses anyway, so for them it's no big deal." Caitlyn said with a sigh.

"You two are handling the divorce better than your mother and I did when you were a kid. I guess we taught you what not to do," he said with a rueful smile.

"Dad, you know as well as I do, that wasn't all on you. There were two people in that marriage, and one of them happens to be Mom. And we all know she is difficult on a good day." She knew it still hurt her Dad. He spent twenty years back and forth with her Mom, and it still broke something inside him to have given up, even if it had made much him happier in the end.

"Trust me, I know. So, did you want to stop for some coffee or anything?" he asked shoving the door on the past firmly closed and changing the subject.

"Nah," pulling the bottle of water out of her purse she showed him, "I'm good. Besides, coffee makes everyone poop, and I'm not trying to be glued to the toilet on the flight, or even worse missing it all together!" They both laughed and settled into a comfortable silence listening to the radio after that. Neither spoke again until the exit sign for the airport came into view.

"Would you like me to sit and wait for your flight with you darling?" her Dad looked over and asked as he turned off on the exit leaving the highway. "I know we didn't really discuss it on the phone the other day."

"Don't worry about it, I've got to go through security first anyway. They won't let you past that to wait with me. I'll be fine." The car pulled up to the curb to unload. Caitlyn jumped out and walked back to the trunk. Her Dad made it back there as she hefted the big case up and out. Setting her carryon bag on top of the other case on the curb she turned with an excited smile for her Dad. "Thanks Dad! See you in two weeks?"

He wrapped his big arms around her and squeezed. "I'll be here to pick you up, don't you worry. Have fun roaming around Ireland, kiddo. And have a pint for me will ya?" Caitlyn pulled out of his embrace with a smile and nodded. She pushed the strap of her carryon bag up her shoulder, grabbed the handle of her rolling suitcase and with a last wave for her Dad she walked into the building.

The airport wasn't very busy at just shy of five in the morning, so it didn't take her long to make it through security. Caitlyn pulled her laptop out, it went nearly everywhere with her anyway, almost like it were an extra appendage. It was second nature for her when she had a free moment to reach for it. She had finished her latest book and sent it off to be edited a few days ago. The plan was to not get involved in a new project until after vacation, since she was hoping to see some sights instead of locking herself in the hotel room and writing for hours on end until the story eased its tight grip on her. However, there were always so many ideas swirling inside of her head that she could purge. Like always the time completely escaped her while she stared at the glowing screen. The world around her melted away until it was like it had never existed in the first place. When the announcement came across the speakers to board her flight it shocked her. She hastily hit save on her work, couldn't lose that! As she jogged to the terminal she was turning off the laptop, and shoving it in her bag. Her brain still trying to clear all the creative fog that had been enshrouding it.

Once she was settled in her seat on the plane, Caitlyn took a deep breath. There was nothing stopping her now. The excitement inside of her was ramping up as the flight attendants went through their spiel before takeoff. By the time the plane was in the air she could have jumped up and down with the rush of emotions swirling around inside her. Reminding herself that she was a grown up, and there was no way she was going to make a fool of herself like that a little giggle slipped out of her mouth. Yeah right, she was on vacation now! As a grown ass woman she was entitled to let loose and have some fun with her life.

# Chapter Two

Caitlyn stepped into the Dublin airport just after ten PM local time feeling both exhausted from the flight and energized to have arrived. It took her nearly another hour to get through customs and collect her things from the baggage claim. With nothing left to do at the airport she took a deep breath and stepped out into the slightly damp Dublin evening. It wasn't raining, which actually disappointed her a tad, but the streets were shimmering with the rain that had fallen in the last few hours. Climbing into one of the taxis that always hover around the entrance of every airport she had ever been to Caitlyn gave the driver a big smile.

"Ha-ware-ya love, where to?" the man asked in his thick accent. He had a pleasant face, and she thought that most travelers coming here surely must appreciate that.

"Tired, but happy to be here! Umm, the Westbury Hotel, hold on, let me look up the address. I've got it written down somewhere," Caitlyn said ruffling through her purse for the little notebook she had all the particulars written down in. It also came in handy for ideas that smacked her upside the head sometimes.

"Don't be troublin' yerself. I know right where that is, bringing people there from the airport all a the time, I am." The taxi driver smiled at her in the rear-view mirror.

"Oh, good! By the time I found it in this bag we might be on the other side of the country," she replied back laughing. It felt so good to be off that airplane, but she was way past ready to unpack her bag and take a nice long shower. The man in the seat in front of her had smelled like the stale remnants of a three-day bender was leaking out through his pores, and she shuddered just thinking about that nasty smell adhering itself to her skin. He had snored louder than a freight train for the last three hours of the flight too. It was pretty damn hard to focus on the paperback book she brought to read. In the end she had just closed her eyes and imagined what adventures the next two weeks were going to bring.

Sitting in the back seat of the taxicab was worlds more comfortable than the airplane had been. Watching Dublin slide past her window with all its charming lights shimmering in the dark eased an ache inside of her soul. The taxi driver was chattering on about all the sights he thought she needed to see while she was here, but conversation seemed too much for her, so she just nodded.

"Been wantin' to come here for a while, haven't

ya?" he asked her, catching on to her overwhelmed silence.

"All my life," came out of her mouth without pause for thought. "I can't remember a time when I didn't want to visit Ireland. It may sound really silly, but she's always called to me."

"Nah, tis not silly at all. She's got a way, our Eire. Sometimes she calls people back. With that hair, yer people definitely came from here at some point." He winked back at her.

"Thanks for not thinking I'm some strange American lunatic. Most people back home just laugh at me when I say things like that," Caitlyn found herself saying.

"Fools, all a dem," he said in his thick accent with a decisive nod of his head. "What is it you do back home, for a living that is?"

"Oh, I write books. Romance novelist would be my proper title, I guess. Mostly I spend a lot of time in my own head daydreaming." Caitlyn laughed at herself. "I've always done that, but I get paid for it now."

He nodded his head as she talked. "Ireland has always been full of dreamers and storytellers, ye'll fit right in here. How long are ye with us for?"

"Two weeks, but not all of it will be in Dublin, I don't think," Caitlyn said as they pulled over in front of what was definitely her hotel. It was a big stone building filled with charming windows, and a black overhang brimming with friendly greenery.

"Ah well, I hope yer holiday is everything yer wanting. Enjoy, and soak it all up to pull out on a rainy day when yer old and gray like meself," he said as he opened the door and stepped out into the night. Thinking about what he said she hadn't yet reached for the door handle when he pulled it open. Looking into his kind, wise eyes she climbed out and surprised the both of them by hugging him.

"Thank you so much." He gave her an affectionate squeeze and stepped back.

"Ah now, don't ye be getting me all mushy, I've got a long night a work yet ahead of me," he said gruffly, but with a wink. Opening the back of the taxi and hauling her bags out he handed them to the young porter who walked up from the front door.

"Welcome to The Westbury ma'am. If you'll come with me, we can get you all checked in," the young man said politely. With a smile and a wave for the taxi driver as he pulled away from the curb she turned and followed him inside.

The lobby looked every bit as luxurious as the pictures on the website had led her to hope it would. Tall tray ceilings with chandeliers were held up by massive wooden pillars. All across the expanse were clever seating arrangements, meant to compel you to wait for a friend, or read the morning paper before heading out to tackle the day. A massive marble front desk taking up one whole wall was where the porter was heading. An older man stood behind the desk, looking with all seriousness as if he were manning the helm of a ship.

"Good evening ma'am, and welcome to The Westbury hotel. Do you have a reservation with us for the night?" She had expected to hear an upper crust English accent to come out of his mouth, but instead she was surprised by the melodic sound of a Dublin one. It shattered some of the stiff impression and had her smiling at him while answering enthusiastically.

"Hello, yes I do! Should be under Caitlyn Reed, I made it a few weeks ago online."

He nodded his head at her, turned slightly and began clicking away on the keys of a discreetly placed computer.

"Ah yes, you have booked the luxury king suite for five nights, with the option for more nights. Good choice, it offers you plenty of space to relax in after a busy day of wandering about the city." He smiled. "Everything is all set, if you could just sign this for me Ms. Reed then Patrick here will show you up to your suite." He gestured his head at the approaching bellhop. Caitlyn quickly signed her name on the paper he passed across the desk to her. "Very good. Have a wonderful stay, if there is anything else you need please don't hesitate to ask," he said as he filed the paper away.

Patrick the bellhop was barely out of his teens at her best guess. Caitlyn followed him across the lobby to the bank of elevators. Figuring he knew better where she was heading than she did, she waited for him to push the button for the elevator. When they were inside, and the doors whooshing softly closed he turned to her and with a smile asked, "First time here in Ireland ma'am?" He had a fairly unremarkable face, until he spoke. His eyes lit up with warmth and humor, making one want to linger and talk with him awhile. Give him a few more years, and he would probably learn to market those lovely laughing eyes of his into lots of dates.

Glancing over at him since he was much the same height as she was, "Mmhmmm, first time."

"We get a good many here on holiday from America for the first time. If ye don't mind me asking, where abouts in the States are ye from? I've been saving up to go there meself," he added with a shy smile.

"I'm from the Midwest. Michigan to be more specific," she told him.

He glanced dubiously at her, "Detroit?"

Letting out a full laugh that threw her head back Caitlyn said, "No. That is probably the only city you would have heard of though." Holding her hand up she pointed to the area Detroit was located. "This is Detroit here. I live all the way over here in West Michigan. I've only been to Detroit twice in my whole life."

He nodded his head. "So what is yer part of Michigan like?"

"I live in a small town filled with apple orchards, and dairy farms." The elevator slowed on the sixth floor, the doors opening with a ding announcing their arrival.

"Do ye live on a farm?" he asked as he wheeled her luggage down the hallway to her suite.

"Good lord no! I can barely keep a houseplant alive let alone a whole orchard." Caitlyn laughed. "I just live in a normal neighborhood. Not everyone there is a grower, only about a dozen families have the orchards." He nodded his head following along. At the door to her room he took a moment to show her how to unlock the door with the fancy key card. He motioned to her to walk in first, and she did so with a smile.

This was her place for the better part of the week, and it was everything she had hoped for. There was a short hallway leading away from the door, one side was the bathroom. Peeking her head in she saw marble sinks, a standalone bathtub, and glass encased shower big enough for a few people to comfortably fit in. The other side had two doors, closets she surmised by the size of the doors. Walking out into the open area she took a slow turn around. Nestled near the windows there was a couch and short coffee table, meant for putting your feet up and hanging out. It faced the dresser which held a decently sized flat screen television. Across the way was a small writing desk and chair, perfect for setting up her laptop and writing all the emails to her boys back home. Lastly the bed was a massive affair. Dark wood, four poster, fluffy white duvet with piles of pillows on top. She knew it was only a king, but it looked so much bigger.

Turning to beam at Patrick she announced, "It's perfect! Absolutely perfect!"

"Very good then. There's a room service menu in the drawer of the desk, along with the channel listing for the telly. Will ye be needing anything else tonight Ms. Reed?"

"Caitlyn please, and no thank you Patrick. I think I'll settle in tonight. I've got a full day planned tomorrow." She handed him a tip, and he smiled a thank you and walked out of the room.

Caitlyn waited until the door closed softly behind the young man before opening her arms wide and spinning in a circle with a not so mature "Yippee!" Then kicking the chucks off her feet she ran to the bed and dove onto it. The duvet was even softer than it looked, and she landed without a sound. Laying there looking as if she were making a snow angel in the expansive bed Caitlyn sighed and whispered to herself, "I'm finally here."

Letting that sink in for a few minutes she just laid there. Finally she stood up and fished her laptop out of her bag. Setting it up on top of the writing desk, she found the Wi-Fi login information in the drawer along with the menu, television sheet, and a half dozen brochures advertising things to do around Dublin. There was a classy note pad with the hotel logo emblazoned across the top, and a couple of pens rolling around in there too. Turning her computer on she logged into her email account. She typed up a quick note letting her sons know she made it safely, the hotel name and phone number, and to be on the lookout for lots of pictures tomorrow. Ending with how much she missed them, and all her love she addressed it to both Wyatt and Mason, and hit send. Sending a similar message to her ex-husband Bryan, although she left out the love part this time.

Logging out of her email account, you can never be too careful, she walked over to her suitcase and opened it up. Living out of a suitcase had always been marginally depressing to Caitlyn. She put all her clothes away in the closet and the dresser. Grabbing her bag of toiletries she headed into the bathroom. Setting her jars and pots of skincare out on the counter, her toothbrush and toothpaste next to the sink. She left the makeup in its own bag, since eyeliners and brushes tended to roll away and get lost forever when left out. The hotel had its own soaps, but her skin was very sensitive, so she always brought along her own. Figuring if she climbed into that bathtub she was likely to fall asleep in it, she stripped down and walked into the shower.

It really was glorious, it had a rain feature in the ceiling, as well as a smaller shower head. It was the handheld kind that you could take down and change the settings to massage if you wanted. Thinking maybe another time, tonight she just wanted to get clean. Turning the taps on and finding the right temperature, just this side of scalding hot, she stood there a moment and let the water sluice down her body. Washing away all of the stale air from the plane, and the stress from travel.

The bathroom was all fogged up with steam by the time she turned the water off and stepped out of the shower. Grabbing a towel off the rack she ran it across her body drying off. Noticing the white bathrobe on the top of the rack she slipped her arms into the holes and pulled it on. It was everything a robe should be. Soft, warm, and it enveloped her in comfort. Using the towel to wring the water out of her hair she picked up the tube of anti-frizz cream and squeezed a dollop out. Running the cream through her hair, taking a little time to scrunch the ends up occasionally before she gave it a little shake. Smearing on her face serum, and night cream she wandered back out into the room.

Walking to the window she looked out into the lights twinkling out of the night darkened city. Thinking tomorrow was going to be a really great day. Not even bothering with the television she was so tired that she turned the lights out and climbed up into the bed still wearing the robe.

# Chapter Three

The sun was streaming into the room in patches bathing the bed in a soft yellow glow when Caitlyn opened her eyes. Reaching her arms out wide with a stretch she sat up. Climbing slowly out of the big bed, her limbs still feeling heavy and sluggish with sleep she padded across the room the windows. Standing in the white bathrobe she looked out at the view, and she laughed out loud at how different it was from the sights she saw from her windows back home. There was red brick building with ornate rounded corners, and people mulling about on the street below. Wondering what it must be like to walk this city every day, for it to be completely normal. Did the locals still see how amazing it was, or were they jaded from a lifetime of experience? They would probably have laughed at her typical tourist musings, that's what, she told herself as she walked to the closet to grab her clothes.

Since she was planning on spending most of her day wandering around the city on foot she figured comfort was key. June back home in Michigan was muggy with humidity already, but it was quite a bit cooler here overseas. Thankfully she studied up on the typical weather patterns, and she packed some pants instead of only shorts. Deciding on a comfortable pair of medium wash skinny jeans and a deep jade colored t shirt for the day she walked into the bathroom. Splashing some water on her face and brushing her teeth she contemplated what to do with her hair. It was a wild mess of auburn curls, but it wasn't frizzy, so she let it be. Vacation hair, don't care and all that. Since she was planning on taking loads of pictures today, some of them inevitably selfies she grabbed her makeup bag. Swiping on a few coats of mascara, dabbing on a tiny bit of cream blush, and shoving her pink lip balm into her pocket she nodded at her reflection.

Grabbing a thin infinity scarf in a gauzy material she wrapped it twice and pulled it on. Tiny little gold hoops in her ears, and a brown leather strapped boyfriend watch completed the accessories. Comfort over fashion won out, and she slipped her feet back into her favorite converse instead of the wedges she also brought. Bending over she rolled her skinny jeans up twice so they stopped just above her ankles. Making sure she had a small umbrella she swiped her purse and headed happily out of the room. Pulling the strap over head to wear it across her body she waited for the elevator. A quick breakfast in the hotel restaurant was all she could manage today, her excitement was too intense to spend time sitting down eating. She gulped downed the remnants of her orange juice needing to get out discover, and explore.

She made her way to Trinity College for a tour. Seeing the Old Library, with its Long Room, and Book of Kells was at the top of her priority list. The sheer magnitude of history awed her. Being an American, especially a Midwesterner nothing back home was this old. The east coast had some old historic buildings and monuments. But her state wasn't even founded until 1837. The Book of Kells was created sometime around the year 800. The years it had seen unfolding were just staggering to think about. It was beyond breathtaking. The colors so vibrant yet beautifully faded from age at the same time. Wondering how many hands touched it before it was put on display, and how many since in restorations boggled her mind. Looking down she noticed her own hands were shaking from such strong emotions coursing through her. The entire Long Room smelled like what Caitlyn thought heaven must, dry old paper, beat up leather bindings, and the promise of knowledge, or adventure to be found between the pages. Nothing on this entire earth smelled like an old book, and a room full of them was nearly overwhelming. The rest of the tour of the college grounds was wonderful, but being in the room with something so priceless clearly topped the list for her.

Caitlyn spent the rest of her afternoon

wandering the National Gallery of Ireland, and the National Museum of Ireland Archaeology. Her sons were one hundred percent right about their mother, she was a complete nerd. Soaking in that much history all day long left her feeling slightly giddy. She was making her way back to the hotel when her stomach rumbled loudly. Realizing she hadn't stopped to have a bite to eat since her rushed breakfast she looked around. Making a quick decision that dinner in a pub surrounded by the happy noise and camaraderie of people sounded better than a quiet meal by herself she walked into the nearest one. The place was already hopping, and a quick glance at the watch on her wrist told her it was later than she originally thought, probably because on the walk back she had seen so many interesting things to take pictures of, she thought laughing at herself.

There was so much noise packed into the space it nearly blanketed her. The smell of beer mingled with the richer tones of meat cooking in savory spices. It was everything she would expect an Irish pub to look like, and that made Caitlyn so happy she walked up to the bar with a giant crooked smile on her face. She absolutely, and immediately loved this place. Snagging an empty bar stool she climbed up and sat. The older man next to her turned and gave her a nod. She beamed at him and nodded back. The bartender, a good-looking man she guessed was somewhere comfortably in his forties, walked over to her.

"Evening, what'll ye have?"

"Good evening. I'd love a pint of Guinness, and whatever that mouthwatering smell is please."

"American huh?" he said with an easy smile.

"Yep, I can't blend in with this accent." She laughed with a shrug and a raise of her eyebrows.

"The hair helps, so long as ye don't open yer mouth," the bartender answered back. "That smell would be the stew, and I can guarantee it tastes even better than it smells."

"That's cause his missus is the one back there making it," the old man next to her leaned in and joked.

"Is that so?" Caitlyn laughed, "Lovely. You are a lucky man then," she said turning back to the bartender.

"That I am. I'll get yer pint, and a bowl of me wife's stew," he said with a wink walking over to the tap to craft her beer.

"What a beautiful day it was," she said to the older man. "I'm Caitlyn."

"Name's Tom." He held his hand out for a shake. "Didn't get soaked to yer skin while ye were walking about."

"I carried an umbrella all day, and the only time it rained was when I was inside the museum, so I didn't even need it. Of course, if I'd forgotten it back at the hotel it would have rained all day."

"Oh, to be sure. Visited the museum today did ye?" He smiled and took a pull of his own drink.

"I started with Trinity College this morning then slowly made my way back here," she said, the excitement still clearly ringing in her voice.

"The Book of Kell's huh?" a deep voice said from beside her. Turning on her stool Caitlyn looked at the man who was sitting on her other side. He most definitely wasn't there when she sat down. There was no way imaginable she would have missed a face like that. He had eyes that couldn't decide if they were meant to be green or blue, and settled with devastating beauty on somewhere in between. His hair was medium brown, with generous golden streaks dancing in the lights. There was the slightest cleft in his chin, and stubble along his jaw that said he hadn't bothered to shave in a few days. He was wearing a simple black t-shirt but had rolled the sleeves up once on his toned arms.

"Absolutely. In all my life I don't know that I've seen anything more beautiful," she answered him, thinking his eyes might just be right up there with the ancient book. If she had been standing at that moment she wouldn't have trusted her knees to hold her upright.

"Ah, but there is a lot of beauty here in Ireland," he said. "Isn't that so Tom?" He looked across her, to the man on her other side.

"Sure is," he answered with a chuckle.

Just then the bartender sat her Guinness down in front of her. "Heya Nolan, wantin' a pint?" he said to the handsome man.

"Sean, when have ye known me to not want a pint?" He laughed. The sound rumbled across her skin and had her heartbeat speeding up. If an attractive man laughing next to her nearly had her moaning, then her love life was far worse off than she ever thought.

"Truer statement. What's the craic? Haven't seen ye in a stretch," Sean the bartender said talking with Nolan.

"Been busy as all hell to be fair." Nolan nodded.

"Glad to see ye in here tonight boyo," Tom added from her other side.

Caitlyn was wondering if she should offer to switch spots with Nolan, or Tom, so they could chat without her in between. Before she could ask a lovely dark-haired woman walked up and sat a steaming bowl of stew in front of her with a generous hunk of bread on the side. "Thank you, it looks great, and I've been told it tastes even better than it smells."

"Damn right it does." She smiled at Caitlyn.

"Keely when're ye gonna leave Sean and run away with me?" Nolan asked her in a loud stage whisper.

"Only in yer dreams Nolan. Are ye after some stew tonight too, or did ye already eat, love?" She patted his hand with clear affection.

"When have I ever come in here not wanting ye to feed me? Never. Since you broke me heart again I guess I will have to make do with yer stew." Nolan sent a grin at Sean as he set the beer down.

"Ye can keep trying, she's never gonna leave me for ye, ya fool." Sean laughed and kissed his wife on the cheek before she headed back into the kitchen.

Caitlyn closed her eyes and let the rest of the pub fade away like white noise in the background. Her first sip of Guinness in Ireland was a moment to be savored. The rich heady taste was everything she expected. When she opened them slowly, she found Nolan staring at her. The look on his face wasn't laughing at her for being idiotic either. "First Guinness in Ireland seemed like a moment. Ya know?" she muttered to him feeling slightly embarrassed.

"I like a woman who knows how to enjoy life," he said, his voice dropping slightly. His eyes burning with intensity into hers.

"Ye just like to enjoy women," Tom added lightening the moment. "Watch yerself with that one Caitlyn, he's trouble."

"I can tell. I'm thinking flirting comes as naturally to Nolan as breathing does." She laughed and spooned up some stew.

"Can't blame him though. If I were younger I'd be giving him a run for his money."

"And if yer wife wasn't expecting you home soon," Sean added laughing as he walked past them carrying a pint in each hand heading for the opposite end of the bar.

"That too. Best be getting back to her then." Tom winked and finished the last of his pint. He climbed off the bar stool and gave Caitlyn a hug. "Hope to see you again darling before yer holiday is over." She hugged him back. He walked over to Nolan, shook his hand, and pulled the younger man into a hug. "Good to see ye again. Don't make it so long next time, eh."

"Do me best," Nolan said with a pat on the old man's back. Tom gave a wave to Sean as he walked out, saying goodbye to a few other people he passed.

"He's in here for a pint every night. Rain or shine. Ye could set yer watch by him," Nolan said sitting back down. His sexy accent only added to his charm.

"I'll definitely come back to see him again then," Caitlyn said. "I liked him."

"Everyone does. Never heard a bad thing about him. So, the States?" he asked. Sean set Nolan's dinner down in front of him before walking away.

"Yeah," she said after she finished chewing.

"Whoa, slow down now. So much information coming at me with that answer." Nolan winked at her. It was a great wink too; he had probably perfected it moments after birth.

Caitlyn laughed in spite of herself. "The Midwest, a small town. Nothing very exciting."

"So tell me, why Ireland in June, and not Hawaii?" he asked.

"Well, if I was thinking Hawaii it would be during the long winter to escape all the snow we get back home. Besides laying around on a beach alone is only fun for a few hours. It's not nearly as relaxing as everyone seems to think. This," she made a gesture encompassing the pub, "is so much better."

"Can't argue there. Although laying around on the beach can have its moments, ye know," he added with a mischievous glint in his eyes.

"True. Maybe my next vacation I'll go somewhere I can pack nothing but bikinis," she tossed back at him, and had the pleasure of watching him gulp the beer he was attempting to swallow.

He recovered fast though. "And sun-cream. Wouldn't want all that lovely skin to get burned."

She was picturing Nolan slathering sunscreen all over her on some beach with palm trees swaying lazily in the warm breeze. An obvious blush swept across her cheeks. Damn her active imagination. She tucked into her stew like her life depended on it for a few minutes.  Nolan let out a laugh and spooned up his own dinner, happy with what he knew without a doubt she was thinking of. She figured having a hot as hell Irishman flirting with her in a pub was probably on everyone's vacation wish list. If not, it damn well should be. It was easy to enjoy since she'd seen him do the same thing to the very married Keely. He clearly meant nothing more than a good time of it.

He asked her how long she was staying for, and Caitlyn found herself telling him her plans for the next two weeks. Everything she wanted to see and experience while she was here. A few other patrons walked over and chatted him up, and he very sweetly, always included her in the conversations. Her food was gone, and her glass empty, the pub was even busier than before. Caitlyn was about to push herself away from the bar and say goodbye when Sean set two new pints down in front of her and Nolan. She looked up at him with surprise, but he was already walking away with their empties.

"I signaled him for another round," Nolan said leaning in closer to be heard.

"Oh, thank you. I know it's habit, or tradition, or maybe custom would be the right word, to buy a round in return. But if I drink three pints with you, I won't make it out of here under my own steam tonight," she laughed. "Sean'll have to make me a bed in the corner to sleep it off."

"No worries, you can get me back next time love." He touched his glass to hers. "Slainte," he said grinning.

"Planning on being here for my upcoming date with Tom?" What the hell she was on vacation she thought, taking a sip staring straight ahead so she didn't gulp nothing but the frothy head.

"To be honest I'd probably tag along the rest of yer holiday if it were an option," he said with all seriousness, looking deep into her eyes.

"Oh, yeah. I'm sure you have nothing better for the next two weeks than playing tour guide to me." They were turned full on facing each other now. Caitlyn's elbow on the edge of the bar, her head resting in her hand. Nolan's foot resting on the pegs of her stool. They made quite the cozy picture to everyone else in the pub.

"To be sure it would be memorable," he said.

"I'm sure. Who wouldn't want a strapping young Irish lad escorting them around? It should be an option when you book your trip." Caitlyn tried joking to ease the building tension between the two of them.

"Age doesn't measure the amount of life one's lived," he said defending his age.

"Spoken like someone in their early twenties," she said laughing so hard she leaned her head back. When she focused on Nolan again, he wasn't smiling at all. The burning intense look from earlier was back in his eyes.

"Being twenty-five just means that I've the energy to keep up as ye traipse all over the countryside." His words seemed innocent enough, but the tone of his voice said he wasn't actually talking about walking around.

"Oh, I've no doubt you would be tons of fun." She admitted with all seriousness finishing her drink. Standing up she waved a goodbye to Sean before this went any further. Intending to thank him for the beer and company she turned back to Nolan. He was off his stool, standing really close to her side.

"Let me walk ye back to yer hotel, Caitlyn. I bought ye the second pint, its only right I make sure ye make it safely." The 'no thank you' she intended to say never made it past her lips. Looking into his eyes she found herself nodding her head before turning to walk out. He was taller than she had expected. Sitting down they were nearly the same height, but he had at least three or four inches on her own five foot five when standing. Thinking that with his height if she wanted to, she wouldn't have to go up on her tippy toes to kiss him, not that she planned on it. Nope.

The sun had set some time ago, and the night was noticeably cooler after the heat from all the people crowding into the pub. Taking a deep breath of the fresh air, she shook the thoughts out of her head sending her hair flying all around for a moment.

"What?" he asked looking down at her with a half-smile.

"I was just thinking...about nothing really." Next time one pint was her stopping point. Telling him she was thinking about kissing him was so not cool.

"Mmmhhhhmmm. Ye have very talkative eyes love, and they were not telling me that ye were thinking about nothing." They were still standing in front of the bar. He wrapped his arm around her, hand resting lightly against the small of her back. She just looked up at him with a smile. "Not telling huh, it's okay, I can guess." He winked. "So where are ye staying?"

"The Westbury. It's just over that way." She gestured with a nod of her head. He started walking them slowly in the direction she had indicated.

"Only two weeks?" he asked. She nodded hoping they never made it to her hotel. "How old are ye Caitlyn?"

"I'll be thirty-five in October. I have fifteen- and thirteen-year-old sons back home," she answered quietly, suddenly not so sure he didn't mean anything by his flirting.

"But no man? Ye say that number like it were three hundred." He stopped them across the street from her hotel. Turning to face her, hand still blazing hot on the small of her back.

"Some days it feels like it is. No, there hasn't been a man in..." She paused looking up at him, and just couldn't tell him how long it had been since she had a man. "I'm divorced," she finally supplied with a shrug.

His other arm wrapped around her, just above the first. His stunning eyes looking pleadingly down into hers. She knew what they were asking, he didn't need to say it out loud. And it was tempting as hell, god knows. But she wasn't about to be someone's grungy night out, no matter how fun it would be. And there was no doubt in her mind it would be good, really good. He just oozed sex. She wasn't inviting him to come up, but she couldn't seem to stop her hand from reaching up. She ran her fingers over the scruff on his jaw, and up into that expanse of burnished brown hair. He stood utterly still staring into her eyes, and she lost herself in their depths, more blue than green now. Pulling his head down to hers she pressed her lips softly to his, and licking her tongue out she tasted him. His arms tightened around her, and he opened his mouth kissing her back with enough passion to melt the soles of her shoes to the sidewalk. Caitlyn let herself savor the kiss for a few minutes before pulling herself back from the edge of desire. Touching his bottom lip with her thumb, still moist from her lips, she stepped away from him knowing that she didn't want to be doing it.

"Definitely memorable, Nolan," she said softly and walked across the street into her hotel before she could change her mind.

# Chapter Four

The next morning it was pissing rain outside. After tossing and turning for hours wondering if she had made the right decision the gloomy weather suited her mood just fine. As soon as her hotel room door had closed behind her all of the previously valid reasons why a one-night stand with a sexy local man was a horrible idea had faded away. So what if he slipped away after? It wasn't as if she had to see him every day at work, or around town. They made condoms for a reason; she could make mistakes without taking risks. Admitting honestly to herself that one kiss had done more for her than any other man ever had. Damn, but Nolan could kiss. It hadn't felt as suave as she expected though. She was sure he was along for the ride with her, just as caught up in the rush as she was. Maybe he wasn't the player she had thought he was. That was a whole new complication to worry over, which she did as she was washing her hair. Telling herself it was pointless to replay it all over again in her head she shoved her arms into the deep blue cardigan. The only thing left to do at this point was to cherish the kiss and get on with the rest of her vacation.

Spending the next hour emailing her sons helped Caitlyn's mood immensely. Telling them all about the cool history she had learned the day before and attaching quite a few pictures. She debated sending a message to her ex-husband but decided against it. Wyatt or Mason would tell him enough about her trip anyway. The boys were fine with their dad, so there really was nothing for her to say to him. Which had her laughing, and instead of feeling the weight of the divorce dragging her down she just felt free. This vacation was exactly what she had needed.

Grabbing her umbrella, she headed out of the hotel feeling much better than when she woke up that morning. Yesterday she had signed up for a Food of Dublin tour. It was supposed to be a great way to get around the city, and she wouldn't have to worry about getting lost because they were all going together in a group of about a dozen.

Meeting up with the guide, and group on Grafton Street their first stop was a fabulous cheese shop. Tasting different varieties of Irish cheese was definitely a great way to start the tour. Their guide Sarah was quite knowledgeable, and everywhere they went she spouted off facts about food, as well as about the city, and Ireland itself. They had bagels in an old Georgian mansion that was converted into a shopping center. They were quite possibly the best bagels she had ever tasted in her entire life, and that's saying a lot. From there they went to a street fair area, and tried all kinds of different foods. There were chocolates flavored with roses, which may or may not have blown her mind. The tour ended in the Temple Bar area, with them taste testing some of the finest Irish whiskey. Not that she was any kind of a connoisseur, but it all seemed lovely to her. That took up all the rest of her morning, and into the afternoon.

Deciding she had enough of walking around town in the rain tucked under her umbrella she stopped into Stephen's Green Shopping Centre. The building itself was simply stunning, especially for a shopping mall. The stores were geared more to locals, so the kitschy tourist stuff was at a minimum, which was perfect. Caitlyn wandered in and out of the shops for a while. Not really needing anything, or more to be honest not wanting to lug an additional suitcase back home she headed towards the food area. Buying herself some chips she sat down and just people watched. This was one of her favorite things. As a writer seeing the way people interacted with each other always told her little stories about their lives.

Like the young couple a few tables to the right. Still in their teens, haven't been dating very long, but not a first date. They were too comfortable with each other for that. The guy looked beyond besotted with the girl, who pretended not to like him as much as her shining eyes and ready laugh said she did. Third date, but no kiss yet Caitlyn guessed. Grabbing the notebook out of her bag she jotted down the way the girl kept biting her lip, she probably didn't even notice she did it, and the way the boy's eyes would zoom in, and he would take a quick breath in. Smiling to herself after a few minutes she looked away, the lad was never going to muster up the guts to kiss that girl if he caught her looking at them.

There was a woman sitting with a young girl eating ice cream a little way in front of her. They had their heads bent together laughing at something the young girl was saying. They're bond was plain to see, and Caitlyn was betting aunt and niece, not mother daughter. Speculating this was a regular habit for them, an outing once a month, she thought about all the places they must have visited. They fed birds in the park, saw the latest cartoon at the theater, rode carousels, and spent hours laughing at all their private jokes.

Finished with her food, and happy with the people watching she wandered out of the mall. The rain had stopped sometime while she was inside of the mall. Grateful she watched the street as the lights came on in the dusk. Taking out her phone she snapped a dozen pictures as she meandered. She had meant to head straight to the hotel and spend her evening in that enormous bathtub. Her feet had a different plan for the night though, and she found herself in front of the same pub from last night. Deciding that she was done thinking, she was on vacation damn it! If she wanted to hang out in a pub why stop herself? There was nobody she answered to.

Pulling the big wooden door open with the old brass handle she stepped inside. The place was already hopping tonight, and there weren't any stools open at the bar. Looking around she found a tall two top and sat down. A young man she didn't recognize from last night walked up to her. "How's it going there? What can I get for ye?"

"Good, good. A pint of Guinness please?" she answered back. He nodded his head, stuck his pencil behind his ear without writing it down and wandered back to the bar. She took a moment and scanned the bar. Tom wasn't sitting on his stool; she must have already missed him tonight while she was at the shopping mall. The door whooshed open and the group of guys she had passed by while they were smoking out front came back in. She watched them walk past her to a larger table. Out for a boy's night no doubt. While she was watching them, she spotted Nolan sitting in the corner, not too far away. He was at a small table like hers. By the way he was looking at her she knew he'd spotted her as soon as she walked in. They sat there staring at each other, the time seeming to stretch out between them. Her waiter walked up with her pint just then, and before she could even say thank you Nolan's voice rang out. "She's with me Danny."

With a slow smile she turned to the smiling waiter and said, "I guess I'm with him, so I'll take my drink over there." Danny laughed and walked over to Nolan's table with her pint.

Setting it down on the table he said, "Sean said ye were in last night tryin a steal Keely again. Good to see ye Nolan." He reached out a hand and they shook. Danny walked away before she got a chance to pay for her drink.

"I didn't pay him yet, where is he going?" Caitlyn asked Nolan as she sat down next to him.

"Caitlyn, love, I told him ye were with me. That meant more than sitting at my table. Danny's a man, he understood," Nolan said lifting her face with a thumb under her chin. He leaned in and placed a soft kiss against her lips, like it was something he did with regularity.

Eyes slowly drifting open from the kiss she smiled. "And am I with you now Nolan?"

"Ye coming in here tonight says that ye know ye are." Nolan slung his arm across the back of her chair, his fingers drawing lazy little shapes on her shoulder, sending chills across her skin.

"I didn't plan on this," she admitted quietly.

"I know."

"I mean any of it. Not being able to stay away

tonight, kissing you last night."

"I know," Nolan said again. "That was the best kiss I've ever had Caitlyn. I couldn't move from that spot for a while. I'm not letting ye walk away from me twice. Not when I know ye don't really want to, ye just think ye should be." His voice was low, and his eyes looked much wiser than the twenty-five years old she knew them to be.

"Tell me that isn't your usual pick-up line." She laughed a little trying to break the tension, but knowing that he meant what he said.

"I don't need pickup lines love, I'm Irish. This accent is all the opening I've ever needed." His deep laugh rumbled out as he leaned his head in even closer to hers.

"Well, it is a damn fine accent," she admitted. "But everyone else in this pub has the same one as you do," she tossed back at him.

"Then I'll consider meself lucky ye liked mine best." He playfully tugged on her hair. "I like it like this."

"Oh, the braid? Thank you. It kept blowing into my face while I was walking around today." When her hair got on her nerves it was inevitably weaved into a side braid, or tossed up in a haphazard bun.

"Well it suits ye. Are ye hungry love?" he asked taking a drink.

"No, I did a food tour today, and had some fries

at the mall a little bit ago. But if you want to get dinner I won't mind," she added wondering if he was asking because he might be hungry.

"I ate before I came here tonight too. What are yer plans tomorrow Caitlyn?" He leaned in and kissed a lazy trail along her neck up her jawline like he just couldn't help himself.

"I...ahhh...I was planning on touring the Guinness Store Room. Other than that...ummm... just wandering about I guess," Caitlyn said struggling to get the words out of her mouth.

"Mind if I tag along?" he whispered softly, his breath tickling her ear.

"I'm sure you've seen the storeroom before," she mumbled. "It's one of the most visited tourist spots in all of Europe," she rambled on, distracted by what Nolan was doing.

He pulled away from her neck, and with a little smirk said, "Not with ye, I haven't."

Caitlyn put her hand up on his chest to stop his forward motion. "If you keep doing that I'm going to melt into a puddle on the floor," she admitted with a raised eyebrow, "instead of drinking the beer you bought me."

"Now how in the hell do ye expect me to hear that and sit here drinking?" he said with an exaggeratedly put upon sigh.

She made a show of taking a slow drink, her

eyes laughing at him over the rim. Sean was walking around stopping at tables to say a word here and there. "Makin' a regular outta ye huh?" He smiled at Caitlyn. "Ye gonna snog her at the table all night lad?" He winked at Nolan.

"I'm not plannin' on it," Nolan said with a grin. "Just waiting for the lady to finish her pint like she asked so I can take her home."

"Cheeky little bastard," Sean said as he walked away his big booming laugh bouncing off the walls.

Caitlyn laughed too. It probably should bother her that everyone in the whole pub knew she was bringing him home with her tonight now. It just didn't. It seemed so natural with Nolan; their chemistry was off the charts. Besides, she was only here for a limited amount of time, and there really was no point in dragging it out. They were both adults who wanted the same thing. He was watching her, an easy smile on his face, but his eyes burned fire. Their drinks were only half gone, but she stood up grabbed his hand and walked away from the table.

"Not as thirsty as ye thought?" he said as soon as they were outside. Caitlyn wrapped her arms around his neck and kissed him. There was no hesitation, the moment her lips touched his he slanted his head and took over. His tongue sliding against hers. Pulling away from him while she could still think she pulled him towards her hotel.

Shaking his head as if to clear the fog he said in a low voice, "Damn, woman." Knowing exactly what he meant she let out a laugh and picked up the pace. Thankfully, the Westbury was close, or she may have broken into a jog, which could prove disastrous with the ankle boots she had on today. Once inside the hotel they didn't have to wait for the elevator, as there was someone leaving it as they walked up to it in a rush.

"Floor?" he asked. She said sixth, he pushed the button and pulled her into a kiss. This one was deeper than the others, with just a touch of desperation. His control wasn't as strong as he wanted her to think. He used his body to push her against the wall. His hands reaching down to cup her ass and pull her against his already evident erection. The full body contact had her moaning into his mouth and rubbing herself against him. Just then the elevator stopped, and the doors opened with a ding. He pulled her out into the hallway and looked down at her.

She just stared at him with big eyes for a heartbeat before remembering that he didn't know which way her room was. Heading down the hallway on unsteady legs she was grateful it was only a few doors away. As Caitlyn pulled the key card out of her purse Nolan stepped up behind her, wrapped his arms around her waist and licked the sensitive skin on the nape of her neck. Desperate to get into her room, hands shaking she couldn't get the little light to turn green. His laugh rumbled against her neck.

"Shut up. I can't think with you doing that."

"I know love. But if ye don't get that door opened soon we're going to get kicked out of this hotel," he said, his hips grinding into her, enunciating the point. Just then the blasted light turned green and he pushed them both into the room. Tossing her purse down she turned around and pushed him back against the door. Looking up into the fire burning in his eyes she kissed him. He pulled the cardigan off her and tossed it somewhere into the room. His hands were everywhere, roaming over her body. Caitlyn's hands found their way into the back of Nolan's white shirt, and she pulled it up. She barely pulled away long enough to get the shirt over his head.

"Nolan," she said in between kisses.

"Mmmm," he answered pulling her tank top off over her head.

"I didn't pack any protection," she said. His nimble hands were in the back unhooking her bra as his mouth moved down the line of her neck. He licked and kissed across her collarbone and down to her nipple. His lips closed around it with a pull and her head fell back on a breathless moan.

"Brought some," he answered as his head made its way over to her other breast. She was so caught up in what he was doing to her that she nearly asked what he brought. Protection, he was saying he had a condom.

"Thank god," she said grabbing handfuls of his hair, as he nibbled her other breast. His laugh rumbled against the nipple caught between his teeth. He reached down and unsnapped her pants.

"Step out of 'em love," he said licking up the side of her breast up towards her neck. His hands holding her hips she lifted first one leg, and then the other out of her boots and the pile of jeans. His tongue found the sensitive spot just behind her ear, and swirled circles. Her hands reached for his belt buckle. "Not yet, don't wanna have to run back here and dig through the pockets," he said as he nibbled her shoulder and walked her backwards further into the hotel room. Caitlyn hadn't left any lights on when she left so the only illumination in the room came from the windows. "Wanna see ye," he said pulling away from her, and turning on the lamp sitting on top of the writing desk.

Nolan stood there staring at Caitlyn in the lacy blue panties that had matched the sweater she wore earlier. He ran his hands through his hair, "Jesus, but yer stunning." With his accent it sounded more like jaysus. Instead of feeling vulnerable and exposed standing in front of him all but nude for the first time, she felt powerful. Staring into the stark hunger evident in his eyes she hooked her hands in the sides of her panties and pulled them down slowly with a little shimmy. He grinned at her as she backed up the couple feet towards the bed.

She could see the hair peppered across his chest and leading down into his jeans. The hair on his head messy from both of their hands. The way he watched her nearly had her trembling with need. "You're too far away from me Nolan."

With a nod he stepped out of his shoes, and walked slowly to her. A few inches away from her, he stopped. Staring into her eyes he reached into his pocket and pulled a strip of condoms out of his pocket and set them on the nightstand. "Now ye can take me pants off love," he said and pulled her in for a kiss. She didn't need to be told twice. Reaching down to undo his belt, instead of pulling it out through the loops she just unsnapped his jeans and pushed them down. He had on a pair of plain white boxers, and for some reason she found that simplicity sexy as hell. She felt him unraveling her braid, as she lifted him out of the boxers. He let out a growl as she ran her hand up and down him. His dick was long and thick in her hand.

Before she could get in more than a few strokes he was pushing her back onto the bed. He climbed up with her, and kissed her so long her toes were curling. His hands roamed over her, finding every sensitive spot. But he wasn't fully on top of her yet, and the need to feel his weight was nearly killing her. She let out a whimpering, "Please, Nolan, I need you."

He pulled away from her and reached for a condom on the nightstand. Leaning back on his knees he stared right into her eyes as he ripped the foil packet open, and smoothed the latex over his hard dick. It was one of the sexiest things she had ever seen in her whole life, and it had her biting her teeth into her bottom lip. He climbed slowly up her body, kissing her hip bone, her nipple and licking up her neck. His gorgeous green blue eyes never leaving hers. Nolan hitched her leg high up on his side and pushed all the way inside of her with one smooth stroke.

He was a tight fit, filling her completely. His breath came out in a whoosh, and he leaned his head down kissing her as he began to move in a steady pace that couldn't be called slow, but was definitely not fast. Nothing had ever felt so good in her entire life. His hips pressed her into the bed, and each upward stroke of his dick had them rubbing against her clit and left her moaning. She met him stroke for stroke, lifting her own hips up into him. He kissed down into her neck and she felt the scrape of his teeth pulling on her ear lobe. She arched her neck and gasped. Her moans were getting more and more breathless as the glorious pressure between her hips built. He quickened the pace, his dick sliding relentlessly in and out of her. Caitlyn's fingers were digging into the back of his shoulder blades, holding onto him for dear life. Her legs started trembling around his hips and he pushed up on his hands to look down at her. Pulling her leg up even further as he deepened his angle.

"Yes. That. Yes. Oh. My. God." She closed her eyes and panted out in time to each thrust of his dick inside of her. Her body starting to buck uncontrollably.

"Eyes on me love." His voice was a low rumble now. "Caitlyn, eyes!" he growled out.

Forcing her eyes to open she looked into his as the giant orgasm ripped through her, and she opened her mouth with a shocked cry. With a hissing sound he pumped into her deliciously harder pushing the orgasm to last even longer. Her back arched up off the bed pressing her nipples into the hair on his chest. "Fuck!" he let out in a gravelly shout and pushed his hips into hers, his dick pulsing with his own release.

She lay there trembling underneath him thinking, '*Wow*.' He leaned down onto his elbows with a satisfied smile and reached his hand into her hair, his thumb caressing her cheek. "That went a good ways past memorable, love." Caitlyn nodded her head agreeing with him.

# Chapter Five

Nolan got up and walked off to the bathroom to dispose of the condom, and sweet baby Jesus, the view as he walked away was enough to have Caitlyn sitting up to watch him go in abject appreciation. The sex had been even better than she thought it would be, which was saying a lot because she was already sure it would good. That intensity in his eyes carried over to everything else he did. Honestly, the best part had been the amazed look on his face as he looked at her. Nolan was clearly a man who took nothing for granted and appreciated every moment to the very fullest. Caitlyn was still lost in her happy afterglow when he came strolling back out to her. His body was toned, but not to the point that he was bulky. He walked like a man who knew full well he had no reason to hide, but he didn't strut arrogantly either.

"A man likes to see the woman he just finished loving with such a smile on her face," he said pulling the covers out from under Caitlyn with a smile, and settling them both underneath them instead. Nolan lay on his back, propped up against the headboard, one arm tucked up, his hand behind his head. With his other arm he pulled Caitlyn in close and she was all too happy to drape herself across his warmth.

Playing lazily with the tufts of hair on his chest she looked up at him. "I'm happy to smile for you anytime you want." The laugh that rumbled through him had little butterflies dancing all through her stomach.

"Mad up for it now, are ye?" he said, his hand stroking her back in long gentle swoops.

"Not usually, it's been a good long while since, well since I've been with a man like this. But it just all seems so easy with you," she confessed to him in a small quiet voice.

"I know." She turned her eyes questioningly up at him. "A man can tell these things if'n he pays attention, and ye can trust I was paying fucking close attention."

"Had to knock the cobwebs back huh?" she joked feeling slightly embarrassed.

"Fucking hell, Caitlyn, watching ye enjoying me was the sexiest thing I've seen in me whole life. The shocked way yer lovely blue eyes cloud over, god only knows any man who could let ye get away must not have any sense left in his head. I meant to take my time, but I just got so damn caught up in ye."

"It's not always like that. It's easy to burn the room down when its new, with all the chemistry frying your brain cells," she said thinking of the heat between the two of them. "But after a few years it just becomes another chore or means to an end," she told him repeating what her ex-husband had said to her.

"The moment having sex with me becomes a chore take me out back and put me out of me bloody misery. That's no fucking way for a man to live." He wrapped both arms around her and rolled her under him. The length of his already growing erection nestled hotly between their bodies.

With hungry eyes she looked up at him, gliding her hands up into his dark hair. He leaned his head slowly down to hers, the heat in his eyes deliciously searing the nerve endings in her whole body. He pressed his lips to hers, his tongue sliding into her mouth to tease her own. When he lifted his head, she was breathless with need already. His thumb traced the skin high on her cheek bone, "I could spend days lost in the way yer looking at me right now," he said with a quiet reverence. Caitlyn didn't know what to say back to that, but before she got a chance to try and figure something out Nolan's mouth tipped up in the sexiest crooked smile. "Such talkative eyes, love."

His head leaned back down, passing her mouth and nibbling on her jaw, just underneath her ear. It felt so good Caitlyn's whole body shivered. Nolan's quick intake of breath told her what her response was doing to him as well. He licked over the sensitive skin he had just loved with his teeth and slid his body slowly down hers. Propped up on his elbows he lifted her legs over his shoulders, his eyes watching her face. He leaned down and licked along the inside of her thigh, the stubble on his jaw scraping against her skin. Her fingers gripped the sheets hard. Taking his time working his way over, it felt like forever before she felt the first touch of his tongue roll against her clit. With a desperate moan she slid her hands into his hair.

He took this as the encouragement it was, and burrowed his head closer to her, his hands reaching under her, holding her pressed to his mouth. He sucked her clit into his mouth, and the whole world narrowed down to what he was doing to her. Nothing else existed but the way he made her feel. He took his time, swirling his tongue around over and over again until she was panting, then he flicked it out with short quick strokes. Caitlyn whimpered and moaned, her fingers gripping his hair with abandon. Every time he brought her to the edge of release, he backed off a heartbeat, just to stoke the fire burning inside of her again.

"Nolan please! For the love of everything holy, please," she begged him, her muscles trembling with the strength of her need for release.

"Mmmm baby, ye taste so fucking good. Did ye need something?" he said his mouth still pressed against her, the air from his breath tickling against her pussy.

"I'm so close, I need to, oh god. Please Nolan!" She struggled to think, panting the words out as he sucked her clit into his mouth again.

"Ye wanna come now baby?" he asked with a teasing flick of his tongue.

"Yes please!" she groaned, rocking her hips against his face, begging for release. Nolan's hands squeezed her ass, and he licked her with a steady, determined rhythm, the pressure against her clit exactly how she liked it. Finally, he let her fly higher and higher until the biggest orgasm of her entire life rushed through her. Caitlyn cried out, her back arching high up off the sheets, her hands holding his head pressed to her as she came. His tongue licked her lazily until the pulsing aftershocks had stilled.

Nolan lifted his head and climbed determinedly back up her body. Tension rolling off his skin. Reaching out to the nightstand he ripped open the foil packet and shoved the condom quickly on with hands she could see were shaking. Caitlyn lifted herself up to kiss him when he pulled back saying, "Yer all over me face baby," stopping her.

Licking his lips and tasting herself there she whispered back, "I don't care," before kissing him like a starving woman. He wrapped his arms around her and pushing off with his legs he rolled them back over again. Caitlyn sat up on her knees with a swivel of her hips she instinctively found his waiting dick and sank down. He filled her completely, stretching her even fuller in this position, and she gasped into the mouth still kissing her. Pressing her hands on his chest she pushed herself up to look down at him. The stark hunger evident in his eyes all the encouragement she needed. She rode him quick and hard, lifting up until he almost slipped out of her then sliding back down into his hips. All she could think was he felt so damn good inside her. His hands were worshiping everywhere on her body. Winding themselves up in her hair, and then stroking down to cup her breasts softly so the nipples rubbed against his palms with her own momentum.

Her body still so sensitive, she came quickly with a surprised cry, stilling on top of him her pussy quaking around his dick. With a growl he grabbed her hips and lifted himself up slamming into her faster and faster, pushing her orgasm on until she couldn't even drag a breath into her lungs before he shouted out and held her hips down. She could feel him twitching deep inside of her in time to her own shudders. Caitlyn collapsed in a boneless heap down onto his chest. Laying there she could hear his heart thundering away, and she tried to remember how to breathe again.

This time when Nolan went to the bathroom to take care of the condom, she couldn't have mustered enough energy to lift her head and watch him if she tried. Her whole body felt like it was made out of molten liquid gold, all glowing and happy. He shut the lamp still illuminating the room off as he passed it and climbed into bed, settling them the same as before with his arms around her, pressing her into his chest.

"Will you still be here when I wake up?" she mumbled sleepily against his skin in the dark.

"I'm yers as long as you'll have me," he whispered into her hair as he kissed the top of her head. Nolan lay there awake long after Caitlyn had drifted off into sleep. He held her close just listening to the pattern of her breathing, the sky was beginning to lighten with the approaching dawn when he finally closed his eyes and went to sleep himself.

# Chapter Six

Late the next morning when Caitlyn woke up, her body felt wonderfully used. Still laying draped across Nolan, his arms holding her pressed to him, she looked up ever so slowly, careful not to wake him. With his face smoothed out in sleep he looked peaceful. In the short time she had known him that wasn't a word she would have chosen to describe him. Charming, up for a laugh, sexy, or intense worked better. Sometime last night she stopped seeing him as younger, and just saw him simply as a man now. It surprised her that it had faded from her consciousness so quickly. Taking stock, she found no morning after guilt. He was still here in the light of day, which undoubtedly helped. But Caitlyn admitted to herself that even if he had fled after she dropped off to sleep it wouldn't have made her regret him. Being with him last night had been absolutely electric. He made her feel things nobody else ever had before.

Stretching, she pulled gently away from him. He rolled onto his side, but didn't wake up. Needing a little time to herself she climbed quietly off the opposite side of the bed. Caitlyn walked into the bathroom and closed the door. Looking at her face in the mirror she realized she had completely forgotten to take off the previous day's makeup, which rarely, if ever happened. Thanking her lucky stars she had only worn a little bit and didn't look like a deranged raccoon, she pulled out a makeup wipe and cleaned up her face. There were occasional red areas on her sensitive skin, most likely from his scruff rubbing against her. There was also a hickey on her thigh, and remembering exactly how it got there had a shameless grin breaking across her face. Walking away from her contemplation in the mirror she turned on the shower. Most mornings she needed the hot water to ease the stiffness left over from sleep, but this morning everything already felt loose and limber.

Caitlyn took the time to shave carefully, thinking she didn't want to wrap stubbly legs around Nolan's waist later. In that moment she knew that she was going to spend the rest of her time in Ireland gobbling up as much time with him as she could. Her son hadn't been too far off the mark about a steamy affair with a younger man. Picturing Nolan as a pool boy in the tropics had her laughing so hard she had to stop running the razor over her legs for fear of cutting herself. After the chuckling died down, she finished the rest of her shower. Going through her typical morning routine, frizz cream in her hair, daily moisturizer with SPF for her face, brushing her teeth she went an indulgent step further and smoothed on the body lotion that smelled like her perfume.

Slipping the robe on she walked out of the bathroom. Expecting to see Nolan still asleep in the bed she was surprised he was sitting on the couch his clothes already on. For a moment the sight had a flicker of panic rising up inside of her. But the cheeky satisfied smile on his face smoothed the doubt away before it had a real chance to take hold.

"Good morning," she said walking over and kissing him softly on the lips. "I tried not to wake you."

"It's good now," he said his lips lingering on hers. "Would've been better if I'd brought more than two condoms, then I woulda been disappointed if you didn't wake me."

"Obtaining more is definitely high up on the list of today's priorities." Caitlyn laughed and sat down next to him. "I was going to order some breakfast, what sounds good to you?" she asked.

"Actually I was thinking that I could run and grab me clothes, and condoms," he added with a wink. "Since yer only here for a short time I plan on being up yer arse the rest of your holiday. Give me an hour and then order us both something, would ye love?" he asked his hand playing with the ties of the robe tempting them both.

"You want to stay with me here for the rest of

the time?" she asked him.

"Beats the hell outta running back and forth for clothes," he replied, still toying with her robe.

"What about your place? I had planned on five nights in Dublin, then I was going to roam about the rest of the country. Last night was night three here." Two more nights with him wasn't going to be long enough. Suddenly seeing castle ruins, and quaint fishing villages lost a little of its sparkle for her.

"Caitlyn, I said I was yers for as long as ye'd have me. I meant it. My place for the next week and a half is with ye. Dublin, Galway, Cork, Kerry, even Mullingar if yer heading there. I've got a car, and I can drive on the left side better than ye can I'm wagering." He was stroking his thumb along her jaw, holding her face now.

"I'd like that Nolan," she said softly.

"I'll see ye in an hour, then it's off to see the famed Guinness storehouse, alright love?" He stood pulling her up with him.

"What do you want for breakfast?"

"I'm probably the least picky eater in the whole of the world. If it's edible I like it. Surprise me." He leaned in and kissed her so thoroughly only remembering the lack of protection stopped her from climbing up his body. He looked down at her and gave her a wink, but she heard the shaky breath he took when his lips left hers.

Nolan walked out of the hotel room and she sat back down with a thud, shaking the haze away for a few minutes. Once her lips stopped buzzing from his kiss she stood up and grabbed some clothes. The sky today looked promising, sun shining brightly. So she pulled on her cropped skinny jeans, and a deep purple shirt with fun crisscross detailing at the neckline. Adding a pair of earrings that dangled with little glass faceted jet beads. Walking back into the bathroom she decided she looked good, but not like she was trying too hard. She didn't want to be the fool wandering around town all done up to impress her new man, and uncomfortable as hell all day long. Besides, Nolan had made it pretty obvious he already liked her, and so far she had been pretty damn casual with her outfits.

Sitting down at the desk after putting on the same makeup as the day before, thinking that if it's not broke don't fix it, she booted up her computer. She transferred her pictures from her phone to the laptop, and logged into her email. The boys' response to yesterday's email was much as she expected. They were having a good time with their dad, and said her pictures were pretty cool. But teenage boys weren't ones to go on for days and days with details. She laughed at the brevity of their email. Clicking reply she told Wyatt and Mason everything about the food tour, and the really cool shopping mall. She mentioned going into a fun pub close by her hotel two nights in a row, how welcoming the owners were, the atmosphere and regulars, but left meeting Nolan out. What else could she do? Ending the letter with how much she missed them, and all her love she hit send.

Glancing at the time on her computer she pulled the room service menu out of the desk drawer. Her stomach was rumbling, starving from all the amazing sex, probably. Deciding it was only right that she try out the world famous full Irish breakfast she ordered two of them. They would get here just after Nolan was due back, so they wouldn't get cold waiting. Making a call down to the front desk she notified them a friend would be staying with her for the remainder of her time with them, and that she would also like to extend her stay to encompass the rest of the two weeks. Driving around with Nolan sounded like fun, but keeping this as their base seemed like the right thing to do. Caitlyn was a woman who followed her instincts, and this time was no different. They informed her of the new cost, and said she could pick up the additional room key card at the front desk at her earliest convenience.

She answered the knock on the door just after hanging up the phone and saw Nolan standing there grinning with a large beat-up brown leather bag grasped in his hand, and black backpack slung comfortably over one shoulder. "Hey love, miss me yet?"

"I was just about to start," she laughingly said reaching up to kiss him. The affectionate greeting came easily to her, like everything else between them. He walked in and set his bags down. "Our food should be here in a few minutes." His hair was still damp from a shower, and he had on an olive green short sleeved Henley. The top two buttons were undone, and she could see his chest hair. His casual masculinity was sexy as all hell. She was betting he didn't even think about it, he just put on the clothes he liked. The green in the shirt drew out the green in his eyes, muting the blue. He smelled so delicious she knew she could spend hours pressed up against him and not even start to get sick of it. She was still staring happily up at him when a knock sounded for the second time this morning on her door.

"Room service," came from out in the hallway. Caitlyn pulled away from Nolan and walked to the door. She held it wide so the man could push the food cart inside the room. Caitlyn pointed out where she wanted him to set up the food, and tipped him.

Nolan took a big sniff. "Smells like ye really did it up."

"I've always wanted to try the full deal. Everyone who visits Ireland always talks about it," she said with a shrug of one shoulder. "Besides, I need something in me to be able to drink at the store house," she said sitting down in front of her plate.

Nolan settled beside her on the couch, his own food on the table next to hers. Making her way through the rashers of bacon, plump sausage, egg, mushrooms, and tomatoes she pushed the beans around the plate with her fork, feeling full. She made herself take a bite of the black pudding, it wasn't as bad as she expected of a sausage made from pork blood, but it couldn't be described as particularly good either.

Nolan noticed the look on her face as she chewed and laughed until tears shimmered in the depths of his eyes. "Good show love, ye don't have to finish it. I was raised on it, and its only just alright," he said pointing out his own half eaten black pudding. He had cleared most of the rest of his plate though. "Other than that, what did ye think?"

"It's an awful lot of food, next time I get it I'll be asking for a half portion." She smiled and drank her orange juice.

"Yeah, but it will carry ye through a full day's work as was intended. Or a long day wandering this fine city of ours." He nudged her with his shoulder and picked up his strong black tea. "Just juice for you?"

"Yeah, I'm not a huge tea drinker, and wasn't in the mood for coffee." She leaned back into the couch cushions.

"I alternate between coffee and tea meself. Ye look absolutely lovely today. I was going to mention it earlier but ye kissed me, and well I forgot me own name momentarily," he said leaning back and draping his arm along the back of the couch.

"I like hearing that. The part about you forgetting your own name," she paused, scrunching her face up as something occurred to her. "Nolan, we don't even know each other's last names."

"Hayes. My surname is Hayes. Ye already know I'm twenty-five, Irish born and bred. I'm not a picky eater, and I like scary movies. And this is the happiest I've ever been," he said laying his other hand on his chest with complete sincerity.

"Caitlyn Reed, from Michigan. My sons are Wyatt and Mason. I'm really happy right now too. I am a big wimp when it comes to scary movies. But I would rather read than watch movies most of the time anyway. Unless it involved some cuddling or making out," she added with a laugh, careful not to mention what she did for a living. It sometimes freaked people out knowing she wrote love stories, and she didn't want to break the spell they were under.

"Ye cuddling into me during the scary bits would be the best part to be sure," he said pulling her in and tickling her neck with his scruff. "Are you ready to go conquer the day now love?" At her giggling nod he continued, "It's a little over 2 kilometers there from here. Would ye like to walk there, or shall I drive us?"

"After that breakfast I'm thinking I need the

walk. Besides, I like wandering about. I get to see more of the city that way, and it's not raining out right now." She said as he stood up and reached a hand down to help her up. They loaded the plates back on to the cart and pushed it out of the room as they exited it. Leaving it in the hall for pick up later they walked to the elevator. Nolan settled a flat tweed newsboy cap on his head as the doors closed behind them. It made him look all the more Irish, if it was even possible to do so. It was a good look on him, and without thinking she dug her phone out of her pocket and snapped his picture. Checking the screen, she saw he had a smile in his eyes, that hadn't quite made it down to the rest of his face yet. It was a perfect moment captured forever.

"What did ye do that fer?" he asked her, the smile now fully formed on his face.

"Because I always want to remember you looking just like that," she said reaching her hand up behind his neck and kissing him with a quick smack.

"Then it's only fair I get to take photos of ye as well," he winked.

"Okay, just don't put them online please," she said without thinking. She had quite a few followers thanks to her books, and she was always careful about what she posted on her social media accounts.

"Ye've my word they will be just for me," he said with a strange look on his face. Before she could ask what he was thinking the elevator doors whooshed open and they walked out into the lobby.

They took their time making their way across the city. Caitlyn kept stopping to take a picture of this or posing with Nolan in front of that. It was at least an hour before they made it to tour the Guinness Storehouse. They signed up for the tasting tour, and Nolan insisted on paying for it. They spent the next two hours exploring the expansive place. The history of the place fascinated Caitlyn. Their guide was an older gentleman who explained all about how the stout was made, from beginning to end. The indoor waterfall had her laughing with complete abandon. The neon glow heading into the tasting rooms bathed them both in a warm red glow. The complete blank whiteness of the tasting room itself was quite a shock after all the blazing color leading in. After that they wandered around the exhibit of the ships that used to carry Guinness overseas. They took pictures next to the famous Guinness harp, smiling like the happiest of fools. The view from the Gravity Bar up on the top floor was nearly magical. Looking out across the whole of Dublin made her say a silent thanks again for being here in Ireland.

Caitlyn looked over to see Nolan watching her as she experienced the view. "Look at this Nolan, isn't it just amazing?" she asked.

"Beyond beautiful," he said his eyes never

leaving her face, and wrapped his arm around her pulling her in tight to his body. They stood there exactly like that for a few minutes until he led them back down to the street. They wandered around the city without any specific destinations after that. Walking with her hand tucked in his she was falling in love with him and didn't even know it yet. Nolan nodded at a lot of people in passing, and Caitlyn figured he must know half of Dublin from the looks of it. Nobody stopped to talk to him, though she was sure his friends would have plenty of questions for him later about her.

They popped into a small restaurant they happened to be passing at dinner time, and ate their meal nestled close together in the corner oblivious to everyone else in the room but each other. The food was good, but the tenor of her vacation had changed. It was no longer just about stacking up experiences in Ireland. It was about making memories with Nolan. The long list of things she thought she absolutely had to see or the trip was a bust shrunk smaller and smaller with every slide of his eyes towards hers, every laugh, every touch. This was what she came here for, to live in full vibrancy. Feeling things with reckless enjoyment. She just hadn't known it yet when she stepped off the airplane.

# Chapter Seven

They were walking back towards the hotel hand in hand in the evening when the sky finally decided to open up pouring rain down on to them. Caitlyn ducked quickly under the nearest building overhang and was rummaging through her purse for the little umbrella stashed in there. She noticed that Nolan was still standing in the rain, and smiling he reached his hand out inviting her to come and join him. "Come dance with me, love," he said grinning even bigger. Helpless to do anything else but go to him she stepped away from the safety of the building and into his arms. He started humming a slow tune and swayed with her in time to the music playing inside his head. Lost in the feeling of his arms around her as they moved in time, and the way his eyes glinted in the dim lighting she felt the rest of the world drift away. People passing by them while tucked safely up under their umbrellas stopped to watch the beautiful couple lost in the magic of each other's arms, getting drenched down to the skin. One woman said in a wistful voice to her husband that they must have been newlyweds to still be so spontaneously romantic.

When Nolan finished humming what she

realized was an actual song, and not just random melodies he leaned down and whispered softly in her ear. "Tucking that memory away forever. I've always wanted to do that."

"Me too, Nolan." She pulled him closer to her, not even noticing the water dripping off her anymore. They walked the rest of the way back to the hotel in the rain happily, never bothering to pull out the umbrella.

The bellhop in the lobby scolded them asking if they had forgotten their umbrella when they walked into the hotel. Nolan just grinned at the man and shook his head as they walked towards the elevator. Caitlyn rode the whole way up to the sixth floor with her head tucked against Nolan's wet chest listening to the sound of his heart beating. There was so much she wanted to say to him, but nothing seemed to come out. Some things were just too precious for words. This time when they stepped out of the elevator onto the floor he led the way to the room. Reaching a hand into his back-pocket Nolan pulled out the second key card they had picked up from the desk earlier. Not wanting to break the connection, his other arm was still holding Caitlyn tight against his body as he swiped the card to unlock the door and let them both into the room.

Caitlyn shucked her purse next to the writing desk and stepped out of her wet shoes, setting them by the heater vents to dry out. Nolan watched her without saying a word and set his own shoes down next to hers. She walked over to him and peeled his wet shirt up and over his head while he watched her, his eyes already simmering with heat. Carefully slipping his belt out from his pants she reached back and set it down on the desk behind her. Unbuttoning his pants, she slowly pushed them down his hips, leaving the boxers in place. He had on another pair of simple white ones, and for some reason that had her smiling. Stepping away from him she crossed her arms in front of her body and pulled the purple shirt up and over her body. The gray lacy bra underneath hid nothing from him, her dark pink nipples clearly visible.

Nolan's hands clenched into fists at his sides, and she knew he was struggling not to touch her, but was letting her lead, for now. Pushing her pants over her hips and down her legs in a smooth bending motion she kept her eyes on him. Walking past him she trailed her hand invitingly across the skin of his abdomen as she headed into the bathroom. She was reaching into the shower to turn it on when she saw his reflection in the mirror. He was leaning casually against the door jam, and everything about his posture said he was enjoying the show, but the heat in his eyes hinted at the effort that control was costing him.

Deciding she wanted to see the moment the chain he was holding himself on snapped she reached behind her and unsnapped her bra, letting it fall away from her full breasts as she stepped up to him. Running her hands up into his gloriously wet brown hair she pulled him down until her teeth grazed lightly along the side of his jaw. She was nibbling on the side of his neck when his arms came around her, reaching behind her she caught them and pulled them off her body. Shaking her head, she headed down to lick one of his flat masculine nipples until it pebbled against her tongue. "Just let me." She said feeling his effort to hold still while she was pressed this close to him. Drinking in the power of that she licked her way down his body until she was kneeling in front of him. She could see his dick straining against the wet fabric, and she rubbed her hand reverently over it before pulling the boxers down. Remembering how much pleasure this had given her last night she wrapped her fingers around the base and licked up the length of him savoring the taste of his skin. Nolan's whole body trembled which had her smiling up at him. Swirling her tongue around the swollen head she watched his jaw tighten until the muscle was actually twitching. Opening her lips she took as much of him into her mouth as she could fit before lifting off him with a popping sound. Licking him slowly she sucked him back into her mouth, moving her hands around the base, she worked him. She watched as the simmering heat in his blue green eyes grew until they were completely ablaze.

A groan bubbled up his throat just before she felt his hands drifting into her wet hair. Lifting her off him he pulled her up and crushed his mouth down on hers. He kissed her like a starving man feasting for the first time in his life, pushing her panties down urgently with one hand and walking them into the shower already full of steam. He pressed her against the wall, and he reached down, unerringly finding her clit. Stroking the already sensitive bud she gasped right into his mouth. Leaning into him she grabbed him and stroked his dick in time to what his nimble fingers were doing to her pussy. She was scant seconds away from coming when Nolan pulled back abruptly.

"Sweet-mother-Mary, hold that thought," he growled and dashed out of the shower leaving the glass door open. Caitlyn stood there so turned on her brain refused to function. Nolan popped back in, shiny foil packet in hand. "Almost forgot," he muttered slightly embarrassed. She didn't bother telling him she had forgotten too, that was pretty obvious. "Now where were we?"

Dropping down he pulled her hips to his face, his tongue darting out to lick her clit. She cried out, bucking against his tongue, the orgasm swiftly ripping through her body. Nolan stood up so quickly that Caitlyn had to lean back against the tiled wall to stay upright as she watched him rip the foil packet open with his teeth. It took him what felt like a lifetime to get the latex rolled onto his length while she waited with anticipation. He stepped back to her and reaching down he grabbed both of her legs lifting them up and opening them wide, his hips pressing her into the tiles as his dick slid all the way inside of her waiting pussy in one smooth stroke. Wrapping her arms around his neck she held on as his body pumped deliciously, and mercilessly into hers. He kissed her breathless as the steam clouded around them, the heels of her feet digging hard into his ass, desperate to pull him in tighter. Crying out into his mouth she came, bucking her hips greedily against him. She felt his rhythm falter, and knew he was almost there. Not giving him time to back away from that edge she bit her teeth into his bottom lip and dragged him into the storm with her. He came with a loud groan stilling deep within her before his head sagged against her shoulder.

They stayed there like that leaning up against the wall while both of their heart beats stopped rushing at breakneck pace as the water rushed out from the shower head next to them. Caitlyn ran her hands in lazy strokes over the top of Nolan's shoulders wondering how she was going to be able to walk away from him when it was time to go back home. He lifted his head and lowered her down slowly until she could touch the floor again and slipped out of her. With a wink he pulled the condom off and stepped out to toss it in the bin. She was pouring shampoo from the bottle into her hand when he made it back into the shower. He leaned against the wall and watched her wash her hair with a satisfied crooked smile.

"Pretty happy with yourself huh?" she asked as she leaned back into the spray rinsing the suds out of her long hair.

"I've no complaints at the moment. How about ye, my love?" he asked with a charming raise of his eyebrows and an adorable laugh.

"I'll let you know when I can actually think again," she laughed back at him as she stepped out of the spray so he could wash off.

# Chapter Eight

They lay tucked up in bed talking about all the little things couples who are discovering each other have a tendency to do. Nolan told her what it had been like for him growing up in Ireland. Turns out they each had only a brother, and that the relationships between them were complicated. Her little brother took after their mother, thought he could do no wrong, and never apologized for anything. She didn't see either one of them if she could help it. Nolan's older brother was always jealous of everything he did, and no matter how hard Nolan tried he couldn't connect to him. He also avoided him whenever he could. Caitlyn told him all about her sons. How much Mason looked like her, and how Wyatt at fifteen was almost grown up and it scared her sometimes.

He asked her in a quiet voice about her divorce. She found herself telling him how there wasn't a big explosion, one mountain they couldn't find a way around. That it was just a million small things pulling them apart for years. The space between them was growing and that she had looked up one day and realized they weren't even a couple anymore. Bryan hadn't seemed bothered by it at all, which was when she knew there was nothing left. She confessed about all the guilt she held onto for too long because she was the one to ask for the divorce. That she was learning to forgive herself, because everyone deserved happiness. She told him how the boys seemed to take it all in stride, thankfully, and they adjusted better than she could have asked for. When she was finished laying it all out, she asked him if there was anyone that had ever ripped him up inside.

He told her about a woman a while ago who kept him on the back burner while she flitted back and forth to another man. That every time he thought it was good between them, she ran back into that other guy's arms. He finally couldn't take the roller coaster anymore and broke it off, realizing that maybe she was only ever with him to make the other man jealous. The woman hadn't even cared when he said goodbye, but she called him crying sometimes now and begged him to come back. He said the first time had nearly undone him, but he knew that it would change nothing, and she probably only reached out to him when she was fighting with her man. The part that bothered him the most now was how she told everyone he had been the one to break her heart.

Caitlyn thought about what a damn fool that woman had been. Nolan was a gift, and to string him along, and jerk him around like that just wasn't forgivable in her mind. She was thinking about it, quietly lost in her own thoughts for a while when he tipped her face up to his.

"What is running through yer mind right now?" he asked smoothing her fiery hair back off her face.

"Just wondering what you're going to tell the next woman that is laying here inside your arms when she asks about me. I can only give you a few days Nolan, and that's not really long enough to make a blip in a lifetime. I can't figure out if I want this to mean nothing, so it doesn't hurt, or to mean everything beautiful and precious. Its messing with my head," she said watching the sadness creep into his beautiful eyes.

"Thinking about another woman being in me arms feels wrong, love. Ye fit so well here," he said softly.

"We both know this has to be just a fun vacation fling," she said feeling her own words slice into her soul like a thousand jagged razor blades.

"Maybe, but yer not going to be an easy woman to replace. I can't imagine anyone being able to top this. It just don't feel right," he admitted.

"I don't want that. I want to be able to close my eyes at night and think of you happy here. Going to the pub and trying to steal Keely from Sean, or wandering the streets looking Irish as hell in your cap. You have so much to give Nolan, so damn much its staggering. You keeping all of that locked inside because of this, and not sharing it would be a real shame," she said running her fingertips over the hair on his jaw.

"Caitlyn, how can ye say that and expect me to pretend it's just casual between us? Ye see things inside of me that no one ever has. I'm good at playing the good time up for a laugh lad, and nobody really bothers to look past that. Thinking of another man wrapping his arms around ye, and holding you pressed close to him in the dark has me stomach filling with fucking rocks. Will he be able to make ye feel what I can? Will he appreciate how honestly ye give yourself, without pretenses? Thinking about someone else being the one to watch yer beautiful eyes while yer body explodes around his might just be the end of me," Nolan said closing his eyes for a few minutes, and missing the tears shining in Caitlyn's.

"I guess we grab all that we can, and wish each other happiness for the rest of it. I don't want you to regret me," she said laying her head down on his chest. "Maybe I shouldn't have walked back into that pub to you."

"I will never regret ye, that's just mental, that. I wouldn't trade the time I've spent with ye for anything in all of heaven or earth."

"Even if this leaves us both hurting? Because I've gotta be honest Nolan, flying away is going to rip a piece of me out." She held her breath in the darkness waiting to hear what his answer would be.

"When I'm old and gray and I count up all my mistakes this won't be one. That piece, I'll happily keep it, and knowing I have it will selfishly make me feel better. We didn't mean for this to be so deep when we took that chance. Best I can figure is this was fated, love. We don't know how our story ends, it may surprise ye," he said pressing a kiss to her temple.

"I don't want to talk about this anymore tonight. I just want to be lost in this moment with you. Just hold me please," she asked him in a shaky voice, wanting to tuck the fears away and soak up the comforting warmth in his arms instead.

"Anytime ye want love," he said wrapping his arms tighter around her body. "What do ye want to see tomorrow?" he asked changing the subject.

"Maybe we could get out of the city and go for a drive into the countryside?" she said quietly.

"That suits me down to da ground. I've somewhere in mind. Go on to sleep now beautiful, and put yer mind at ease," he said, his fingers rubbing soothingly down her back. He started humming the same thing he had been when they were dancing earlier. Caitlyn meant to ask him what song it was, but sleep claimed her before the words ever made it out. Nolan lay there thinking he was already completely defenseless when it came to her and being powerless had never felt so right to him before.

## Chapter Nine

Eyes drifting slowly open, Caitlyn soaked up the feel of Nolan's warmth pressed up tight against her back. One of his arms was slung around her, holding her securely to him. Something told her that if she were to move away from him he would just tug her right back into his body. A small smile on her face she pulled away, testing her theory she put a small space in between them. Nolan didn't disappoint her, bringing her right back towards him as he scooted forward to meet her. Thinking about him chasing her all over the bed while she slept had a swarm of butterflies tickling her insides again. Finding a man who cuddled you after sex wasn't difficult, but one who held you close all night long, that was a rarity indeed.

"Mornin' beautiful. Where do you think yer going?" His voice still deep and gravelly from sleep.

Filing the sound of it away in the recesses of her brain she leaned back into him shrugging her shoulders. The action itself had been casual, but the words she said were anything but. "Nowhere, Nolan. I'm not going anywhere."

He moved the hair off her shoulder. "Good, I

like right where ye are meself. In fact, I'd be a damn fool not to take full advantage of the bounty laid in front of me," he said while laying kisses across the top of her shoulder.

Caitlyn's breath caught in her throat as his hand slid knowingly down her body. His fingers slowly teased the patch of short red curls until goosebumps broke out over her skin.

"Jesus, love," he breathed into her ear and slid a finger up inside of her. She was wet, and already aching hungrily for him. From this angle his palm pressed deliciously up against her clit while his finger stroked deep inside her pussy. Within moments she was gasping for breath her body racing towards that first peak. Crying out she reached back tunneling her fingers into his hair. Nolan added a second finger to the first one still working inside her. "One more time. I love how ye feel when yer breaking apart around me," he said scraping his teeth along her skin. Helpless to do anything else with his hand doing that to her she moaned as the aftershocks from the first orgasm built, and built until she was shuddering as another one crashed through her.

Nolan leaned away from her a moment, and she heard the condom packet ripping open before he pressed against her again. Reaching down he hooked her leg in the crook of his elbow giving him better access, and slid slowly inside her still trembling pussy.

"Fucking hell ye feel good," he said holding still, his dick all the way inside her absorbing all the little spasms as her quaking body milked his. Caitlyn pushed back into him, silently begging him to move, and he gave a teasing rotation of his hips. "Need me?" he asked her, knowing the answer.

"Oh god, yes," she whimpered.

"I'm all yers love," he said and finally rocked his hips, moving his dick. Hitting the perfect spot.

Crying out a thankful gasp she closed her eyes lost in the way his body made hers feel. Every time he was buried deep inside of her the rest of the world just faded away. The room could burn up in flames around them, and as long as he kept making love to her everything would be okay. The sound of his breathing, deep and excited in her ear, his chest hair tickling her back, his fingers gripping her leg as he held it up, was all too much. She could feel the effort it was taking him to keep moving steady, and needing to feel him come with her as she raced towards the edge, dug her fingers into his scalp. "Come with me Nolan...I want...together." She heard his growl in her ear, his hips stuttered as she came apart around him with a breathless moan.

They lay there tangled in each other while their hearts slowed down. "Love?" Nolan asked.

"Hhmm?" she answered sounding content.

"Still wanting a drive today?" he asked stroking

his fingers softly over her skin.

"Yes. I want you to show me somewhere. I want to remember for the rest of my life, this is where Nolan took me."

"I'd like to take ye everywhere," he said sitting up and looking down at her. "Caitlyn, I..." he started before she quickly put her fingers up to his mouth stopping what he was going to say.

"I'm, uh, I'm going to get dressed and send my kids an email. Want to order us some breakfast?" she said with an edge of terror in her voice. Whatever it was he was about to say was something she knew she could not handle hearing this morning. The intense look in his eyes told her that much.

"Alright love," he said flopping back down on to the bed as she got up and walked away.

Grateful he didn't push she checked outside and saw it was raining softly, but the sun was somehow still managing to shine. It gave the morning a dreamy, ethereal quality. Although being in his arms could have added to that magic. Opening the closet, she pulled out a pair of black skinny jeans, and a white t shirt that had slim horizontal black stripes on it. Pulling out her lacy white bra and matching underwear from the dresser drawer she headed into the bathroom. After she was dressed, face washed and had a little makeup on she pulled her hair up and off her neck in a messy ponytail, strands floating carelessly around her face. Walking back out into the room she saw Nolan was just pulling his shirt on. It took her a full minute to remember how to breathe seeing him in the deep blue color. He was so effortlessly sexy that it was literally a punch to her solar plexus.

Catching her watching he winked. "A man could get used to ye watching him like that, love."

Shaking her head at him she let out a shaky laugh and picked up her laptop carrying it over to the couch to type up her email, leaving the desk for Nolan to make the call to room service. There was an email in her inbox from Bryan. Dreading what it would say she opened it. He was asking her why she was staying the whole time in Dublin now, instead of moving around like she originally planned. One of the boys must have mentioned it to him after her last email. As a rule Caitlyn didn't like to lie, but telling her ex-husband about the exciting affair she was currently enjoying didn't seem like the best idea in the world. She told him instead how she loved her hotel room and didn't feel like packing and unpacking over and over. That getting to the places she wanted to see wasn't that hard, nothing seemed too far from here. After that she sent off one to her boys, making sure to include pictures she took in the Guinness Storehouse yesterday. She asked how they were doing, told them she missed them, and to be good for their Dad.

Ending it with all her love she sent it off.

By the time they were done eating their breakfasts Caitlyn was practically buzzing to get going. Shrugging her shoulders into her well-loved denim jacket she grabbed her purse, checking for an umbrella. She turned to ask if he was ready when she saw the way he was looking at her. "What?" she asked, tilting her head quizzically to the side.

"Damn, I'm a fuckin' lucky man," he said with his blue eyes like waves dancing in the sun. She loved that he looked thunderstruck and was so willing to show her how he was feeling.

Walking over to him she ran her hands up his chest and leaned up to kiss him. Telling him with her lips and tongue what she couldn't manage with her words. His arms wrapped tightly around her, pulling her in as close as he could. She kissed him until she was damn sure he understood what she was saying. Then she pulled away and with a beaming smile said, "Show me your country Nolan."

Downstairs the valet brought his car around for them. He watched her face closely when the black Range Rover pulled up to the curb. He held the door open for her, and she climbed up inside the passenger seat. Wondering why he had been looking at her that way she watched him round the hood and walk to his door. Not coming up with any reasons that made any sense at all to her, she gave up and enjoyed the ride out of the city, glad she wasn't the one driving. Nolan reached over and laced his fingers through hers like it was something he had always done when they rode together. Nothing ever seemed like it was the first time with him, it all came so naturally to them.

Once they were free of the hectic hustle and bustle of the city the openness comforted Caitlyn. It was always like that for her. The buildings had a way of crowding in, and making you feel surrounded. Once the horizon cleared it always eased something down deep inside of her. Caitlyn was enjoying her time in Dublin but seeing the vast green rolling past the window was enough to have her sighing in relief.

"This place is so beautiful. I would never be able to name all the different shades of green in front of me if I tried. There just aren't words," she said still looking out the window.

"All that rain is good fer something then," he joked, his thumb rubbing across her hand. He took her to the lovely Powerscourt Gardens, in County Wicklow. The massive forty-seven-acre estate was full of statues, formal gardens, with lakes and walking trails. They strolled for hours lost in each other. Caitlyn took a million pictures of the stately old house, and wondrous gardens. The ever-present sprinkling of rain not even bothering them. Tucked up close to each other underneath the umbrella, it felt like they were the only ones there.

A little while later a bored looking blonde teenage girl walking with her parents near them stopped and openly stared, not seeming to notice that her parents kept walking on. Her young, freckled face turning a deep shade of scarlet with her blushing, before a giant grin spread across her face showing off the multicolored braces on her teeth. She gave an excited little wave of her hand, before running away to catch up with her parents. Caitlyn remembered what it felt like to be that young, and if she had happened across Nolan, in all his easy masculine beauty, well she would have probably had the same response too. Looking up at him she wasn't even sure he had noticed the girl's reaction though, since he was staring intently down at Caitlyn. So many thoughts flitting across his ocean eyes, too fast for her to interpret any of them. Then he smirked at her, in the way only a man who knows exactly what you taste like can. Now she was the one who's cheeks were blushing.

He reached down holding her face in his hand, caressing her cheek reverently. "Are ye enjoying making memories, my love?" he touched his lips softly to hers a moment.

Gazing up into his eyes she admitted, "This is definitely memorable, Nolan." The smile he rewarded her with was bright enough to blind, and she basked in its warmth as they made their way back towards his car.

He took her to a small restaurant that looked like the kind of place tourists usually passed by, but that the locals knew was really the best place around to eat. They were seated in a quiet spot Nolan facing her, and away from the rest of the room. Caitlyn knew she had his complete and undivided attention. Having Nolan focus so intently on her like she was the only woman in the whole place was dizzying. After she finished eating, she excused herself to go to the restroom while he paid the bill. The woman looking back at her in the mirror as she washed her hands over the sinks was hardly recognizable to her. She looked so carefree, happy, and completely besotted. Caitlyn wasn't sure when she had ever seen herself look like this before, but she liked it.

There were a few people around Nolan when she walked out, talking excitedly. As she approached, she heard snippets about goals scored, and what everyone thought about it. She guessed he was finding out what the score was on a game he missed out on, she walked up smiling, thinking nothing more of it. He said goodbye politely and walked them out of the restaurant and to the car with a hand lightly on her back.

The long, exciting nights spent in Nolan's arms, followed by days out exploring finally caught up to Caitlyn on the ride back to Dublin. Unable to fight the drugging pull of the quietly humming engine, and smooth motion of the miles speeding past she curled up in her seat, resting her head on her arm laying on the leather center console she fell asleep.

"Love, we're here. C'mon baby, let's get ye up to bed," Nolan said as he ran his fingers over her hair.

Caitlyn blinked at him bewildered for a moment while her brain worked to fight free of the wonderful hold sleep had on it. "We're here?" she asked with a yawn.

"Yeah, ye slept the whole way back. Want me to carry ye up?" he asked as she fumbled with the seat belt.

"No, I can walk. I don't need to be carried up to bed like a baby," she said grumpily.

Nolan disguised his laugh as a cough, opening his door and climbing out. Handing the valet his keys he walked over and opened her door. Leaning in he held out his hand for her. Caitlyn used him to pull herself out of the car and stepped onto the pavement. Nolan's arm came around her, guiding her into the lobby. "Wait, my purse," she said.

"Don't worry, I've got it love," he said leading her into the elevator. Leaning on Nolan was the only thing keeping Caitlyn upright the whole way up to their floor. The doors dinged and she took a clumsy step forward. Nolan caught her before she weaved into the doorway. Scooping her up with an arm under her legs, the other behind her shoulders he walked them towards the room.

"I'm not that sleepy," she protested, her words mumbled as she pressed her face into his chest. They stopped at the door, and he tucked her in close to his body leaning back a bit as he reached for the key card in his back pocket. He managed to get them successfully into the room and closed the door with his foot. He carried her straight to the big four poster bed. Setting Caitlyn down on the soft expanse of white comforter Nolan squatted down and took her shoes off. Caitlyn sat there frozen watching him take care of her like it came so naturally to him. He gently lifted her striped t-shirt up off her, then unbuttoned her pants. Caitlyn sleepily helped him tug the jeans off her. Once she was in her lacy white bra and panties, he pulled the covers back and tucked her in gently.

"I'm still wired from the drive, love. I'm gonna check me emails and come to bed in a bit," he said in a whisper as he leaned down pressing a kiss on her forehead. Caitlyn watched, through heavy lidded eyes as Nolan walked over to the couch pulling his phone out of his pocket and sat down. Thinking that it was nice to have someone take care of her like that, she burrowed into the covers and dropped off to sleep.

## Chapter Ten

After falling asleep so soon the night before, Caitlyn woke up especially early. Nolan was curled all around her once again, but she managed to slip out from under his arm without waking him. Locating the big fluffy white bathrobe, she pulled it on and stood gazing out the window. She watched as the darkened city began to lighten with the first rays of dawn. The sunrise bathed the sky in blazing hues of pink and orange. Feeling inspired she walked over to the desk and turned on her laptop. She was still busy clicking away, words flying on to the page in rapid fire succession when Nolan woke up. So caught up in what she was doing Caitlyn didn't notice Nolan until he came up behind her leaned down, and wrapped his arms around her in a hug.

"Morning. Whatcha doing love?" he asked, his morning voice sexy as hell, all rough and crackly.

"Purging. Hold on, hold on, I'm almost done," she said distractedly. He stood there patiently holding her as she got the last of the thoughts racing through her head out. Once her work was safely saved it finally filtered through that he was really there, standing behind her. Leaning her head back she looked at him.

"Hi," she said feeling a little insecure now.

"Ello. Ye with me now?" he asked laughing softly. She nodded her head up and down at him. "So, purging?"

"Yeah, that's kind of what I call what I do when I'm not working on a specific project, but something inspiring hits me. I unload all of it to come back to later. I watched the sun coming up over the Dublin skyline today, and the beauty of it almost hurt my soul," she said with a shrug. He was still looking at her. "I'm a writer," she confessed, holding her breath.

"A journalist?" he asked, pulling away from her slowly with a raised eyebrow.

"No, a novelist, umm romance novelist, technically. I write love stories," she said turning in the chair instead of leaning back to look at him.

"The Book of Kells," he said remembering back to her awe when she was talking about it that first night in the pub.

"Yep. I'm a big ol' nerd," she admitted smiling sheepishly at him. He laughed, the sound building until he threw his head back releasing it. It was a sight even more beautiful than the sunrise had been. His whole face lit up, his dancing eyes sparkling like gems in the sky. Thinking that she would keep him laughing every day for the rest of his life if she could she reached up and held his face between her hands. He looked down at her, his eyes still full of life and kissed her pouring his joy into her.

Nolan pulled back, his eyes still smiling at her. "Do you wanna..." Caitlyn interrupted whatever he was about to ask her by pulling his head back down to hers, the sudden need to drink him in burning through her veins. Her hands roamed all over his sleep warmed skin. Nolan reached between them and untied the robe, pushing it quickly off her shoulders as she reached her hand inside his boxers. She stroked the already hard length of his dick, walking him backward to the couch, and pushing him down onto it. Darting back across the room, feeling his eyes blazing on her the whole time she grabbed a condom from the box on the nightstand. Thinking maybe they should strategically leave boxes out every few feet all over the room she rushed back to him with a knowing grin.

Dropping down to kneel in front of him she took his dick in her hands bringing her mouth down greedily. Not bothering to spend her time slowly teasing him she bobbed her head up and down quickly. "Holy fuck!" he shouted grabbing her head in his hands. The feel of his dick in her mouth was really working for her, and she moaned around him. "Come here, baby," he said pulling her head up, his dick sliding wetly out of her mouth. She stood up, ripping the condom open. As she unrolled it down his length Nolan shoved her panties down her hips. Stepping out of them she climbed up onto the couch straddling him. As she sank down on his waiting dick, he yanked the bra straps off her shoulders and down her arms. Her breasts spilled out of the cups and he leaned his head down, pulling her to him with his hands on her back. His mouth closed over the first nipple and she threw her head back with the sensations shooting through her body.

"Oh god, Nolan, that's so good. It's always so good," she chanted as she rode him with abandon. Hands fisted in his hair, holding him to her as his mouth lavished attention on her, his busy mouth licking and sucking. When his teeth bit down on her nipple, just this side of pain she gasped, her pussy clenching in response. Always observant, Nolan caught on, and licked his tongue soothingly over the sensitive bud, before catching it with his teeth again. Crying out, her fingers gripping his hair she came in a hot rush around his dick.

"Shit," he hissed out through his teeth as her hips rocked against him in time to the aftershocks trembling inside her. "Fuck!" he shouted his hips thrusting up to meet her as his dick, locked deep inside of her twitched.

Caitlyn sat there, still on top of him, her heart racing. Knowing deep down that no matter how many times she made love to him she was never, ever, going to get enough of Nolan. With a bittersweet smile she climbed up off him. "Wanna share the water with me?" she asked jerking her head towards the bathroom.

"Yeah, go ahead and start it love, I'll be along when I can remember how me legs work," he said with a little laugh. Looking down at him, a sheen of sweat glistening on his skin, hair mussed from her hands, and satisfied ocean eyes her heart stuttered.

"Okay, Nolan," she said, wanting to say so much else, but knowing she shouldn't. She walked into the bathroom pulling her bra the rest of the way off. Caitlyn was halfway through shaving when Nolan walked in. She watched through the steam as he took care of the condom before opening the glass door. He stepped right up into the water, closing his eyes and letting it run over his head. She watched him wishing she could take a picture of him right at this moment. He turned around and slicked his hair back off his face with one hand, and reached for his shampoo with the other. Watching him do something so ordinary had her picturing what it would be like to have him with her always. Shaking her head, she shoved that thought deep, deep down, and locked it away.

Not wanting to ruin the whole day breaking her own heart she asked, "Wanna go with me to the Dublin Zoo in Phoenix Park today?"

"I haven't been there since I was young. Lots of people there," he said as he rinsed his hair.

"Yeah, especially with the sun out today," she

said.

"Hope you brought yer sunnies," he joked.

"Sunnies?" she tossed over her shoulder at him as she wrapped herself in a towel.

"Sunglasses, you silly American of mine," he said kissing her shoulder, his hair dripping down onto her. She laughed at him as she walked to the counter. He stood there, a towel slung low on his hips watching her go through the motions of her routine. She walked out to get dressed leaving him the counter to do his thing.

Excited for the day ahead she pulled a teal sundress out of the closet. Putting on the strapless bra she brought, she slipped the dress over her head and smoothed it into place. It went to just above her knees, so she could move around comfortably in it, and there were spaghetti straps that crossed each other on her back. Deciding that she would leave her hair down for added protection from the sun's rays she slipped her feet into the leather sandals she brought.

Nolan walked out of the bathroom and stopped. "Jesus, love. I've seen ye without a stitch of clothing on and yet ye keep managing to get more beautiful every time I look at ye."

Without thinking she walked over and laid her lips softly on his. "Thank you," she breathed against his mouth before she walked back into the bathroom.

Slathering sunscreen all over her shoulders and putting her makeup on, there was a silly love-struck grin plastered across her face the whole time. She added the little gold hoop earrings, thinking she was happy Nolan hadn't shaved. His scruff was approaching actual beard level now, and she hoped he left it the rest of their time together. He was dressed in a heather gray t-shirt, and khaki shorts, and was stepping into white sneakers when she walked back out. She tossed the bottle of sunscreen into a slouchy brown bag that matched her sandals and carried it over to where her other purse was sitting on the desk. Caitlyn transferred over all the contents to the new bag, including the pair of sunglasses she hadn't needed yet so far this vacation.

"Wanna walk, or shall I drive milady?" Nolan asked as she grabbed the denim jacket and they walked out of the room.

"How far is it, good sir?" she tossed back joking with him.

"About three kilometers I'd say." He pushed the button for the lobby once they were inside the elevator.

"Hhhhmmm. We're going to be walking all around the zoo too. Might be a good idea to drive," she answered.

"Less time for yer lovely shoulders to get fried in the sun too." He winked at her putting a navy ball cap on his head, his sunglasses already tucked into the neck of his shirt.

They spent the whole day wandering around the gigantic sixty-nine acre zoo. Caitlyn took pictures of every single animal to send home to her boys. The history of the place fascinated her too. First opening in 1831, it was one of the oldest, and most popular zoos in the entire world. She talked Nolan into posing with her for a few selfies, her favorite one being the one where he unexpectedly kissed her cheek. The smile in her eyes was genuine and they looked so good together. They got dinner at one of the cafe's inside the zoo, and ate at a little outdoor table while he had her cracking up telling her all about when he came there as a kid.

Nolan asked her as they left the zoo if she wanted to head back to the hotel, but the sun was still shining in the sky and she didn't want to miss a moment. "I'd really like to see the Ha'penny Bridge Nol," she said shortening his name without even thinking about it.

He looked over at her from his spot in the driver's seat with a goofy grin on his face. "Alright baby," he said in a soft voice with that grin still on his face.

Caitlyn took that as an encouraging sign he liked the nickname she had accidentally called him and smiled herself. Nolan parked the rover and she pulled on her denim jacket as they got out to wander the Temple Bar area and make their way slowly over to the bridge. Watching all the people bustling around Caitlyn told him about how she sometimes liked to people watch and make up scenarios. She told him about the day in the shopping center, thinking it had been so long ago, but it had only been a few days. They had only spent a short time together, but it felt like she had always known him, he was taking up space so perfectly in her life.

By the time they made their way onto the white painted cast iron pedestrian bridge the last rays of the sun were blazing fire across the sky. Caitlyn pushed her glasses up into her hair as they stood in the center leaning against the rails, his arm around her watching the sun sink down over the horizon. Nolan leaned in and kissed Caitlyn, so lost in each other they didn't notice as the bridge's lights came blazing to life all around them.

# Chapter Eleven

The room was still blanketed in darkness when Nolan woke Caitlyn. "C'mon love, the day is waiting for us," he said brushing her wild red curls softly away from her face.

"Nolan, it's still dark out," she mumbled sleepily.

"It won't be when we get there. Unless yer not wanting an adventure, that is," he said nuzzling in and tickling her neck with his still growing beard scruff.

"Where are we going?" she asked sitting up, excitement chasing the last vestiges of sleep away.

"Not tellin' ye," he said climbing out of the bed.

"Well how will I know what to wear?" she asked sounding confused.

"Dress for walking about outside. Bring yer umbrella, this is Ireland after all," he said pulling out clothes from the dresser.

Caitlyn stretched her arms out, arching her back thinking through what clothes she brought. Climbing out of the warm bed she padded across the soft carpet to the closet gathering what she figured she needed, and walked into the bathroom. "If you want me to go adventuring with you at the ass crack of dawn after making love to me half the night, I'm gonna need coffee," she called out, hearing Nolan's laughing response as she closed the bathroom door.

Washing her face, she looked at the state of her hair. Nolan liked to run his hands through it when he was buried inside of her, between that and rolling enthusiastically around in the bed made it an absolute mess. A lion would be jealous of the size of her mane today. Not feeling up to washing it she tossed it up in a tortoise shell clip and hopped in the shower to quickly wash her body. Drying off she shrugged into her favorite pair of jeans, so well-loved they looked like she had a go at them with some sandpaper in spots. People paid good money to buy jeans this distressed. After pulling on the mint green v-neck t-shirt she brushed her teeth and swiped a coat of mascara on, but said to hell with the rest of her makeup. Walking back out into the room she pulled on her converse sneakers and grabbed a navy zip front hooded sweatshirt out of the closet. Turning she presented herself to him, "I'm ready if you are."

"C'mon my grumpy love, let's get some coffee in ye," he said handing her purse to her and kissing her cheek. Instead of leaving the lobby immediately he turned them to the restaurant and picked up the large to-go cups he must have called down and ordered while she was in the bathroom. Thinking that was an incredibly thoughtful gesture she smiled gratefully at him she took a slow sip of the beautiful, life giving elixir.

Quirking her eyebrow up at him she said, "It's absolutely perfect."

"I pay close attention, remember love," he said giving her a cheeky wink. He wasn't joking with that statement. Once he figured out she liked something he used that to his full advantage, usually with completely devastating accuracy. Shaking her head with a smile on her face she drank some more coffee as they walked outside to the car.

"Maybe I should be paying for some of your gasoline, you're carting me around and all." she said when they were pulling away from the hotel. "This thing probably guzzles it."

He sent her a completely male, insulted expression. "Yer not paying for the petrol in me car Caitlyn."

Thinking about it she realized he had paid for every single meal they had eaten together. "I just don't know that its fair of me, I'm the one who planned on paying for this vacation. You kind of stumbled into it."

"Way I was raised, a man pays for his woman when he takes her out on a date. I'd be filling the tank anyway, so that's neither here nor there," he said with a shake of his head.

"Just don't try and pay my hotel bill, and we'll call it even then," she said laying her hand on top of where his was resting between them on the center console. Understanding all about male pride thanks to being outnumbered by them at home she wisely let it go. There weren't that many cars on the road at this ungodly hour of the morning, so he didn't have to fight traffic as they left the city. Caitlyn tried to pay attention to the road signs as they passed to figure out where it was they were heading, but gave up about twenty minutes into the ride because she was enjoying it too much. "Nol, got any music?" She asked him.

He smiled with a little insecure half laugh. "I dunno, whatcha want?"

"Something that you like."

"Oooo, good one. A person's taste in music tells ye a hell of a lot about them," he answered. Letting go of her hand he pulled his phone out of his pocket. "This is me driving playlist." He said turning the volume up, having synced it with the Bluetooth in his car. The first song playing was *Take It Easy* by The Eagles. He glanced over at her to gauge her reaction, but she was smiling, her head already bopping along to the beat.

"I love this song. Everyone loves *Hotel California*, but this one is my absolute favorite by them." He let out the breath he must have been holding in with a soft whoosh and started singing quietly along. He had a nice voice, and thankfully he knew all the words. Nothing was more annoying than someone who sang along but didn't actually know the words, so they just made random noises. It wasn't long before she was joining in, her voice mingling softly with his. Caitlyn knew she wouldn't wow anyone with her voice, but she could carry a tune easily enough.

Nolan looked over at her as the song was ending, a strange look in his eyes, and a giant grin on his face "Love, ye suit me right down to da fuckin' ground." The next song up was Bruce Springsteen's *Dancing in The Dark*, and grinning from ear to ear she figured this ride might end up being the best idea ever.

They stopped at a cafe in a small village outside of Athlone after the sun was up to have some breakfast. They had been driving for a while at this point and it was nice to get out in the fresh air. Sitting at the table in the early morning sunshine Caitlyn couldn't help but stare at Nolan. His brunette hair shone in the light, shot through with tones varying from light gold to deep bronze. He was a man always comfortable in his own skin, and that ease seemed to radiate off him. The memories she was making, and experiences she was racking up with him didn't seem like they would even be possible with another man. She found herself wondering what had made him so self-possessed and sure of who he was already at only twenty-five. Maybe he was one of those rare people who always knew exactly who they were, and what they were meant to do with their lives? After all, she had always loved books, and that love had thrown her naturally into writing them.

"Want to wander about, or are ye keen to find out where I'm taking ye?" Nolan asked as they finished up their breakfast.

Looking around her thinking she would be happy absolutely anywhere in this lovely country, as long as she was next to him she stood up with a smile. "Let's go."

"OK, me lady is mad up for it," he laughed hooking his arm around her as they walked back to his rover.

He asked her about the boys back in the car, and she told him all about her sons staring with varying degrees of awe at the scenery rolling past the windows. Nolan was surprised to learn that they played soccer instead of American football, telling her about how he had played all throughout school while he was growing up. She asked him if he had ever been to the states, and he said he had done a fair bit of traveling here and there including some in the states. She told him all about the last author signing event she went to, and how much fun that had been. After the day spent sitting behind a table meeting a bunch of her readers they had all gone out for drinks and partied the night away. Caitlyn pulled her phone out and showed him pictures of the boys. Wyatt all serious sitting behind the wheel ready for drivers training, Mason grinning at her covered in mud after the last soccer game of the season. No matter how many pictures she showed him he never looked bored.

Completely distracted by the pictures, and stories behind them, when the rover turned into a car park Caitlyn looked around and realized where it was he had brought her. "Nolan! Oh my God! Do you know where we are?" she exclaimed, her voice squeaking with all her excitement.

"I sure as hell hope so, as I drove us here after all," he said pulling her into a quick laughing kiss. Caitlyn jumped out of the car before Nolan had a chance to come around and open her door. Closing her eyes a moment she took in a big breath of the sea air, tasting the salt. When she finally opened her eyes, Nolan was holding out her jacket, the happiness etched clearly on his face. The wind coming off the Atlantic Ocean was a bit cooler here. She pulled on the jacket, her nerves practically humming with all the excitement coursing through her veins. Nolan put on a gray jacket over the black shirt he was wearing and added the navy ball cap he wore to the zoo yesterday. Hand in hand they walked away from the car.

The Cliffs of Moher are without a doubt one of the most photographed locations in all of Ireland for a good reason. Millions of years old, rising some five hundred feet above the crashing waves below, there was a thrumming power running underneath her feet. Imagining all the people who had walked this exact path over the rugged ground since the dawn of time had her hand shaking within Nolan's grip. Seeming to understand she wasn't scared, just moved beyond words he rubbed his thumb knowingly across her knuckles. Blocking out the sound of people talking around her Caitlyn focused on the sound of the sea birds calling out to each other in the air, waves thundering as the met they solid rock face, grass rustling in the breeze, the rest just faded away. Looking out across the beauty in front of her she could barely breathe.

It was a clear day, and you could see for miles out to sea. Glancing over at Nolan she found him staring at her, not at the stunning vista spread before them. "Even if I live to be a hundred and five, I'll never forget this moment. You standing there with strands of yer beautiful hair dancing in the breeze, and eyes shining like the midday sky. Jesus, Caitlyn." He leaned down and kissed her, the emotions crashing back and forth between them. He held her face in his hands, his thumbs stroking her cheeks and she knew what he was telling her with his eyes. Laying her head on his chest she took a moment soaking it in.

An older couple, their hair long since gone to white walked up to them, no doubt having witnessed their passionate kiss. The man turned to Nolan and asked. "Would you like me to take a picture of you and your girl, son?"

"I'd be a sight grateful for that," he said pulling his phone out and unlocking it before handing it over to the man. Nolan reached up and snatched the hat off his head, pulling Caitlyn up close to him, wrapping his arms tight around her.

The nice man backed away a few feet before pointing the phone at them. Looking over at his wife she nodded her head and said, "Cheese!" He walked the phone back to them as Nolan put the cap back on his head and took it.

"Thank you, shall we take one of you guys?" Caitlyn asked. The woman handed Caitlyn a digital camera and took a minute posing with her husband. Giving them the countdown she always used with her sons she said, "One, two, three, cheese!" Checking the screen to make sure it turned out she smiled and walked it back over to the nice couple. They thanked her walking away talking about what a nice young couple they were.

The two of them wandered around for hours, Caitlyn taking pictures of every single thing. At least a dozen of the view out over the sea, more of the cliffs themselves. She managed to snap a couple of Nolan while he was unawares. She liked those ones the best, when he was completely natural. She got a few silly faced selfies with him, but her favorite was the one with him standing behind her, his head tipped down against hers. They both had giant grins on their faces, and the water glittered prettily out behind them.

When they left Nolan made a bit of a detour and drove them into Limerick. He showed her the gloriously medieval St. Mary's Cathedral, and they ate a simple dinner of fish and chips while walking along the legendary River Shannon as the sun went slowly down. "Today was perfect Nol, thank you so much," she told him once they were back in his rover heading east towards Dublin.

"I didn't want ye to miss out on the cliffs. I'm sure they were on yer plans before I happened along," he said bringing their joined hands to his mouth and kissing her knuckles.

"My list was a mile long. I never would have gotten to see everything on it and still had time to breathe. I've loved everything I've seen here, but if I spent the rest of my stay up in that hotel room with you, I would have no regrets," she said with all honesty.

"That's mental, that. But I'm glad to hear it," he said to her in the dark car. They turned the music on lower this time, until it was just soft noise playing in the background. The day felt so big that neither of them said much, lost happily inside of themselves for most of the two-hour drive back.

It was late when they walked into the hotel

room. Caitlyn set her purse down and tossed her coat on top of it. Kicking off her shoes she flopped herself down onto the couch. Nolan was in the bathroom, and as he walked out she heard the rushing sound of water. "Come take a bath with me love." He said pulling off his shoes. Standing up off the couch Caitlyn pulled her mint green shirt up over her head, tossing it, not caring where it landed. Pulling her worn jeans off her hips and stepping out of them she walked into the bathroom, with Nolan trailing behind her.

The water was already halfway up the sides of the giant tub, tendrils of steam rising into the air. Standing behind her Nolan unsnapped Caitlyn's bra, pulling it slowly off. His hands immediately reaching around to cup her breasts, thumbs sliding teasingly across her nipples. She bent over pushing her panties down and rubbing her ass suggestively against his growing erection. Taking one hand away from her he shoved his boxers down and stepped out of them up into the tub, bringing her along. The water wasn't quite as hot as she would have made it, but it was damn close. Nolan sat down and pulled Caitlyn in front of him, her back pressing up against his chest. The water relaxed her after the long day, and she pulled the clip out of her hair before leaning her head back onto him. He peppered lingering kisses along her shoulder as his hands glided slowly over her body, igniting a slow, steady burn. When he finally reached a hand down between her legs she sighed in relief. His fingers slowly circled her clit, while his other hand gently rolled her nipple. Opening her legs invitingly wider in the water she moaned. He was whispering in her ear, it was so low she couldn't be sure, but she thought he was speaking in Gaelic. But her body was climbing, and she couldn't hold onto a single thought to ask him what he was saying. Gasping she reached down and held his hand to her as she came. Nolan's fingers stilled as she shuddered against his hand.

He stood up in the water a minute, stretching a condom over himself. One he sat back down she turned around and running her fingers up into his hair kissed him. She may not have known what he was whispering to her, but she knew that it had meant a lot to him. He pulled her down onto his dick, as she told him everything with her mouth that words couldn't explain. His hands gripped her hips as she rode him with exquisite slowness, barely rippling the water. Lost in the way his body felt inside of her she didn't even notice the water cooling around them. Nolan was trembling underneath her when she finally broke apart around him. The first rumbling quakes of her body gripping his tightly. His hands snaked their way up into her hair holding her to him as his mouth devoured her, his hips bucked his own orgasm up into her.

They stayed like that in the water kissing even

after their bodies were sated. He reached down and hit drain releasing the cold water around them. Standing up Nolan lifted Caitlyn carefully out of the tub and set her down on the rug. Grabbing a fluffy towel off the rack he gently dried her off, before running it over his own wet body. Taking her hand, he led them out of the bathroom towards the waiting bed.

# Chapter Twelve

The sound of Nolan talking quietly off in the distance pulled Caitlyn from a deep sleep. Slowly raising an eyelid, she saw the room was already bright with the day. He was sitting on the far side of the room in his boxer shorts on the couch, hair a beautiful, sleepy mess, with his phone up to his ear. She could tell by the way he was still keeping his voice down low he hadn't noticed that she was awake yet.

"I can see it in her eyes, yeah it's obvious. Mum, if ye coulda saw her face, ye'd understand. Her eyes say everything she's thinkin', damn but they're gorgeous. No, she won't even let me come close to bringing it up. I'll come 'round for tea once she's off to da states. I dunno, its gonna fuckin' hurt, I can tell ye that. No, no I'm sure. I know, I love ya. Bye, Mum." Caitlyn watched his profile as he talked. The emotions playing across his face told her more about the conversation that the bits and pieces she was catching. Nolan was really close to his mother, probably confessed all his problems to her, but she was getting the impression he hadn't mentioned this to her yet. He sat there staring at his phone looking like he wasn't seeing it, for a few minutes before thankfully getting up and walking into the bathroom. She was starting to feel like a creeper pretending to still be asleep. The thundering sound of the shower turning on echoed through the room.

Caitlyn was sitting at the desk writing to her sons when Nolan walked out with a towel wrapped carelessly around his hips, hair still dripping wetly down his shoulders. "Good morning. I heard the shower start, so I figured while I wait my turn I should send my boys all the cool pictures from the cliffs yesterday."

"Ye could've joined me love," he leaned down and laid a sweet kiss on her temple before walking away to get dressed.

"I'll keep that in mind for next time," she said while she typed. Transferring the pictures from her phone onto the laptop, she put all the ones of Nolan into their own folder labeling it 'N.' She was staring at the one from yesterday, with his head resting on hers when he walked back over.

"That's a good one, that." He rubbed his hands over her shoulders, fingers massaging the muscles. He was a man who gave his affections freely, always touching her.

"Yeah, it really is. They all are, have you ever even taken a bad picture in your life Nolan?" she joked.

"A time or two I'd guess," he said pulling

abruptly away and tucking his hands down in his pockets. "I was gonna send some clothes out to be washed, if ye'd gather up yers I can take care of that while ye take a shower."

"Uh, yeah, thanks. I've been putting everything in the bag the hotel provided for that, it's in the bottom of the closet. Let me make sure I didn't forget anything," she said standing up to scan the room, thinking something she said had hit on a nerve. Nolan didn't look mad, but something had closed down in his whole demeanor. He didn't say much as he grabbed the bag out of the closet, and with a little wave walked out of the room.

Caitlyn stood under the hot spray wondering what had happened. Maybe he was insecure about his picture being taken? But he had posed happily for it. No, he had even said he liked how the picture looked. Maybe what she said reminded him of something that someone had said to hurt him before? She couldn't even apologize, since he didn't seem upset. Just shut down, pulled back from her. It left a loneliness deep inside of Caitlyn that she knew was only just hinting at how she was going to feel when this was all over in a few short days. Stepping out of the shower she did her usual routine mindlessly on autopilot. She was dressed for the day in a fitted white t-shirt, and dark rinse cropped skinny jeans. She had cuff bracelet with turquoise stones in a pretty design, and a pair of matching turquoise dangles hanging down from her ears. Her hair was down and drying in wild curls all over the place. The weather looked like it wasn't sure yet if it was going to rain but wasn't all the way sunny either. She was stepping into the cute ballet flats when Nolan walked back into the room.

Watching his eyes closely she said, "Thanks Nol, I appreciate it. I've been meaning to get around to that before I run out of clean clothes."

"Mmmm, and that would be such a tragedy, spending the whole day naked with ye." He sent her a cheeky grin. Whatever had been bothering him was gone now, her charmingly easy Nolan was back. The dull aching tension in her chest slipped away.

Walking over and wrapping her arms around him she laid her head against him, inhaling his familiar scent. Warm, and slightly spicy. Locking it deep within her mind. "I don't want to be a tourist today," she said into his chest.

"Oh, so yer a local bird now? Well beautiful Caitlyn from Dublin, whatcha wanna do today?" Nolan said his hand stroking a lazy pattern on her back.

"Let's go to the movies!" she said feeling inspired.

"The cinema, yeah, we could catch a picture. I'll even share me popcorn with ye for a kiss," he said playfully, as his fingers tickled into the sides of her rib cage. Caitlyn squirmed in his arms and laughed full on, head tipping back before Nolan leaned down and kissed her. They decided to walk, so Caitlyn grabbed a thin cherry popsicle red cardigan before heading out.

They had all day in front of them, and soaking up the moments felt like the right thing to do as wandered the streets of Dublin. In no hurry they made their way slowly to the cinema, as Nolan had called it. Deciding between the silly frat boy comedy, the sappy romantic comedy, the explosion heavy action, or the zombie horror movie was surprisingly easy. Caitlyn wasn't in the mood to watch people pretend to fall in love when her feelings were swimming just barely under the surface. The longer she spent with Nolan, the harder it was not to tell him how much he was coming to mean to her. Remembering he said he loved scary movies she voted for the zombie flick, and he was all too happy to agree with her.

Nolan paid for their tickets, and they got two drinks and a large popcorn to share. Like her, he preferred to sit way in the back, and since it was only midday, the theater wasn't overly crowded. Setting their drinks in the outer cup holders, Nolan lifted up the arm rest between them, and wrapped his arm around Caitlyn, pulling her full against his side. "No need to be scared, I'd never let anything happen to ye," he whispered in her ear as the lights went down. Their giant popcorn was completely gone within the first half hour, which was a good thing because that's about the time things in the film started getting intense. Caitlyn wasn't sure how much popcorn she could have eaten watching the zombies rip savagely into people and gobble down their organs.

One scene where a small group of people were fighting off a dozen of the hungry zombies had her burrowing her face into Nolan. He pulled her even closer and whispered when that part was over, and she could open her eyes again. He hadn't laughed at her or made her feel like a baby for getting freaked out. He just held her and let her know when it had passed. This man was a serious treasure, and she was almost pissed off at the fates for dropping him all the way on the other side of the world from her. But she had to admit he would be missing some of that appealing charm without that irresistible Irish accent. It was such a part of Nolan, that she couldn't even picture him without it. She was laughing thinking about him with her own accent as they walked out of the movies.

"What?" he asked with a confused little laugh of his own.

"I was thinking what it would have been like if you were from my neck of the woods. Its hard to imagine you without that sexy accent though," she shared, laughing again looking up at him.

"Oh, I can sound like I'm from wherever you

want me to, babe," he said in a completely flawless American accent with a wink.

"Holy shit!" she said stopping and staring up at him with a dumbstruck look on her face. He laughed, raised an eyebrow at her, and proceeded to knock her the rest of the way on her ass. He could do an Australian, Spanish, British, Scottish, and Russian one as well. All she could do was stand there shaking her head in disbelief. "That's fucking incredible! How are you so good at that?" she asked completely impressed.

"Always have been, really. It just comes naturally to me," he said back to his natural Irish accent. "I used to bug the hell outta me Mum with it growing up," he admitted with a shrug.

Thinking of the multitude of ways her own sons found to get under her skin she said knowingly, "Oh, I just bet you did."

He linked hands with her as they started walking again. They wandered into a few random shops. The kind most tourists passed right by and didn't even notice, but people who lived here loved. In one while he used the toilet, she saw a navy newsboy flat cap that she knew would look awesome on Nolan. She quickly brought it up to the counter and bought it before he came back out. As they left the shop he didn't ask her what she bought, and she figured he assumed it was some trinket for herself.

They passed a few restaurants, their scents teasing the air, and he asked her what she was in the mood to eat for dinner.

"Remember Nol, I'm a local gal, I want dinner in our favorite pub tonight," she said with a wink.

"C'mon then," he said, his eyes twinkling with humor he swung their hands happily between them.

When they walked into the pub Sean called out a booming greeting. "Heya Caitlyn, still bummin' around with this lad, eh? Nolan, whats the craic?" Caitlyn saw Tom was sitting on his designated stool, and she made a beeline right up to him and hugged him.

"Tom! I'm so glad we didn't miss you. When I came in here the other night you had already left."

"Aren't you a sight? Sean mentioned our boy Nolan here had caught yer fancy," he said patting her back comfortingly as he hugged her back. Nolan chatted away with Sean, and she filled Tom in on everything she had seen. Pulling out her phone she showed him a dozen different pictures when Danny the waiter from the other night came up.

"Give it here now, I'll take yer picture." He held out his hand for her phone.

Looking over to see Nolan was grinning from ear to ear she said, "We have to get Sean and Keely in it too." Sean yelled loudly for his wife, who walked out looking happily annoyed.

"Caitlyn wants her photo with the lot of us. God only knows why," Sean laughed pulling his wife in close and leaning them into the picture.

"Well, hold on Danny, I'm after a shot too," she said handing him her phone. They all pulled in tight, faces alight with happiness for a second picture.

"Anyone else?" he asked cheekily as he handed Keely her phone back before heading off to wait on his tables.

"Smells like bangers and mash tonight Keely," Nolan said leaning across the bar to flirt shamelessly with Keely.

"It is, and if ye leave me be I'll send some out for ye. Caitlyn, are ye wanting some too?" she asked her after sending a wink at Nolan and patting his cheek affectionately.

"Absolutely, I wouldn't miss out on that after having your stew," Caitlyn said as Sean set pints of Guinness down in front of her and Nolan. Keely nodded and walked back into the kitchen through the swinging door.

Once again, the food didn't disappoint, it was comforting and delicious. Keely sure had a way. Tom said his goodbyes after their first pints were gone, heading on home to his wife waiting there. Sean kept a steady supply of drinks in front of them, as they chatted and laughed with the regulars and flirted with each other. The room was swaying pleasantly by the time they climbed off their stools and headed out of the loud comfortable pub into the dim night.

"Nol, I think I might be a little drunk," Caitlyn whispered to him as they walked arm in arm back to the hotel.

"Oh, we're right pissed, love. Ye wanted to be a local, remember." His accent was even thicker with the help of all the Guinness.

"Pissed? I'm not mad," Caitlyn said quite confused.

"It means drunk here in Ireland baby," he said as they walked through the lobby towards the elevator, Caitlyn swinging the bag with his hat tucked safely inside. They made their way into the room, after a few failed attempts with the key card. Caitlyn threw her stuff down in a heap, and pulled herself up kissing him. It started out as a simple kiss, but the heat whooshed up, quickly engulfing them both. Moaning into her mouth Nolan yanked her shirt up over her head. Caught up in the urgency Caitlyn followed his lead, tearing clothes off him as fast as she could. His hands were racing hotly all over her body, as he backed them clumsily toward the bed. Touching her everywhere she needed, but still not easing the starving ache inside. The backs of her legs hit the bed, and without thinking she turned around bending down, pressing her breasts into the soft white comforter.

Nolan leaned down low over her kissing a scorching line down her spine. Caitlyn lifted her ass towards him, in desperate unspoken invitation. Grabbing her hips, fingers digging in, he held her tight as he swung his hips forward burying his dick deep inside of her. Caitlyn let out a thankful moan, happy to finally have him exactly where she wanted him. Nolan pumped into her pussy in a steadily devastating rhythm. Driving them both madly towards the end, as she cried out encouragingly with every stroke. She could hear his labored breathing, as her body clenched deliciously around his and she flew over the edge screaming out her orgasm. Nolan stuttered twice before burying himself deeply, his dick twitching hotly.

Caitlyn leaned there against the foot of the bed feeling wonderfully boneless, having lost all the feeling in her legs. Nolan helped her up into the bed and they collapsed completely spent in each other's arms, falling asleep.

# Chapter Thirteen

Her head was pounding mercilessly before she even opened her eyes, and when she did manage to peel them open the sunlight all but scorched her retinas, even as watery as it was outside. Moaning Caitlyn rolled over in Nolan's arms burying her face in the ready comfort of his chest. His answering grumble told her he was feeling just as miserable as she was.

"I'm never drinking again. Ever. Just thinking about drinking makes me wanna throw up," she said, her voice scratchy in her dry throat.

"Bloody, fucking hangovers. Nature's way of kicking ye in the arse for having fun," Nolan said, his voice cracking. "Need food, and water. It'll help, trust me."

"Deal with a lot of hangovers, do you?" Caitlyn asked as Nolan bravely climbed out of the bed.

"I'm Irish, love," he said as if that explained everything, while he walked over to the phone and ordered them some breakfast. None of it sounding remotely appetizing to her. After he hung up the phone, he pulled some gray workout shorts out of the dresser drawer and stepped into them. Caitlyn decided she may never move again in the whole of her entire life, as she laid there feeling like death warmed over. Nolan sat down on the couch. "If I crawl back in that bed with you I'm not gettin back up." The knock on the door announcing the arrival of their food came a short time later. Nolan lumbered over to the door and instead of letting the waiter push the food cart in he thanked the man and wheeled it into the room himself. Caitlyn thought that was probably a good idea since she was still naked and sprawled across the expansive bed.

The smell of food hit her then, and instead of turning her stomach like she expected it to it kind of smelled surprisingly good. Crawling out of bed with sloth like speed she snagged the shirt Nolan had worn the night before and pulled it over her head. It hit her mid-thigh, covering everything as long as she didn't move around much, which was just fine by her. Plopping ungracefully down on the couch she watched Nolan lay out their food. He ordered them each tall glasses of orange juice and waters. Feeling like she had traveled the vast desert and half of it was still lingering in her mouth she grabbed the water gulping it down in big, grateful swallows. There was toast, and scrambled eggs. Simple, easy, and wouldn't be too terrible if it happened to come back up later. Nibbling on her toast she looked over at Nolan determinedly scooping eggs into his mouth like it had to be done, even if he didn't much like it. Laughing at the pair of them she said, "We're absolute messes this morning Nol."

He leaned over and kissed her temple, "Yer not a mess, just beautiful, and maybe a wee bit pale," he said with a wink. She wasn't brave enough to eat more than half a toast, and a few bites of the eggs, but the orange juice tasted like the nectar of the gods to her. They sat there for a while next to each other, her body curled into his larger one looking through yesterday's pictures on her phone.

Finally her bladder protesting its fullness had Caitlyn making her way into the bathroom. Glancing at her reflection in the mirror she winced. Mascara smudges under her bloodshot eyes, her hair looked like a demented bird had attempted to build a nest but was unable to tame it. If Nolan could see her looking this rough and still tell her she was beautiful he was either blind as all hell, or a complete goner over her. Sitting on the toilet she reached for the toilet paper after peeing. Glancing down she noticed there was something shiny on her thighs. Touching it tentatively with the tips of her fingertips it felt sticky. Standing up quickly in a panic she said, "No. No, no, no, NO! Nolan!" Her volume increasing from a shaky whisper to yelling out his name. He came rushing in the bathroom a bewildered look on his face.

"What's wrong, love?" he asked looking around

for the problem.

"Everything!" She pointed down at herself. "I'm all sticky. I'm pretty sure its cum, shit, shit, shit! Please tell me we remembered a condom last night!" she said, tears already welling up in her eyes.

Nolan stood there completely still for a few long seconds before slowly shaking his head back and forth. Ripping his shirt up and over her head Caitlyn stumbled into the shower turning the water on. Feeling completely stupid she scrubbed the stickiness off her thighs, knowing it didn't change a damn thing at this point. When she stepped out of the shower, she saw Nolan sitting on the floor, exactly where he had been standing. He must have just dropped like a stone there. His knees bent, head hanging low, hands in his hair. He reached a hand up and caught hers as she walked past him heading for her clothes.

"Caitlyn I'm so sorry, I wasn't thinking. I've never in me whole fucking life forgotten to wear protection, ever. I'm clean, I get meself tested regularly." His eyes looked like the light shining up from a frozen lake, and even now she was struck by how beautiful he was. "Are ye on the pill?" he asked her, a glimmer of hope in his voice.

"Nope. I didn't need to be. You were the first man since my ex-husband. It's not like I expected to come over here and stumble into a steamy affair Nolan," she said, her voice shaking with the tears she was trying to hold back from falling.

"Okay, okay... No matter what happens, I'm yer man, and I've got ye," he said. She knew he meant that if she ended up pregnant, he would stand by her. There was no shred of doubt in his eyes, plenty of apology, a little regret, but no doubt. He would one hundred percent, without a doubt change his entire life because of one night of irresponsible sex. He was the best kind of man, and knowing that she pulled her hand gently out of his.

"I'm going to go for a walk. I'm not mad at you, Nolan. I didn't think about it either. I just need some time alone." She pulled on a soft pair of black leggings, white tank top, and the long gray cardigan. Grabbing her purse she walked out of the room, her hair still hanging wetly down her back.

Caitlyn walked aimlessly for a while, lost in her own thoughts racing through her head. Emotionally exhausted, she sat down on a bench in the park and hugged her knees up to her chest as tears streaked slowly down her face. How could she have been so stupid? She wasn't young and naive anymore. At thirty-five years old, with two teenage sons she knew better, dammit. And the look on Nolan's face, she just couldn't do it. This was not going to be the story of his life. Dragging him away from his country, ruining his whole life. He might think he was doing the right thing now, but eventually he would come to resent her, she was sure of it. The thought of Nolan ever looking at her like she was everything wrong in his life would kill her. Pulling out her phone, Caitlyn made up her mind.

The sun was going down by the time she made it back to the hotel. Her tears having finally stopped once her decision was made. She found Nolan pacing the room when she walked in. He was still in the athletic shorts from earlier, but he had added a shirt sometime during the day. The lost look on his face told her the day had been a long one for him too. Walking up to him she wrapped her arms around his waist, and laid her head on his chest, listening to the soft thumping of his heart.

"I don't want to talk about it, please. We don't know for sure there is even anything to discuss right now. Can we worry about all of that later? Just be with me tonight Nolan, please," she whispered. "I need that."

"Anything for ye, my love," he said softly back. She tipped up her face, meeting his lips as his head came down. Reaching up into his hair she held him to her as she poured everything she felt inside of her soul into him. Walking him backwards she led them towards the giant four poster bed. When he was standing next to it she slid her hands up into his shirt lifting it up and off of him. Pulling down his shorts she pushed him gently back onto the bed. As he climbed up she carefully took her own clothes off, setting them in a little pile on the floor. Kneeling next to him on the bed she leaned over kissing him. Running her hands along his body she kissed a path slowly down low, and lower until she could see his chest heaving with anticipation.

Taking her time, she licked up one side of his dick, and down the other. Tracing the veins with her tongue before she swirled it around the swollen head, just like she knew he liked. His toes were curling by the time she finally took him in her mouth and sucked him deep. When she felt him swell even bigger in her mouth, she quickened her slow pace and cupped his balls gently in her hand. Nolan gripped her hair and letting out a low groan came in hot spurts down the back of Caitlyn's throat. She swallowed it all down, slowly sucking him clean before lifting her head.

Laying next to him she ran her hands in lazy patterns on his chest. When he made to pull her up to his face and return the favor, she leaned down and licked along his shoulder instead. It didn't take long before her mouth tracing patterns all over his shoulders and chest had his dick growing hard again. Grabbing a condom, she told him to lay back and let her put it on him. She took her time rolling it down his length slowly, teasing him. Throwing a leg over his hips she leaned down, her hair creating a red curtain around their faces, blocking out the rest of the world.

Sliding down his dick slowly, and inch at a time she watched his eyes as his body filled hers. Stealing pieces of his heart she rode him exquisitely slow. Making love to him for hours, every time she felt him getting close, she slowed down easing him off the edge. Caitlyn had lost count of how many times her own body trembled and bucked on top of his when he finally couldn't take any more. As she arched way back, her long hair tickling the top of his thighs his fingers dug into her hips holding her in place. As she cried out her orgasm, she could feel him twitching deep inside of her, finally finding his own release. Leaning down she kissed his lips rocking her hips softly, milking every bit of pleasure out of their orgasms.

Finally, she climbed off him, and he stumbled into the bathroom and took care of the condom. Nolan climbed back into bed, and she pressed up close to his side, wrapping her arm around his middle. "Caitlyn, it's gonna be okay," he said his fingers drifting into her hair. Not having the words to say to him, she nodded her head and counted his heartbeats as his breathing deepened. Nolan drifted off into a deep, exhausted sleep.

Caitlyn eased slowly out of the bed, feeling like she was ripping the skin away from her body with every inch between them. Standing there she almost gave in and crawled back next to him, but instead she forced herself to turn away. Picking the clothes up from the pile she made earlier she pulled them on. Walking quietly around the room she packed her suitcases, afraid he would wake up any moment. Pulling out her purse she ripped the note, out of her always present notebook, she had written him in the park hours before. She set it down on the desk, setting the navy-blue flat cap she had bought him the day before next to it. Unable to help herself she tiptoed back over to him, smoothed his soft brown hair off his forehead and laid a soft kiss there.

Grabbing all her luggage she walked out of the room while she still could. The whole time she was waiting by the elevator she stared down at her room door willing it to burst open, and Nolan to come running out stopping her from leaving. She was still staring at the door when the elevator doors closed, stealing it from her sight. As the floors dinged by down to the lobby there didn't seem to be enough air, and she struggled to drag breaths into her lungs. Handing the man at the front desk her key card with a shaking hand she asked for a delayed check out, letting him know that although her train left soon, her friend needed the room until tomorrow morning. He must see all kinds of strange things in this business, so he just nodded, passed paperwork over to her to sign, and wished her safe travels to her destination.

The valet called a taxi for her, and she sat

silently numb the whole ride to the train station. It wasn't until Caitlyn was sitting on the train heading north that the tears streaked hotly down her face in a never-ending stream.

# Chapter Fourteen

*Nolan,*

*The time I've shared with you has gone a ways past memorable, it's been completely unforgettable. I've found more happiness in your arms than I have ever known before. Thank you for showing me your country, and your beautiful heart. My only regret is that I have to say goodbye to you, sooner than I had planned, and that I know it's going to hurt you. I'm so sorry. I know you would give up everything here if I asked you to, but how could I do that to you? I would never be able to forgive myself for costing you that. You are a treasure, and you deserve so much more. Remember I'm leaving my heart there with you. Take care of it please.*

*Caitlyn*

# Chapter Fifteen

It was still dark outside when Caitlyn stepped off the train in Belfast, Northern Ireland. She had tried, while crying on the park bench in Dublin, to switch her flight home to something sooner, but was unable to. Knowing that if she stayed in Dublin she wasn't going to be able to make herself stay away from Nolan, even though she knew she should. She just wasn't strong enough for that. So after hanging up with the airline, she booked a hotel, and bought a train ticket up to Belfast. Telling herself it was better this way. After all, how could she explain to her family back home she abruptly cut her trip short, the trip she had spent a lifetime wanting to take. No, that wasn't a conversation she planned on having. *'So kids, I fell in love with a handsome man I met in a pub. Everything was going great until we idiotically forgot to use a condom, and it burst my stupidly happy bubble, making me realize I could be ruining his life, so I ran away from him in the middle of the night.'* Yeah, right.

The sun was just beginning to lighten the sky when she walked into the hotel. Thinking it was a real shame all the splendor of the place was wasted on her at the moment she walked into the lobby. She barely managed to hold it together until she was up in her room, with the door closed behind her. Her luggage still sitting stacked where the porter had set it, she crumpled to a heap on the floor. She curled into a ball and started sobbing. The wild pain filled, keening sounds ripped up from the very depths of her soul. Nothing had ever hurt Caitlyn this much, not even the dissolution of her marriage. Thinking about Nolan waking up alone, imagining his face when he realized she was gone, tore through her bringing another round of sobs wracking her body. She cried for hours, until she finally sobbed herself to sleep, still on the floor barely inside the room.

She dreamed of Nolan, running after her, and no matter how much she tried to turn around or stop, her feet just kept pounding the pavement sending her further and further away from him. His voice so full of pain echoed out as he yelled her name, begging and pleading with her to come back. Waking up with a start she sat up on the floor. Reaching a hand up she felt the tears already racing down her cheeks. Looking around she saw the late afternoon sun burning in the sky outside of her window. Crawling to her luggage she pulled her laptop out and sat back down, leaning with her back against the wall. Turning it on she let her sons know she was up in Belfast now, and the name of the hotel she was staying in. There was no need to worry them should they try and get a hold of her at The Westbury back in Dublin. Logging back out of her email account she turned off her computer and set it down next to her.

She stared numbly out the window her mind replaying every moment spent with Nolan over and over again on a heart crushing loop. She meant what she had said to him. No matter how much pain she was feeling right now, she would never regret him. Hugging her knees to her chest, she laid her face down on them and watched the light fade from the room through the watery veil of her tears. Sometime later when there seemed to be no tears left inside of her she trudged woodenly to the bed and laid down, still fully clothed. Curling herself into a tight ball she wondered what Nolan was doing. Knowing that each tear that fell from his beautiful ocean eyes was her fault. She hoped selfishly that he didn't feel as much for her as she did for him, if it saved him from the pain she was feeling. It was hours before she drifted to sleep feeling cold without Nolan's warmth pressed against her body.

She dreamed of him again. He was standing out on the cliffs, his voice raw, screaming her name out to the open sea. Bringing his hands up he clenched desperately at his hair and fell to his knees in the grass, tears flowing unheeded down his face. Caitlyn tried to take him in her arms to offer some comfort to him, but her hands passed right through his body. She sat there next to him crying as she watched him suffer unable to do a damn thing to make it better.

Caitlyn woke up with the covers tangled all around her, from restlessly tossing and turning no doubt. The dream had a fresh surge of guilt bubbling up to the surface. She laid in the bed, her face pressed into the pillow screaming, her tears soaking into it. When the tears ran dry once more she wandered into the bathroom. Seeing her reflection in the mirror she knew it was a good thing she hadn't been able to get home sooner. Even she could see the pain etched onto her face, the hollows under her red-rimmed eyes, her red hair hanging in limp tangles all over the place. She surely would have terrified her sons if they saw her like this. How had she managed to keep it together throughout her entire divorce, but losing a man she had in her life for only a week was bringing her to the lowest of lows?

Suddenly feeling pissed off at herself for wallowing when it was her fault in the first place she turned the shower on. Walking back out she rummaged angrily through her suitcase until she found her bathroom stuff. Carrying it into the bathroom she took a much-needed shower ignoring the tears that fell mingling with the water down the drain. "How much can one person cry anyway? I don't have the right to these tears, dammit!" she yelled at herself. Thinking that since she had broken Nolan's heart, her own pain was the rightful punishment.

Stepping out of the shower she stood there, her hair dripping water everywhere staring into the mirror. There were still patches of red where Nolan's beard had rubbed against her sensitive skin as he made love to her. She still had a little hickey marking the side of one breast. Ripping the towel off her she threw it with an angry shriek at the mirror not wanting to look at herself anymore. Walking out of the bathroom she put on the first clothes she pulled out of her bag, not caring one bit what she looked like.

Sitting back in the bed she pulled her laptop onto her lap. Checking her email she saw there was one from her boys, and one from her ex-husband. She read the boys letter, and replied back, as cheerfully as she was able to. Taking a deep breath, she opened the one from Bryan. She expected him to be upset with her for changing her plans yet again. Instead, she was surprised by what he had to say. He told her to have fun and take some pictures of the Giant's Causeway for him since she was up in Northern Ireland. Not really planning on going out to see the area she realized that if she didn't everyone back home would wonder why she hadn't. Every other day of her vacation she had basically inundated them with pictures, they would definitely notice now if she didn't.

Pissed off at herself again she logged out and powered down her computer. Pulling on her sneakers she picked up her purse and begrudgingly left the room. Down in the lobby she asked if they could book her on a guided day trip tour to the causeway for the next day. Once that was settled, she headed out of the hotel.

Caitlyn wandered around the city for hours, taking pictures of everything, but not really seeing anything. A few times she thought she saw Nolan, but when she got closer they were always just strangers. Realizing she was probably freaking random men out rushing up to them like a pathetically deranged woman she made herself stop. After all, what the hell would she even say to Nolan? 'I'm sorry. I still live on the other side of the world. I still have to leave you no matter how much I love you.' Feeling like she had never been more alone in her whole life she walked back towards her hotel in the fading light. It was dark by the time she made it into her room, and she collapsed onto the bed, crying herself to sleep again.

The next morning feeling as bad as she looked she met the tour guide, and the rest of her group in the Belfast city center. She sat in the back of the crowded bus and stared out the window at county Antrim rolling past, struggling not to cry. Everyone could clearly tell she wasn't going to be worth talking to and thankfully left her alone, chatting among themselves. Getting out at the first stop she took pictures of the Causeway Coast, including one of the Scottish coast off in the distance since it was a clear day. When they stopped in the Dark Hedges, everyone but Caitlyn posed for pictures among the impressive trees. Deciding that crossing the Carrick-a-Rede rope bridge wasn't for her she sat quietly inside having tea with half of their group while the rest braved the walk. After that they finally made it to the Giants Causeway, and as beautiful as it was, all the amazing hexagonal rocks, and the stunning view, she just couldn't clear the haze of pain away enough to enjoy it. She found herself remembering standing in Nolan's arms at the Cliffs of Moher, as tears poured from her eyes. Unable to stop them she wished Nolan was here with her.

An older woman from their group walked over and without bothering to ask pulled Caitlyn into her arms, rubbing her back soothingly as she cried. Caitlyn laid her head on the woman's shoulder, her body shaking uncontrollably with her sobs. She let it all go, everything she had been struggling to hold in since leaving the hotel room that morning. "It will never be the same, but you will get over him honey," the lady said to her. Caitlyn pulled away to look questioningly into the kind brown eyes. "I know that look. Hollowed out face, lost eyes. Your heart is broken, and you can barely breathe through the pain. I'm not going to lie to you though dear, it won't all be alright. But it will get better than it is right now." She took a tissue out of her large purse and handed it over to Caitlyn to wipe her tears.

"Thank you. I guess I probably shouldn't have come today, it just all got to be too much," she admitted.

"Nonsense, you're trying to put the pieces back together, no shame in tears. The direction is what matters, moving forward, not the pace. I'm Gloria, you can sit with me on the bus, and if you cry the whole way back to Belfast I won't mind in the least. I've got a daughter your age, and I just couldn't let you cry alone like that."

"Caitlyn," she said gesturing to herself. "Thank you Gloria, I appreciate it, so much. Its been killing me trying to be strong," she admitted.

"It may feel that way right now, but someday it won't," Gloria said leading them back towards the bus.

"I left him. I shouldn't be such a mess," Caitlyn confessed guiltily.

"Oh, pish-posh! I'm sure you had your reasons, and they're probably good ones. But that doesn't mean you didn't love him. You gave him a part of yourself, walking away doesn't change that," Gloria said wisely patting Caitlyn's hand.

The ride back to Belfast was easier sitting next

to Gloria. She didn't expect Caitlyn to talk much, and filled the silence easily. She told her all about her daughter back home in Oklahoma, and all of the grandchildren she had there. Pulling a small photo album out of the large purse she showed her dozens of pictures. When their tour van arrived back in Belfast Caitlyn hugged Gloria and thanked her, knowing she wouldn't ever forget the kindness. Heading back to her hotel room Caitlyn decided that she wasn't going to pretend to be a tourist for the remaining two days in Belfast.

# Chapter Sixteen

Spending her time sitting up inside of her hotel room Caitlyn alternated between sobbing for long stretches, getting angry railing at herself, and sleeping in spurts. Every time she closed her eyes though, vivid dreams of Nolan assaulted her mind, and had her jerking awake crying again. It didn't even occur to her to eat most of the time, and when she did remember to order food, she spent most of the time staring at it while she poked it with her fork. Nothing looked good, and when she forced it down it felt like cement sitting heavily in her stomach. In a weak moment she called down to The Westbury in Dublin and asked the woman who answered if Nolan had checked out yet. She happily told Caitlyn that he had left the hotel a short time after she herself had. Misunderstanding her reasons for calling, the woman told her reassuringly there would be no surprise charges on her card, everything went as it should. Thanking her Caitlyn hung up the phone wondering if she had even made it to Belfast before Nolan woke up. Probably not, she decided, a fresh wave of guilt enveloping her again in its crushing weight.

Sitting on the messy bed in the dark room, her

hair sticking up in wild tufts she opened her laptop. Feeling raw she transferred the pictures she had taken that last night in the pub from her phone. Clicking on the folder that held all the pictures of Nolan she sat there watching a slideshow of them all pass slowly by. Touching his face on the screen as the images shuffled past, she wondered if she should delete them all. Realizing it wouldn't make her miss him any less, in fact stealing these moments from herself would probably have her hurting even worse. She sent her boys one last email letting them know she was about to set off on the long journey home, and she would text them from her cell phone when she landed.

Gathering up all her belongings, making herself walk the room twice to be sure she wasn't forgetting anything she stacked her bags on top of the large suitcase, grabbed her purse and wheeled everything out to the elevator. Caitlyn nodded her head at everything the clerk said as she signed the papers checking out, not really hearing any of it. She waited out front in the dim light of dawn for the taxi the hotel had called to take her to the train station. This was the last sunrise she would see in Ireland and realizing that tomorrow morning she would be waking up in her own bed filled her with a striking sense of loss. Once she was back home in Michigan Nolan would truly be forever out of her grasp. They hadn't thought to exchange phone numbers, or email addresses. Maybe they thought there was time, and there probably would have been if she hadn't left him. But what good would that do anyway? Calling each other would only prolong the inevitable. This break hurt, so much that standing upright was hard for her at times. But watching him drift away from her would be just as heartbreaking, maybe even more so with the hope fading away slowly.

Once she was sitting on the mostly empty train Caitlyn took the ear buds out of her purse, popped them in, and turning her music onto shuffle she willed it to dull the pain. As the miles flew past the window, bringing her closer to Dublin she found herself afraid. Would Nolan be at the airport? He knew what day she was supposed to head home, they had talked about it enough, although she couldn't recall telling him the exact time of her flight. Would he be standing there waiting for her? Could she walk onto that airplane while he watched her? As the train slowed to a stop in Dublin the weight that settled on her chest made breathing almost impossible. Making that final taxi ride from the train station to the airport had her anxiety ramping up to near panic levels. Unable to decide if she wanted Nolan to be waiting for her, or if she was hoping he wouldn't be there. Everything that flew past her window in the city reminded her of him. This city would always be Nolan's, he was intertwined so thoroughly into the very fabric of this place for her.

Walking inside the airport Caitlyn looked frantically around her. For one breathless moment she thought she saw Nolan, but it was only her sleep deprived imagination working overtime. Feeling both thankful and heartbroken that he wasn't actually waiting for her she passed through security and checked her bags. Sitting there with only her carry on and purse she stared unseeingly off into the distance. When they finally called for her flight, she stood up saying a silent goodbye to Ireland, and to Nolan, she walked with everyone else to board.  As the plane lifted off the ground Caitlyn felt the weight lift off her chest, leaving a pronounced emptiness in its wake that was just painful.

She spent most of the flight pretending to read a book. The words on the page held no magic for her, but she wasn't in the mood for conversation either. She only dozed off once, and this time when she dreamed of Nolan he was walking broodingly through a verdant field. His hands were tucked deep in his pockets and he walked with a steady pace. His eyes looked empty, but he wasn't crying or screaming her name into the breeze. Thinking as she woke up that maybe going home would help her forgive herself.

Caitlyn was one of the last to disembark when they landed. She took a few minutes in the bathroom to splash cold water on her face knowing how she must look. Hopefully, she wouldn't alarm her family when they saw her. Taking a deep breath, she headed out to get her bag. She found her Dad waiting for her, and she rushed into his waiting embrace.

"Caitlyn, honey! I'm so glad you're home!" he said squeezing her tight.

"I'm so glad to see you," she answered back breathing in his familiar and comforting scent.

"So tell me, how was it? I want to hear everything on the ride home," he said pulling back to look at her. "Cait, honey, are you alright?" He stared down at her, concern etched in his features.

"Yeah, Dad, I'll be OK. I sent the pictures to get printed up before I left, want to stop at the store and pick them up on the way?" she asked him while walking out to his waiting car. "Then you can see them all."

"We can do that, when are the boys coming home?" he asked settling behind the wheel.

"Not until tomorrow morning, but I texted them already letting them know I'm back stateside." Turning towards him in the seat she told him all about her adventures on autopilot. Careful to leave Nolan out. She told him about the stunning splendor of the country, rattled off cool facts she had learned from everywhere she had visited. After they picked up her pictures, they sat in the parking lot of the store looking through them all. He listened intently, asking questions about this or that along the way. He helped her carry all her bags inside the house. She had just given him the t-shirt she had bought for him at the Guinness Storehouse before he finally said, "I can see something is tearing you up inside. I don't know what it is, and I know you don't want to talk about it right now, but honey, when you do...I'm here. You know that, right?" he asked pulling her into a hug and patting her back.

"Thanks Dad, I know. I just can't... I can't talk about it. I need it locked away for now," she said in a small voice.

"I understand, believe me I do. Do you want me to stay with you for a while?" he asked her.

With the five-hour time difference, even after the long flight it was only late afternoon. "Nah, I'm going to unpack and wash all my clothes. Then probably run to the store and grab some food before the boys get here tomorrow since they're always half starved." He nodded his head at her, probably well aware she was hoping to hide behind the normalcy. Her dad knew her better than just about anyone else, but he wouldn't push, instead trusting her to come to him when she needed. Saying goodbye and thanking him for picking her up she waved as he pulled away.

Walking back into the house she sat down on the living room floor methodically pulling everything out of her bags. Setting aside the trinkets and souvenirs she carried all the clothes into the laundry room. Sorting by color she discovered she had one of Nolan's t-shirts. It was the one he had on that last night. It was probably in her pile of clothes and in her rush to grab everything she hadn't noticed. Standing there in front of the washing machine she held his shirt up to her face and sniffed deep. It still smelled like him, warm and spicy like making love in front of a fireplace. It looked really well worn, a light gray color with the word IRELAND in faded green across the chest. Setting it aside she tossed the last of the load in, added the liquid detergent, and started the washing machine. Carrying the shirt to her room she set it with careful reverence on her bed for later.

Taking care of everything and putting her suitcases in the back of her closet she grabbed her pad of paper and a pen, and  walked into the kitchen. Looking through her empty cupboards, refrigerator, and freezer she methodically made a list. Heading to the store she stocked up on everything they needed. Walking through the isles her mind three thousand miles away, Caitlyn zoned out. It was a good thing she knew the store like the back of her hand. Her sons wouldn't appreciate it if there wasn't any food in the house for them. Teenage boys could eat like nobody's business.

Back home when the groceries were put away, and her clean clothes stacked neatly in drawers or hanging in the closet Caitlyn finally let out the breath she had been holding. Pulling Nolan's t-shirt over her head she turned off the lights and climbed into bed. It wasn't as good as feeling his arms around her, but it was better than nothing. Laying in her bed, Caitlyn cried quietly, her tears soaking into the pillowcase.

The next morning, she was sitting on a stool at her kitchen island drinking coffee when her sons burst in. Their energy exploding into the quiet house. She barely had time to make it off her stool before Mason was crushing her to him in a fierce hug. "Missed you Mom!" he said loudly as if she wasn't in his arms.

"Missed you too baby," she said stroking a hand across his hair. Turning she reached for Wyatt pulling him into her other arm. He squeezed her tightly to him for a precious heartbeat before pulling away.

"So, what did ya get us?" he asked her.

"I set it in your rooms, go on take a look," she said barely getting the words out before they were dashing off.

"Hey Cait. You look tired," Bryan said finally walking over.

"Yeah, jet lag. I couldn't sleep very well last night either, with the time difference my body is all off kilter," she said with a shrug.

He nodded his head at her answer. "I've got some tickets to the baseball game this weekend. I know it's your weekend, but I was thinking the boys might want to come if that's alright with you," he asked.

"I don't mind Bryan, they're your sons all of the time not just every other weekend. Besides I've got to get going on the next book anyways," she told him.

"Right. I'll grab them Saturday afternoon then and leave it up to them if they want to stay over at my place after or come back here," he said. She nodded at him. He looked so different than Nolan, although the comparison wasn't a fair one since he was over a decade older. She couldn't help but wonder what Bryan would think if he had met Nolan. Big, tall all-American guy and the shorter, but devastatingly charming sexy Irishman. It was almost laughable, and completely ridiculous since they would never meet. Bryan called out a goodbye to their sons as he left.

It didn't take long to get settled into their summer routine. Caitlyn cried herself quietly to sleep every single night and was already writing when the boys woke up late each morning. They would all inevitably end up around the pool in the backyard soaking up the sunshine. Caitlyn sitting under the shade of the umbrella at the table typing away as Wyatt and Mason splashed around, their music blasting. When the boys were with their dad Caitlyn didn't have to pretend though, and she poured herself into her work, barely coming up for air. When she was writing the pain inside of her didn't scream so loudly, so she eased the ache the only way she knew how. About a week after she got home, she woke up one morning to the tell-tale blood of her period. Sitting on the floor of her shower as the water rained down on her blocking out the sound Caitlyn sobbed. A baby was a complication she definitely didn't need in her life right now, but it would have been Nolan's baby. A part of him, made out of the magic happiness they shared. She didn't realize how much that would have meant to her until she knew she wasn't pregnant. Now all she had of him were the pictures she couldn't make herself look at, and the shirt that didn't smell like him anymore after so many nights on her.

# Chapter Seventeen

June marched relentlessly on into July. Caitlyn spent her days lost in the words pouring out onto the page, and her nights suffocating beneath the heart ache and grief she let out when she was finally alone. If her sons noticed anything was wrong, they didn't ask her about it. She had finally put some of the pictures from her vacation in frames around the house. Some people decorated with art, big paintings on the walls. Caitlyn painted her home with snapshots and memories. Nolan wasn't in any of the pictures, but she saw him everywhere she looked. The picture she had up on the refrigerator of her smiling in the park next to the sculpture of Oscar Wilde, he was the one who took it. The stunning view of the Cliffs of Moher framed on her mantle in the family room, he had stood beside her as she snapped the picture.

She hosted a big cook out for the fourth of July every year, inviting all of their family and friends. Caitlyn made a real effort, wearing a pretty flowing floral tank top, and cuffed jean shorts, her hair flying wild and free. Her Dad happily manned the grill while the boys had a bunch of friends jumping in and out of the pool all day. She sat with a glass of wine telling the women gathered around the table all about her vacation. Conversation turned, as it usually did to everyone's love lives. With one cousin fast approaching her wedding day, another still single, and Caitlyn herself divorced, so single. They all talked about what they wanted to wear to the February wedding, before her Aunt Maura leaned in saying, "Maybe you'll meet a nice man there. You need to get back out there, deary. Life didn't end when your marriage did."

"I know that Aunt Maura, I'm over Bryan, honestly. I'm happy with where my life is at the moment," Caitlyn said with a dismissive wave of her hand.

"You don't look happy Cait. Oh, sure you're enjoying your writing, and raising those delightful scamps of yours. But I can see the purple smudges underneath your eyes, even hiding behind those sunglasses. You've lost some weight too, and by the way you're pushing food around your plate without eating I don't think that was on purpose." Maura tucked the hair behind Caitlyn's shoulder. "I worry about you honey, especially since my sister hasn't been much of a mother to you."

"I know you do Aunt Maura. I've been deep into a project since getting back from Ireland, that's all." Needing a moment Caitlyn took a sip of the cool white wine in her glass. "I don't want to date right now," she said thinking nobody would be able to hold a candle next to Nolan anyway. Excusing herself from the table she walked inside the house. She walked up the steps and past everyone inside enjoying the cool air of the living room and kitchen. She headed into her room and closed the door quietly behind her. Leaning her back against the wood she dragged air into her lungs. She knew her aunt meant well and loved her dearly. But even thinking of another man's hands on her skin was enough to make her hands shake and had the bottom of her stomach dropping out. Caitlyn needed a few minutes to settle herself and added a touch of concealer under her eyes to cover the circles there.

She sat on the side of the pool after that, away from the gossip. Dangling her feet in the water she watched her sons horse around and found herself laughing at their crazy antics. Pulling her phone out she took pictures of everyone. After the sun went down, they all loaded into their vehicles and headed into town for the fireworks. Sitting curled up on a blanket in the field as the fireworks exploded in the air, their boom echoing deep in her chest she wished Nolan was here beside her. She took a video of the finale, posting it on her Instagram. She had quite a few followers, her readers keeping up with her. Caitlyn tried to make sure she posted regularly, but always careful not to post any of her sons. It had been hard lately though, just another chore on her list. She had only posted once since getting back from Ireland, a collage of her trip.

They made it back home late, and she sent the boys off to bed. Caitlyn spent hours cleaning up the mess from the party exhausting herself before climbing into her bed. It didn't matter though, she always dreamed of Nolan. Tonight was no different. He sat in a crowded coffee shop staring out the window at people walking past. A pretty blonde woman walked over and tried to chat him up, but he must not have heard her because he never looked over. The woman walked away disappointment written clearly all over her face. Nolan took his phone out and stared at the screen. Caitlyn looked down and saw a picture of her face looking back at her. Waking up to the sun shining in her windows she curled into a ball until the ache in her chest loosened.

The rest of July passed by with each day blending into the previous one. She brought Wyatt to drivers' education up at the school every day, picking him back up a few hours later. He started dating Alex, one of the girls in their neighborhood, and they spent the afternoons together hanging out at one house or the other. Mason thought they were annoying with all of their flirting, so he usually went into his room and played video games when she was over. Caitlyn spent hours writing. Lost in the love story she was creating, instead of her own sadness.

Bryan took the boys camping up north for a week at the beginning of August. Left by herself, Caitlyn let the mask fall. She didn't have to pretend every day that nothing was wrong. She curled up on the couch in an old t-shirt and her comfiest shorts, her hair wound up in a bun, no makeup on, and wrote all day. She fully realized she was just going through the motions, not actually living, but couldn't seem to crawl back to life.

When the boys came home from camping, the back-to-school frenzy started. Spending hours trudging around at the mall while the boys picked out and endless supply of clothes and shoes. Then they had to stock up on all the pencils, pens, binders, notebooks and all the other supplies that the teachers claimed they needed. Wyatt was in high school, but Mason still had one more year of middle school left, so there were two different school orientation nights to attend, and a handful of teachers to meet.

The school year started with the usual early morning grumpiness. In the final stretch Caitlyn wrote like a demon during the day to finish the book. Wyatt, and Mason were both doing soccer again this fall. Wyatt played through the school, but Mason was still on the youth league for another year yet. Thankfully, she took turns with Bryan getting the boys to their practices all week long. Halfway through September she finally sent the finished book off to her editor. After bringing the boys to school one morning she turned the television on. She always fell into a hole when she wrote, but this time it was worse than usual, for obvious reasons.

Flipping it to a popular national morning news program she sat down with her coffee.

The anchors were talking to an older actress Caitlyn liked. She apparently had a new movie coming out soon and was doing promotions for that. After the interview was done, she got up walking into the kitchen to make herself a second cup of coffee. The commercials ended and the sound of screaming echoed out of the television. The anchor was struggling to be heard over all the excitement.

"Finally, the man of the hour, here to play us his brand new single *And You Don't Know* live on television for the first time ever, the one and only Nolan Hayes!" Hearing the name Caitlyn dropped her mug, the ceramic shattering everywhere on the kitchen floor as she stumbled back into the living room. Standing there frozen she watched as his handsome face filled the screen. His hair was styled up off his face in purposeful disarray, and he had shaved his beard off. But there was no mistaking, she spent too much time staring into that face, this was her Nolan. He was holding a guitar in front of him, fingers dancing over the strings as the music started. The screaming hushed, the crowd in front of him filled with breathless anticipation. The camera zoomed in tight on his face when he sang the first line. She could see the pain swimming in his eyes, clear as day. He sang slowly into the microphone, his low voice pouring everything he was feeling into the words.

> *My love such a beauty hurts to see*
> *My love left and took the best of me*
> *I love you still baby*
> *And you don't know*
> *You got the best of me*
> *Still holding the heart you gave me to keep*
> *Your love was the best I ever had baby*
> *And you don't know*
> *That you're leaving me half a man*

Caitlyn sat down hard on the couch with a thump watching him sing the rest of the song. He politely thanked the crowd when he was done, and another of the anchors announced, "Nolan's highly anticipated new album *Definitely Memorable* will be out next month, he's spent a long time writing it, but you won't have to wait too much longer to get your hands on it!" They cut to some news story that Caitlyn didn't even bother to pay attention to.

Sitting there on the couch she picked her phone

up and called her dad, asking him to come over. She was still sitting there when he walked in the door twenty minutes later. The broken coffee mug still on the kitchen floor, television still playing. He had to call her name twice before Caitlyn realized he was even there.

"Darling, what's wrong?" he asked, the concern clearly written all over his face.

"Dad, remember when you said I could tell you what happened to me in Ireland when I was ready? I think I need to tell you now." Caitlyn told him everything in a rush, barely breathing between words. Every day spent with Nolan, all the magical little moments. She even told him how much chemistry they had without giving him too many details about the sex that he wouldn't appreciate. She told him about stupidly forgetting to use a condom when they'd had too many pints. How she left him still asleep, hightailing it all the way up to Belfast when she couldn't fly home sooner. He listened to the whole thing without interrupting once.

"That's why you have been wandering around like a zombie for the last few months?" Caitlyn nodded at him, tears shimmering in her eyes.

"What happened this morning?" he asked gesturing at the spilled coffee on the floor.

"I finished the book I was working on late last night, sent it off to editing. After bringing the boys to school this morning I turned on the morning news. Easy enough, drink my coffee and catch up on what's been happening in the world while I was locked away in a book." With a frustrated little laugh, she added, "Except he was on the TV Dad!"

"Nolan?" he asked.

"Apparently so. He told me his name, and I guess thinking about it now, maybe it was a test, but I had no idea who the hell he was."

"Honey, even I know who Nolan Hayes is. You must've been living under a rock," he said pulling out his phone showing her that he had some of Nolan's songs. "Although I probably wouldn't recognize him on sight, I like his sound, but his good looks are lost on me," he laughed.

"I'm such a fool. Who falls in love with a rock star?" She shook her head. "I thought he was some normal guy from Dublin, Dad." She stood up stalking into the kitchen, grabbing a broom and cleaned the mess up ranting the whole time. Her Dad followed her, settling himself on a stool while she got it all out. Finally, she looked over at him. "What am I supposed to do?'

"Well, do you love him?" he asked her already knowing the answer.

"So much, I can't breathe sometimes it hurts so bad to be away from him," she said rubbing a hand over the ever-present ache in her chest.

"Then I suggest you tell him. This time let him decide if it's too crazy to jump into this. From what you said about the song he was singing I'm thinking he's been missing you too darling."

# Chapter Eighteen

After her dad left Caitlyn decided it might be a good idea to educate herself. Pulling out her phone she downloaded both of Nolan's previous albums, his self-titled debut, and the follow up one called *Not Done Yet*. Sitting at the island while her phone played song after song of his she was busy reading all about him on her laptop. The first link she clicked on was a fan page, and strangely enough it seemed to be dedicated to the cleft in his chin. There were dozens of posts detailing everything the owner of the page wanted to do to Nolan's chin, some of them not quite physically possible. Laughing she clicked back out. That was not a road she planned on going any further down. Although in all fairness, the girl hadn't been too far off about how earth shattering it would be to sit on his face.

It surprised Caitlyn that although there were plenty of rumors about his love life he had kept it all quietly under wraps. It seemed that if Nolan was in the vicinity of a female celebrity, he must be dating her according to the media. There were hundreds of tabloid pictures taken by paparazzi, hungry for the next big scandal. Mostly he was doing mundane everyday things, getting groceries, pumping gas, Christmas shopping. He had the exact same expression in every single one of those pictures. His eyes had a distinct blankness, his jaw was noticeably tense, and there was an annoyance easily readable in the set of his shoulders. This man hated being hounded by the press. Caitlyn remembered the look on his face when she had joked about never taking a bad picture. She understood now that he must feel like there were too many pictures of him floating around, and he couldn't do a damn thing to change it.

Finding herself bopping along to his music still playing, she clicked on his official website and read his biography. Surprisingly, she knew most of it already. He had been honest with her about himself, he just left out the tiny detail that he was a mega famous rock star. Although he seemed to describe himself as a singer/songwriter. Looking into it she found he wrote all of his own songs, and plenty for other artists as well. Everyone who had ever worked with him said that he was a great guy. Nobody seemed to have any ongoing feuds with him, which was a rarity in the world of A-list celebrities.

His debut album ended, and his second one started playing. He had definitely matured in between, his sound changing enough to reflect that. A few songs in the title track, *Not Done Yet,* started playing, and she instantly recognized it. She had heard it literally everywhere about two years ago, it was inescapable. But as Caitlyn sat back, she was transported back to Ireland. This was the song Nolan had hummed as he held her in his arms, the rain soaking them through to the skin. He had hummed his own hit song in her ear while he danced with her. That moment took on a whole new meaning now that she knew he was sharing an important piece of himself with her. Lyrically speaking the song was about falling in love with a woman who he knew didn't love him enough, but even though he knew she didn't he wasn't done falling yet. It was simply beautiful and leaned more towards hopefulness rather than sadness.

After the second album was done playing, she looked up his new song *And You Don't Know*. It had been released to radio the week prior, and Nolan was doing a few interviews at the different stations to promote it. Her hands shaking Caitlyn clicked on the video of the first interview with a well known nationally syndicated radio DJ.

"Welcome back to the show Nolan, good to see you again man. It's been what, two years?"

"Good to be back. Yeah, it's been, just shy of two years, I think. I had the world tour, and then took some time off back home recently to write me new album," Nolan replied easily.

"That new single of yours is already burning up the charts, it's gonna be another smash hit I'm sure."

"Thanks bud," Nolan said with a genuine smile.

"Oh, yeah yeah, it's true. You seem to write a lot of love songs though for a man who is always single, Nolan. How does that work exactly?" the DJ asked.

"Well, in this business I've always thought it was best to be single." Nolan held his fingers up making air quotes around single. "Kinda like the forms ye fill out, choices are married, or single. Not been married last I checked, so single it is," he chuckled.

"But that doesn't really mean single then," the DJ pushed.

"I mean, I'm a twenty-five-year-old man, I've obviously dated here and there of course." Nolan said with a nervous laugh.

"I'm sure women are all over you with that accent man, it's gotta be like catnip."

"I've heard some are fond of the sound of it, sure," Nolan said taking a sip of water from the bottle in front of him.

Changing tactics, he asked Nolan, "So, everyone's already buzzing about the inspiration for *And You Don't Know*. I've heard a few theories. I hate to ask, but you know I gotta, you know I do. What is it about?" the DJ asked with a smile that said he didn't hate asking at all, not in the least. In fact, Caitlyn thought the man was enjoying watching Nolan squirm.

"C'mon now. All that yer asking is who I've been shaggin'. When have I ever answered that about any of me other tunes?" Nolan said uncomfortably.

"That's true, you've always been very closed mouthed about women in your life who may have inspired your songs. You're not one to air dirty laundry like that," the DJ said visibly disappointed.

"A real man never kisses and tells. He'd never convince another woman to kiss him again if'n he did that," Nolan said with a little laugh, and Caitlyn could tell it was an answer he used often.

"You've got the new album that is coming out next month, what's the name? And is the vibe of the rest of it like the single you just brought out?" the DJ asked.

"Ah, yeah next month. I've called it *Definitely Memorable*. Well, if all the songs sounded exactly like *And You Don't Know* then it would get pretty boring to listen to I'd think? I try to make sure there is a good mix of up-tempo songs thrown in there with the more sappy ones," Nolan said fidgeting.

"Why *Definitely Memorable*, is that a song on it?" the DJ asked homing in on Nolan's comfort level. This man was relentless.

"No, it's a line in one of the songs though. I, ah, was about half finished with the album when I took a break back home. The songs I wrote after that are pretty personal to me, but I want people to listen to me songs and interpret them through their own experiences. I wrote them from mine, but if I assign my meaning to them for everyone that's not what music should be about." Nolan was biting his thumb nail now.

"Are you planning to tour this album?"

"I've got some shows in the next few months, along with this promo, yeah. I like touring though, being up on a stage, suits me right down to the ground. Nothing better," Nolan said laying a hand up on his chest and grinning.

The DJ wrapped the interview up then launching into the news of the day before the video ended. Caitlyn couldn't watch any more, listening to him grill Nolan made her skin crawl. She thought that was probably tame compared to some of the questioning he had to have faced before. Seeing this side of him was certainly enlightening though. He was always so open with her, full of charm and affection ready to give. But to the rest of the public, he came across as a deeply private man. He didn't discuss his personal life, didn't parade models around town on his arm. And he most definitely could have, he was certainly handsome enough, which honestly wouldn't have even mattered with his level of fame.

Realizing it was time to get her sons from their schools, the day had flown by while she all but stalked

Nolan. Today was her day to get the kids to soccer practice too. Wyatt walked to the field from school. It was all part of the same complex, but he would need a ride home at five thirty. Mason had practice across town until five. That left her with about two hours to kill. Usually that wasn't a big deal, because she would bring her computer along and get some work done. But with her latest project off being edited she was at a bit of a loss. Sitting in the bleachers with a few of the other soccer moms while Mason ran drills she logged on to her Instagram, to check her notifications. Unable to help herself while on there though, she searched Nolan's page out. It was easy enough to find him, what with him having millions of followers and all. The man could probably take over the world if the urge hit him. "Jesus," she whispered to herself. If Nolan was private in interviews, then his social media accounts were his outlet. He posted frequently. His page was full of selfies with the guys in his band, cool places he visited in his travels, and some official photographs for this or that event. He seemed genuinely accessible, and his fans clearly loved it.

Going back, she saw that he didn't post at all during June. That entire month was missing from his timeline, which seemed to be unusual for him. The next picture he posted wasn't until the fourth of July. He was standing with his hands in his pockets in front of a soundboard in a studio somewhere. The caption said, *"Working on this album for ya, happy independence day America, have a good one."* There were firework and beer emojis after that. He was wearing the navy flat cap she had bought him. In fact, every picture he posted of himself since then seemed to have that hat on his head. As she was scrolling through, he posted a picture of the view out over the Atlantic from the Cliffs of Moher. With it he said, *"Missing June sunshine in Ireland."* There were no silly faces, or hashtags this time. But Caitlyn just knew without a doubt that he meant her.

Tears welled in her eyes as she excused herself from the group of moms, rushing to her car. Sitting in the driver's seat she rode the roller coaster of emotions flying through her. Laughing with tears streaking down her face. Nolan still thought about her, he missed her. As soon as she soaked that in, she thought, *"But what the hell does that matter? I was worried about complicating his life before when I thought it was an ordinary one. Now it's even more complicated."*

Drying her tears as Mason flopped into the car asking "Mom, are you alright? You've been kinda weird since you got back from Ireland. I mean you're always a little strange being a writer and all, but crying in the car? That's definitely a new level of weird."

"You're right Mason, I was hoping you kids

didn't notice, but it would be impossible not to I guess," Caitlyn said as she drove them the short distance across town to get Wyatt.

"So what gives?" Mason asked her before chugging big thirsty gulps of his water.

"I think this is probably a conversation your brother should be here for," she sighed.

Mason nodded and started playing on his phone killing time until Wyatt was done with his practice. Wyatt was busy talking on the phone to his girlfriend Alex on the way home though. It wasn't until later when they were sitting around the table eating dinner that Mason brought it up again.

"Mom was crying in the car while I was at practice. So I asked her what's been up with her," Mason said around the large bite of chicken in his mouth.

"Mase! I thought we agreed to leave it alone?" Wyatt said his blonde head whipping over to look at his brother.

"Wait, what? You guys had a conversation deciding not to ask me what's been going on?" Caitlyn asked shocked.

"Yeah. Well, we aren't blind Mom," Mason said like he was stating the obvious.

"And we're not little kids anymore either. I can tell you've been crying at night, but I didn't think you wanted to talk about it," Wyatt admitted shrugging his shoulders.

"I guess I owe you both an apology. I didn't know you guys noticed. Maybe I should have, I guess. Thank you for respecting my privacy like that though, it was quite mature," she said.

"Like I said, we're not little kids Mom," Wyatt said. Mason nodded his head as he shoveled more food into his mouth.

"I, ah, I met someone while I was in Ireland. Almost as soon as I got there," she confessed uncomfortably.

"By someone you mean a man?" Wyatt supplied.

"Yes, smart alec, I mean a man. We had a wonderful, exciting love affair. I had to end it, for a lot of reasons that made complete sense at the time. Now, spending the last three months crying I'm not really sure anymore," Caitlyn said summing it up the best she could while resting her head in her hand.

"Maybe you made a mistake Mom," Mason said.

"Were you happy?" Wyatt asked before she could answer Mason.

She sat there staring at her fifteen-year-old thinking that he was maturing faster than she gave him credit for. Nodding her head, she finally said, "I really was."

"What about him?" Mason asked.

"Yeah, I think he was too," Caitlyn said quietly.

"I think you should try and give it another chance," Wyatt replied wisely.

"I don't know that I can guys, it's not always that simple." She stood up clearing her plate.

"Why not Mom?" Mason asked, helping himself to another chicken breast.

"There's something she isn't telling us." Wyatt said to Mason. Her oldest son was always quick to cut through the bullshit.

Standing there in the kitchen leaning exasperatedly against the sink she said, "You wouldn't believe me." The boys looked at each other sharing the kind of look only siblings could. Figuring what the hell, she shrugged her shoulders and walked into her bedroom grabbing her laptop. Carrying it back out to the table she held a finger up to ward off the boy's questions. Opening the folder, she had stashed all the pictures of her and Nolan in she turned it so they could see the slide show.

"Holy frigging crap Mom! That's Nolan Hayes, THE Nolan Hayes! Like, Grammy award winning, uber famous Nolan Hayes!" Mason yelled, nearly choking on his food. Wyatt's face showed nothing as he studied each picture that slid past the screen with complete focus. When they had seen all the pictures Mason asked excitedly, "Why didn't you get him to autograph something for us?"

"Because, you moron, she didn't know. Couldn't you tell?" After insulting his little brother, Wyatt turned to her, his face still unreadable. "Do you love him?"

Standing there with both of her sons staring at her she nodded her head slowly. "I really do. You're right Wy, I didn't know who he was. Not until I saw him on TV this morning. I didn't want to ask him to leave Ireland for me." She avoided the pregnancy scare, thinking it really didn't set the best example for her sons. "Turns out that he left Ireland for the rest of the world a long time ago."

"What would one of the character's in your books do?" Wyatt asked her. "Don't worry though, we're not going to tell anyone," he added with a menacing look towards his brother. "I've got a butt load of homework to get done," he said walking off towards his room.

Later as she lay in bed staring at the ceiling in the dark, she thought what the hell. Grabbing her phone off the nightstand next to the bed she followed Nolan on both her Twitter, and her Instagram accounts. Setting her phone back down before she could undo what she had just done she rolled over and willed herself to fall asleep.

# Chapter Nineteen

A week trudged ever so slowly past. Caitlyn didn't know what she had expected. With millions of followers around the world why would Nolan notice that she had followed him? He probably didn't even have notifications turned on, or his phone would be blowing up all hours of the day and night. She herself, had no clue who most of her followers were, and she had barely a fraction that he did. She started typing out messages to him so many times that she lost count. It never sounded right though, and she deleted them all before she could muster up the courage to send them. Telling him she missed him seemed like stating the obvious. Asking him why he never told her what he did for a living seemed bitchy, or worse yet like she was some kind of fortune hunting gold digger. Saying a casual 'hey how's it going' just didn't feel like enough either.

Getting annoyed with how indecisively desperate she was being she left the temptation of her phone at home for the day and went to her hair appointment. The same woman had been cutting it for years now, and Caitlyn trusted nobody else. Sitting in the chair while her stylist Jen snipped busily away at the mass of auburn curls Caitlyn relaxed and did her best to put Nolan out of her mind. Chatting with an old friend had this magical way of putting things in perspective for you, especially when you weren't even thinking about your problems. She took Jen out to lunch after her hair was trimmed and layered to curling perfection. There was this tiny Mexican restaurant in town that could do no wrong as far as she was concerned. Everything on the menu tasted like a slice of caloric heaven on a plate. Jen decided on a wet burrito, and Caitlyn got a massive plate of nachos this time. They talked about Jen's fourteen-year-old daughter Ava, how her boys' soccer was going, Caitlyn's new book, and all the happenings in their small town while they ate. It was a perfectly normal afternoon, and exactly what Caitlyn needed.

She was in a great mood when she picked the boys up from school. Neither of them had practice that day, and there was already a crew of teenagers hanging out on her front porch, and spilling into the lawn when she pulled in. Her sons tossed their backpacks in the garage after she parked, and Wyatt picked up one of the ever-present basketballs and they headed out to play a game with their friends on the hoop in the driveway. There always seemed to be boys hanging around her house, splashing around the pool out back in the summer, playing ball, or having video game tournaments during the winter. From experience she knew she was going to end up feeding at least half of them dinner. Looking through her pantry she gathered the ingredients for spaghetti. It was the kind of meal that she always kept on hand since it could be stretched a long way, especially when you added meat balls and a few loaves of garlic bread.

Walking past her phone she snagged it off the counter. She had a few texts to answer back, but nothing major. Plopping down on the living room couch, feet up on the arm, laying down holding her phone up she opened her Twitter. Not obsessing about what to say to Nolan all day she knew exactly what she needed to say to him now. Opening her direct messages, she typed out...

*"Nol? That drunken mistake didn't get me pregnant."*

Thinking if nothing else he deserved to know that. Hitting send before she could change her mind, she got up to make dinner for the kids before they tore through the house like a pack of starved wolves. They would clear her out of every crumb in the house if she didn't have food ready for them when they finished up their game. As predicted, three extra boys ended up eating spaghetti and meatballs with them for dinner, and there wasn't a single noodle left when she cleared the table. The boys said their goodbyes to their friends and headed to their bedrooms to get their homework done. Caitlyn turned on some music and cleaned up the kitchen. She was wiping down the counter tops when her phone lit up with a notification.

*"But it made you run away from me,"* Nolan had written back. That he responded at all had a surge of adrenaline coursing through her veins, making her hands shake and her head feel light.

*"I didn't want to ruin your whole life,"* she replied back to him, sitting down at the kitchen island.

*"Bang up job you did, that. Saving me from the unimaginable horror of happiness."* She could almost hear his voice as she read his words.

*"I deserved that,"* Caitlyn sent without even thinking. Then added a second message, *"I broke my heart you know."* He didn't answer for a long time. Caitlyn was laying in bed, thinking that was it, the end of it. The sound of her phone buzzing on the nightstand nearly had her jumping out of her skin.

*"Mine too,"* Nolan finally said.

*"I have nightmares about that."* Her thumbs flying across the phone.

*"About me? Just what every man wants to hear,"* came his response within moments.

*"Well, about breaking your heart more specifically. In the dreams I have to watch you suffer and can't fix it. Every night, all summer long,"* Caitlyn told him rolling over onto her side.

*"Sounds like you're feeling guilty,"* Nolan said.

*"For hurting you yes, I feel like shit about that*

189

part. *I don't know Nolan, I couldn't stay, and if I didn't go right then I wouldn't be able to leave you. Falling so hard for the guy you met at a pub on vacation was never going to end well. I said goodbye the only way I could manage,"* she replied. There was a long pause again as Caitlyn stared at the glowing screen.

*"Leaving me like that didn't help. You poured yourself into me all night, Caitlyn. I felt it,"* he sent her. Then another message appeared beneath that one. *"I wasn't going to let it end when you went home you know. I'd been trying to figure out how to tell you everything. I know you thought I was some bloke with his whole life in Dublin,"* he finally said.

*"Yeah, I probably looked like a total fool. Everyone else knew who you were, and I had no clue."* She hit send.

*"I thought you looked like the rest of my life."* Reading what he sent had a sharp pain slicing through Caitlyn. She wasn't sure what she had expected him to say to her, but this hurt. There was nothing to say back to that, so she set her phone down. Staring at the moon out of her bedroom window she felt lost as tears slowly slipped down her face.

Her alarm woke her the next morning, blaring incessantly. Turning it off Caitlyn walked to her son's rooms to make sure they were getting up. They had their own alarms, but that only got them up about half of the time. Once they were both up and moving around, she went back to her room and hopped in the shower. She had people scheduled to come over and close the pool out for the year, now that it was getting cooler, and they would be here a few minutes after she got back from dropping the boys at school. They were all three grumpy this morning, so the boys were snipping at each other, and Caitlyn had a headache from crying the night before. After the boys were dropped off at their respective schools Caitlyn stopped to buy a massive coffee before leaving town to drive home.

A white van from the pool company was already in her driveway when she pulled in. Two guys got out as she parked. Climbing out of her own car she walked over meeting them halfway. After double checking everything she wanted them to do they went around back with their equipment. Walking into the house Caitlyn heard her phone buzzing on the counter, where she must have left it. Scowling she picked it up. Nolan had messaged her. Opening her twitter app, she saw he had sent her a few of them.

*"Truth is I've been lost without you."*

*"Can we figure out a way to fix this?"*

*"I'm still holding on to your heart. You can't have it back love."*

Standing there in her kitchen grinning like a fool she sent him her phone number. It rang less than a minute later.

"Nolan?" she asked, her voice breathless with excitement.

"Yeah, love, its me." His voice came through the phone lower than she remembered, his accent heavier.

"Oh god, Nolan I'm so sorry," she blurted out. "I was so scared, it was so dumb. I know that now."

"I get it, honestly I do. But we can't change it. I was pissed at ye for a while, my heart a fuckin' mess. Writing the album helped take the edge off it though. I forgave you ages ago. It's so good to hear your voice love." Caitlyn closed her eyes and absorbed his words, feeling them fit into all the places left broken deep inside of her.

She told him all about the book she just finished, and he told her about his new album. The conversation flowed just as easily between them as it always had. Eventually he had to let her go to do a soundcheck for a late-night talk show he was playing on. Telling her to watch the show tonight they hung up.

Looking at her phone she realized they were talking for over two hours. She spent the rest of the day floating around in a happy bubble. Bryan got the boys from school, and to practice that afternoon. He texted Caitlyn to let her know they were going out for pizza after and asked if she wanted to meet them.

Texting him back she declined his offer but told him to have fun with their boys. Caitlyn had a big Caesar salad for dinner, while emailing back and forth with her editor about the book. Bryan dropped the boys off, this time not coming inside.

Later, sitting propped up in bed, pillows stacked behind her Caitlyn turned on her television across the room. The show was about to start. Other than Nolan there were two actors on tonight. One talking up his movie coming out, the other one spilling secrets about the newest season of her highly anticipated show. They announced after the commercial break they were coming back with Nolan's new song. The anticipation ramping up inside of her Caitlyn watched the damn commercials drag by, impatiently. Finally, the talk show came back on, the host holding up a copy of Nolan's single as he introduced him. The camera panned over to the stage where Nolan stood with a big smile in front of his band.

"This one's for me love," he said into the microphone as he began singing *And You Don't Know*. He looked killer in black tailored dress pants, and a white button-down shirt that fit him impeccably. He managed to look casual and comfortable in the restrictive clothing, wearing them with practiced ease. When his song ended, he thanked the audience and handing his guitar off to someone he walked off the stage heading over to sit on the couch and chat with the host.

"Love that song Nolan!" he said shaking Nolan's hand.

"Thanks, I think it's alright meself," Nolan laughed with a shrug.

"Couldn't miss that dedication though. Someone out there's gotta be very happy right about now. And if you listen closely, you'll catch the sound of millions of young girls' hearts breaking," the host joked holding his hand up to his ear to listen.

"I hope she is. Happy that is. I told her to watch," Nolan said smiling and ducking his head slightly embarrassed.

"This is new territory for you, letting the world into your personal life like this," the host said.

"Well, I'm not waving her picture around, telling ye all the details. But I guess it was time," Nolan laughed. They touched on when the album was set to release after that. Caitlyn sat there a smile lighting up her face. Less than ten minutes after the show ended her phone rang. Looking over she saw Nolan's name lighting the screen up.

"Whatcha think?" he asked her, the smile in his voice sending goosebumps over her skin.

# Chapter Twenty

"I miss ye so fuckin' much Caitlyn," Nolan said into the phone a week later. Laying in her bed listening to him she knew exactly what he meant. They had spent hours talking to each other and sent hundreds of texts back and forth. As good as hearing his voice on the other line was, she needed to touch him, feel his arms wrap around her body.

"Me too Nol," she said softly into the phone staring over at the frame she had put on her nightstand. It was the picture of Nolan she had impulsively snapped in the elevator at The Westbury. He was looking at her, his ocean eyes smiling, stuck in that moment just before the grin spread on to the rest of his face. Looking at it now, she couldn't believe she had ever been able to walk away from that man. She could see all his heart glimmering inside of the blue depths of his eyes.

"Have ye got yer son's this coming weekend?" Nolan asked.

"No, this is the weekend they go to Bryan's. Why?" Caitlyn asked sitting herself up in bed, hope surging through her.

"It just so happens I have a bit of a break from work this weekend. I'm supposed to be in Chicago, not too far from ye. I can hop a flight up," Nolan said hopefully.

"Chicago is less than an hour flight from here!" Caitlyn exclaimed.

"That's nothing at all, and I need to see ye." Nolan's laugh rumbled into her ear.

"Won't you cause a bit of a scene though?" Caitlyn asked picturing him getting mobbed by excited fans at the airport.

"Not always," Nolan said, the mirth gone from his voice. The lack of freedom was his least favorite part of his job. Everything else was great, but he had told her sometimes he just wanted to be a regular guy and not a brand.

"What if I came down there to you instead?" Caitlyn said thinking it would just be easier all around that way.

"I'd like that," he said.

"I would too," Caitlyn said with a smile, thinking about how good it would be.

"First thing in the morning, I'll have Mags, me assistant, get on it." She could hear rustling around and knew that he had to get ready to go. He was shooting the video for the new single overseas right now. It was hours later over there, and he should have been asleep a while ago.

"I can get it," she said.

"Let me take care of it. I'll text ye the details as soon as I get 'em. Talk to you tomorrow love," he said sleepily.

"Night Nol," she whispered before hanging up. Plugging her phone into the charger she made sure the alarm was set. Hugging a pillow to her chest she drifted off to sleep happily in Nolan's shirt.

Amid the morning chaos her phone dinged letting her know she had a text. It was Nolan telling her good morning and letting her know what time to be at the airport Friday. She told him to have a good day on set and drove the boys to their schools. Back home she spent a while going back and forth with her editor deciding on a cover model for her book. Spending her morning looking through a dozen pictures of male models wasn't much of a hardship though. She had used a few of them on previous books, and it was always interesting to Caitlyn to see the new tattoos, or hairstyle changes as they grew and evolved. Narrowing it down to her favorite one they sent them off to design the artwork. It would take a few more days until she had to pick which she liked best.

After hanging up with her editor she sat down at the counter and opened a new document on her laptop. Taking a deep breath in, she flung herself into another story. This one was rooted in all the ideas she had purged while she was in Ireland, and Caitlyn got lost in her work for hours. The alarm on her phone pulled her out of her imaginary world reminding her she had to pick Wyatt and Mason up from school. Meticulously saving her progress and backing it up she closed her computer. Looking at her phone she noticed a handful of texts from Nolan. He was sending her pictures from the set, showing her behind the scenes stuff he thought was cool. She texted him back as she was slipping her feet into shoes.

*"Hey babe, cool pictures. Looks like a lot of fun! Sorry I didn't respond sooner, I was writing."* She tossed her phone into the depths of her purse pulled on a jacket and walked out to her car. His response came while she was waiting in the pickup line at Mason's school.

*"No worries. I get that my woman is busy. You're not always sitting around waiting on me to call. You got your own shit going. I like that,"* his text read. She was smiling like a loon when Mason climbed into the car.

"Hey Mom, can we have take-out for dinner tonight?" Mason asked as he settled in the back seat.

"Chinese?" Caitlyn laughed knowing her son.

"Oh yeah!" Came his excited answer. When Wyatt plopped down in the front passenger seat Mason leaned forward letting his brother know their dinner plans.

"Cool," Wyatt said before pulling his phone out to text his girlfriend.

"Oh, hey guys, I'm going to make a quick trip down to Chicago this weekend while you're at Dad's house," she said as they drove towards home.

"To see Nolan?" Mason immediately asked from the back.

"Yeah, as you have probably noticed we've been talking. But I'd like to see him, and Chicago is pretty close to Michigan," Caitlyn said glancing back at her son in the rear-view mirror.

"So, are you guys back together now?" Wyatt asked turning in his seat to watch her.

"Yeah, I think so. Is that alright with you guys? I know I haven't really dated since the divorce; I don't want you to be upset about it," she said suddenly worried.

"I think it's cool Mom," Mason said as they got out of the car.

"As long as your happy Mom, that's all that matters," Wyatt said bumping his shoulder affectionately into hers as they walked in the house. "But I would like to meet him, since he is so important to you then we should get to know him. Right?" he added making a beeline for the refrigerator to find something to hold him over until dinner time.

"Well, he is pretty busy right now gearing up to bring out his new album, but I'm sure he will make time somewhere. I'll bring it up to him this weekend," she said happy that her boys were taking this so well, hoping that it stayed that way.

Walking into her room Caitlyn dialed Bryan. He picked up on the second ring. "Hey," he said.

"Hi, so I'm going out of town this weekend when you've got the boys," she said looking through her closet picking out what to pack even though it was only Tuesday.

"Where?" he asked.

"Just to Chicago. But if you could keep them Sunday night and get them to school Monday morning, I would appreciate it," she said absentmindedly.

"A book thing?"

"Ahh, no," Caitlyn said realizing she was going to have to tell him about Nolan.

"So why are you driving down to Chicago for the weekend?" he said sounding annoyed.

"First of all, I'm flying down to see a friend. Secondly what I do with my time while you have the kids isn't really your business, that's what it means to be divorced. If you can't keep them an extra night just let me know," she said sitting on the foot of her bed, running a hand through her hair in frustration.

"Are you seeing someone Caitlyn?" Bryan asked in a tight voice.

"What happened to the whole 'what your

mother does is none of our business' line you told the kids in June before I left for Ireland?"

"I don't know. It's just strange, I guess. We were married for a long time," Bryan said sounding a little lost.

"I know, but we have been divorced for a while now. You can't expect me to stay single for the rest of my life Bryan. I'm only thirty-five, I've got a lot of living left to do. I don't ask you about your love life," Caitlyn said sighing.

"Have Wyatt and Mason met him?" Bryan asked stubbornly. But she noticed he ignored the comment about him dating. Go figure.

"No, they haven't. It's still fairly new. But they know about him. What's it gonna be Bryan? Can you keep them an extra night or not?" Caitlyn asked feeling over having this conversation.

"Yeah, I'll get them to school Monday." She could still hear that he wasn't happy about it in his voice.

"Thanks. I'll let them know," she said ending the phone call before it turned into an argument. Caitlyn wondered why Bryan was suddenly so concerned with what she did with her time. He hadn't begged her not to divorce him, or anything like that. And she knew he had been dating for a while. Shaking her head, she stood up determinedly not allowing his attitude to tarnish the shining excitement of her upcoming weekend she walked out to the living room to order the previously requested Chinese takeout.

She told the boys while they sat around the table munching on egg rolls, crab Rangoon, sweet and sour chicken, and lo mien noodles. Neither of them seemed to be bothered by an additional night at their father's house. It helped soothe the remnants of her annoyance with Bryan. He could think what he wanted, like she said it wasn't his business, and it was pretty late now to start being jealous. After dinner Mason got his homework started, and Wyatt went to his room to face-time his girlfriend since he didn't have any homework tonight. Her phone rang while she was sitting down about to turn the television on. Seeing it was Nolan she sat in the living room talking to him while Mason finished his homework up at the table. He was happy with the footage they had shot that day, but he sounded completely exhausted. There was one more day left to shoot, then he had an appearance to make in London Thursday before flying back to the states. He would arrive in Chicago a few hours before she would get there. She let him go, telling him to get some sleep after only a half an hour of talking.

Caitlyn stayed up until the wee hours writing. Wednesday and Thursday, she spent furiously working, trying to get a running start before she took a break for the weekend. She was too excited to see

Nolan to kid herself that she would actually make time for writing. The months since she had seen him last felt more like years. She was up before her alarm Friday morning, unable to sleep. There was time to take a shower and pack the rest of her bathroom supplies into her suitcase before she woke the kids up for school. Caitlyn let them know she would be staying at The Peninsula Chicago and would let them know the room number once she got there. Mason gave her a big hug before climbing into the car. Wyatt joked on the way to school that he hoped she didn't end up splashed across the front page of gossip magazines. Poking him in the ribs before he got out Caitlyn laughed.

The information Nolan had sent her via his assistant Mags told her that she was due to fly out at noon. Caitlyn was going to leave her car parked at the airport and drive herself. It was only a weekend; she didn't want to bother her Dad for that. Parking her car in one of the lots meant specifically for travelers she walked into the airport with a bounce in her step. Being the end of September, it was quite chilly, and it would probably be even more so with the wind in Chicago. She had on a thin plum sweater; dark skinny jeans tucked into cognac colored riding boots with her moss green military style utility jacket. Her auburn curls flying wild and free. A few heads turned appreciatively as she passed by, but she never noticed that kind of thing.

This was Caitlyn's first time on a private jet, and she felt fancy as all get out. Along with the pilots there was a single flight attendant. But after getting her settled in, and offering her champagne, which she declined, he made himself scarce. Which she considered quite the talent since the plane wasn't very big. She took pictures to send her boys once they got out of school. And one shameless selfie, after all it was a pretty damn cool mode of travel. They were landing in Chicago before she knew it. Disembarking when she was the only passenger was a whole new experience for her. No impatient people pushing as they jostled slowly off the crowded airplane.

Nolan's assistant Mags was waiting for her. She was a petite woman somewhere around forty. Her dark hair was worn in an incredibly flattering pixie cut, that set off her liquid brown eyes to perfection. She was a ball of harnessed energy and efficiency. Caitlyn liked her immediately. Mags was responding to emails on a tablet next to her in the backseat of the car on the ride to the hotel.

"How long have you worked with Nolan?" Caitlyn asked.

"Almost from the beginning," Mags said while typing.

Caitlyn nodded her head wondering how much Nolan shared with his assistant. "From what I understand you two have a somewhat complicated history, but you should know that you're the first woman he has ever flown out to see him. Way I figure, that means something. His family doesn't count," she added.

"The whole week I've been so excited, but now that he is so close, I'm nervous as hell. I didn't know about all of this," Caitlyn gestured with her hand encompassing everything, "before."

"He's the same person he has always been from the moment I met him. I don't think you have anything to worry about. He's been buzzing about seeing you too," Mags said putting the tablet away. "I'll be here in town in case he needs me, but Nolan is officially off work until Monday afternoon." She winked at Caitlyn.

# Chapter Twenty-One

The beautiful lobby of The Peninsula hotel flew by her in an opulent blur as Mags walked them hurriedly to the elevator, which was fine by Caitlyn. She hadn't flown down here to admire the hotel. Mags herself was staying a few floors below where Nolan was waiting. Handing her a key card with the room number Mags told Caitlyn to keep him occupied so she could go get a pedicure and maybe a massage too. Caitlyn was laughing as the doors closed behind the spunky woman. Keep Nolan busy huh? That sounded pretty damn good to her. The elevator spilled her into a luxurious corridor, and she headed off to find their suite pulling her suitcase along behind her. Standing outside of the door with their numbers on it she wasn't sure if she should knock or use the key card when the door opened before she could make a decision. Nolan was standing there in faded blue jeans and a long-sleeved red thermal that just happened to show off every one of his muscles to perfection. His hair was disheveled, probably from running his hands through it like he habitually did. It was only his eyes though, that Caitlyn saw. Blue fading into green around the pupil, like waves on the ocean. They were filled with so much happiness she wondered how it didn't beam out of him in rays of sunshine.

Caitlyn launched herself into his ready arms. Burying her head in his chest she breathed the scent of him deep down into her lungs. Locked in his arms felt like coming home again, and she just held on as it all crashed through her system. "Nolan." She exhaled the breath that felt like she had been holding in since that last night with him in Ireland.

"Caitlyn, my love," he said his hands stroking down her back. "God, I've missed ye so." All she could do was nod her head and agree with him. Reaching out he grabbed her bag with one hand, and he pulled them inside of the room.

"How did you know I was here?" she asked still not letting go of him.

"Mags called letting me know she was off the elevator and ye were heading up to me. I hung up and walked to the door, saw ye standing out there. Looking so unsure, and I wasn't about to let ye walk away from me again," he said kissing the top of her head.

"I wasn't sure if I should knock or use the key card she gave me. I won't leave you again Nolan, I can't survive that twice," Caitlyn confessed looking up into his eyes. The slow smile that spread across his face all but turned her knees into jelly. He was so damn beautiful it nearly hurt to see.

He leaned down pressing his lips to hers, and heat snapped to life between them instantly. Slipping her hands under his shirt she felt the warm skin of his back. Reaching an arm up, Nolan yanked his shirt over his head impatiently. Freed from his lips Caitlyn ripped the zippers down her boots and kicked them flying off. He was pulling her sweater up and over her head as she peeled the jeans down her legs. He rained kisses down her neck, across her collarbone and lifting her up against the wall he brought her breasts up to his mouth. Caitlyn wrapped her legs around his waist as Nolan laved his tongue over and over across one nipple before switching to the other one. Desperate to feel all of him Caitlyn tried to reach between them and undo his pants.

"Condoms are in da bedroom," he said around her nipple. His accent thicker with the desire burning through him.

"I've been on the pill since July," Caitlyn moaned. His mouth was an absolute wonder.

Nolan's head pulled back, his eyes searching hers. "Why?"

"So no matter what I'm always covered," she answered him honestly.

"Only I get to touch ye like this," he said resting his forehead against hers.

"No other man has existed for me since I saw

you Nolan," she whispered, watching his eyes blaze right in front of hers.

"Thank god for dat," he said his mouth devouring hers like a starving man finally able to feast.

Wrapping her arms around his neck, fingers playing in his hair she rocked her hips against his. Pressing her to the wall with his torso he reached between them and she heard the sound of his zipper ripping down. Then she felt the heat of his skin pressing against hers.

"Be sure, love. We can go in the bedroom," he said in between kisses. His dick rubbing temptingly against her clit, bathing himself in her wetness. She knew that no matter how turned on he was, if she asked him to wait until there was a condom between them, he would without hesitation.

"I'm sure Nolan, I want you. Here, just like this," she said pulling his mouth back to hers. As her tongue teased along his he moved his hips up, finally sliding his dick deep inside of her aching pussy. He felt even better moving inside of her than Caitlyn remembered.

"Fuckin' unbelievable," he growled against her mouth, his hands pulling her legs open even further. Nolan pounded her into the wall with a savageness born out of desperation, and Caitlyn loved every intense second of it. Her breathless moaning turning to cries as his hips sped up. Leaning her head back against the wall she closed her eyes, the storm deep inside of her body gathering. "Eyes love, give me yer eyes," Nolan said pumping in and out of her harder and harder. Opening her eyes, she looked into his, screaming as the orgasm ripped through her. Nolan's breath quickened, his teeth clenched, and he slammed into her. His dick locked deep inside of her quaking pussy, she felt the hot gush as he came.

"I love you Nolan," Caitlyn whispered, her voice shaking, still staring into his eyes.

"I know, baby. I love ye too," Nolan said stepping away from the wall, still locked deep inside of her, and carried Caitlyn off into the bedroom.

# Chapter Twenty-Two

A giant window took up one whole wall of the bedroom, looking out to sky-rises. There was a giant king-sized bed topped with an opulent comforter, and piles of pillows against the massive headboard. Nolan tossed Caitlyn down on to the bed with a grin and jumped on top of her, kissing her. Coming up for air he asked her how the flight down had been, and she told him how she had been so impressed she even took a selfie. Nolan pushed up on his arms and laughed. It was a full throat-ed sounding, eyes crinkling, face glowing laugh. Caitlyn just stared up at him stunned breathless. Reaching up she laid a hand against his cheek, and just absorbed some of the joy pouring off him.

"Thank you," Caitlyn whispered, her hand still cupping his face as he stared down at her with so much happiness swimming in his eyes.

"What fer?" he asked her. God, how she loved the sound of his accent.

"Forgiving me. Why did I let you go?" She tried saying more, but the words clogged up in her throat. Shaking her head against the bed she repeated, "You didn't have to forgive me."

Nolan turned his head and laid a kiss on the hand still resting on his face, before leaning down and kissing her sweetly on the tip of her nose. "That's what ye do when ye love someone. Caitlyn, ye lit up me world from the moment ye turned and looked at me sitting on the stool in that pub. Why would I wander alone in the dark when I can walk with ye in the light?"

Wrapping her arms around him she pulled him down and hugged his body tightly to her. "I've spent months imagining your face waking up without me there, and I don't think I will ever be able to let that image go," she confessed.

Rolling to his back so he didn't crush her with his weight, he pulled Caitlyn up on his chest. Smoothing her hair back from her face with his hand it took him a moment to arrange his words, as she watched his face. "I'll not lie to ye, I was fuckin' crushed. However yer picturing it, twas probably worse, truth be told." Tears shimmered in her eyes, and she tried to pull away from him. He held her still and continued, "I called every damn hotel in all of Ireland trying to find ye, but couldn't. Then I called the airport, but they wouldn't tell me any damn thing. Not sure what else to do, I drove to me Mum's. I told her everything, the whole of our story up and until that moment. She told me to give ye time, that ye must be scared as hell, and rightfully so, but not to doubt that ye loved me. When I asked how she knew, she told me that if ye didn't there woulda not been a note. I sat there, thinking out in her back garden for hours. Long after the sun set. The next morning, I grabbed me guitar and didn't stop writing until all the sharp edges of the pain dulled." Caitlyn stared down at his chest listening. Using a finger Nolan tipped her face up, not allowing her to hide it. "Where did ye go?" he asked.

"I couldn't get an earlier flight home, I caught a train up to Belfast. I couldn't have stayed away from you in Dublin," she told him. "I'm so sorry Nolan, all I did was break both of our hearts."

"Pouring all of that into my songs, I've nothing left to hold against ye. Like I said, I understand, really baby I do. And I see that ye suffered just as much as I did. Years from now, it will just be another chapter in our love story, it'll not define us. You'll see."

Gazing down at the truth she could see in his eyes, his body warm underneath hers, she let his words sink in. Leaning down she pressed a kiss against his lips. Pulling back, she asked him, "How did I get so lucky? Time and time again you show me that you're just the best man, Nolan. There aren't enough stars in the sky to thank." She laid her head back down on his chest.

"I dunno about ye being the lucky one. I've got a gorgeous woman here on me chest. She happens to have eyes that make me hands shake with their beauty, lips that taste better 'en anything else in the whole of the world, and a body that would tempt a saint. Best part, is I've somehow managed to charm her into handing me her heart." He kissed her long and deep. Drifting over to her neck he whispered in her ear, "I'll not be handing it back, not ever."

Caitlyn nodded her head at his words. Then let out a shaking breath as he sucked her ear lobe into his mouth, biting it tenderly. "God, I could stay right here all day," she breathed as his hand gripped her hair turning her head to give him better access to the other side of her neck.

"Suits me right down to da fuckin' ground," he said, his breath brushing her heated skin. "I've not had ye in me arms for far too long."

Caitlyn climbed up, straddling his hips. Rubbing her clit over his semi-soft dick she felt him growing hard as she moved. He sat up kissing her mouth hungrily, his hands moving her hips, guiding her pussy over his now fully hard dick until he slid smoothly inside. Holding on to his shoulders she rode him slowly. He wrapped one arm around her back, holding her so close against his chest that the hair sprinkled there scraped her nipples as she moved. His mouth against hers he swallowed her cries as she found a rhythm that dragged the thick head against that glorious spot inside of her pussy. Moving up and down only inches, she chased the bright light of pleasure building inside of her. Body strung tight as a bow, shuddering she came in a hot rush that drenched his dick. Nolan watched her eyes as her body all but broke apart around him, gripping his dick in quaking spasms.

"Jesus Christ love, breathe," he said as her body finally let her gulp in air.

"Holy fucking hell Nolan," she gasped still trembling on top of him. "I don't think I can move anymore."

With a flirty wink Nolan held her to him, lifted up onto his knees and laid them down at the foot of the bed. Pushing up on his hands he looked down at her as he pulled his dick all the way out of her and slid deliciously back into her pussy. "Drenched me baby." All Caitlyn could do was arch her neck back and gasp with each surge of his hips, so lost in the way he was making her feel. He found a steady rhythm, slowly out, rocking quickly back in. She watched him look down at his body disappearing inside of hers, and the heat in his eyes nearly burned her. The pressure deep inside of her was ramping up again, and she reached her hands up around him. Whimpering with each slide of his dick inside of her she gripped his hips with her legs as they started shaking. Caitlyn scratched her nails down his back, her pussy pulsing rapidly around his dick. Slamming his hips down he groaned, "Fuck," her orgasm pushing him violently into his own release.

Nolan collapsed on top of her, their bodies slick with sweat as his heartbeat thundered against her chest. "That was...I've never..." Caitlyn struggled to think through the lazy bliss shrouding her brain.

"Came like that before? Ye always come hard, love. But ye damn near broke me dick off squeezing it so hard. It was fuckin' magnificent," he said into her neck, breathing heavily.

"It's always going to be this good between us isn't it?" Caitlyn asked.

Pulling himself up onto his elbows he held her eyes as he said, "I'll not ever get bored of being inside ye, Caitlyn. It'll never be a chore to me. It is the best I've ever had; every single time blows me mind. Amazing."

Riding the wave of pride inside of her she said, "It's not amazing Nol. It's definitely memorable, get it right." She leaned up and kissed his now smirking face.

"How could I forget?" he asked chuckling as he buried his face in her neck.

"Nice album name by the way," she said as he rolled off her, disconnecting their bodies.

"Since half of the album is about ye it only seemed right." He got up walking out the bedroom door into the living room of the large suite. He walked back in, looking better than any man had the right to, taking a long drink out of a bottle of water. Setting down next to her on the bed he handed the bottle over to her.

Caitlyn swallowed thirstily and handed it back to Nolan to put the cap on. "Half of it? Half of your album is about me?" she asked in disbelief.

"Mmmhhmmm," he said, his fingers tracing patterns on the skin of her thigh.

"Are all of them about me breaking your heart?" she asked a little worried.

"No. Wanna hear it? I've just got the final mix, I listened to it on the flight here." When she nodded her head, he walked back out of the room, coming back in with his phone. Setting it on the nightstand he pulled the covers back. They spent an hour laying in bed listening to his songs. He was wrong, of the fourteen tracks, eight of them were about her, so over half. Only three of them were sad, and Caitlyn felt guilty hearing them. But the other five soothed the guilt. He sang an entire song about the way her eyes broke apart as he moved with her in the dark. If ever she doubted his feelings for her, this album was proof. In fact, he was shouting it to the world loud and clear he was madly in love. The other songs didn't seem to be about personal experiences, just observations, or made-up scenarios.

"It's just incredible Nol, even better than your

other two, and that's saying a lot," she said cuddling against him propped up by a mountain of pillows.

"Thanks, love. I'm pretty proud of it meself," he said linking his fingers through hers and bringing it up to his mouth for a kiss.

"My kids thought I was pretty stupid for not recognizing you, ya know," she confessed to him.

"Oh yeah? I actually really liked that ye didn't have a damn clue. That way I knew a hundred percent what was happening between us was genuine, and real." His thumb tracing along her knuckles. "When did ye figure it out?"

"When you sang *And You Don't Know* on the morning news. Dropped my coffee shattering the mug all over the floor. I called my Dad freaking out about the whole thing, by the way he is a huge fan too," she laughed.

"Is that so?" he laughed. "That gives me a leg up then. Yer Dad already likes me, takes some of the stress off. What about yer sons? Other than thinking ye should've recognized me of course," he asked chewing on his bottom lip.

Recognizing the nervous habit, she traced her thumb along the lip before laying a kiss there. "Mason thinks the whole thing is cool. Wyatt said he just wants me happy; I guess I had them worried all summer. Although he did ask me to figure out when they get a chance to meet you," she said.

"I'll get Mags to email over my schedule. I'd like to meet them too. I plan on being around for ages," Nolan said before holding her chin, his eyes searching hers, and asked, "Worried them how?"

Caitlyn took a deep breath and said, "Honestly?" Nolan quirked an eyebrow up in response. "Okay, I cried myself to sleep every night while wearing a shirt of yours. During the day I flung myself into my work because it was the only thing that eased the pain. I tried so damn hard to not show it, but everyone saw it anyway," she told him in a rush.

"Oh love." He pressed his forehead against hers. "Never again." She nodded her head. "I've a crazy job sometimes, so I'll not be the man that's able to hold ye every night while ye sleep. But I'll give ye everything I've got inside." He kissed her softly, and then she felt his lips curl up in a smile. "What shirt?" He asked as he rolled to her back. Caitlyn was laughing as she answered him, his mouth on a determined journey down her body.

# Chapter Twenty-Three

Rolling around in the giant bed Caitlyn and Nolan made up for all of the lost time. They made love, talked, and cuddled, or dozed, just to wake up starving for each other all over again. It was late afternoon on Saturday before they finally came up for air, crawling out of the bed. Nolan pulled on a pair of simple white boxers, and black basketball shorts.

"Are all your boxers white?" Caitlyn asked watching him feeling deliciously loose and limber.

"I'm a simple man," he said shrugging his shoulders.

"Well, I happen to find it irresistibly sexy." She got out of bed reaching her arms up high and stretching her back.

"Yeah? Any time you wanna see me in them ye just let me know love," Nolan said with a cheeky wink before he walked out of the bedroom to call down and order them some food.

Caitlyn's luggage hadn't made it any further into the suite since Nolan had dragged her inside the door pulling it along with her. They had been a little busy devouring each other since then, and clothes weren't required. In fact, Caitlyn couldn't remember ever spending a whole day like that before. Thinking she could get used to it she walked into the living room area looking for her luggage. Nolan's eyes never left her as she crossed the room towards her suitcase. The satisfied smile that spread across his face had her insides clenching in response.

"Love? Anytime ye wanna walk about in nothing but yer skin consider me mad up for it. Damn, but that's a sight I'll not be getting sick of seeing for at least a hundred years." Walking to him, still rolling her suitcase behind her she pressed her body snug against his and kissed his lips sweetly.

"I love you Nolan, but if you don't feed me soon, I might pass out," she joked with him.

He wrapped his arms around her comfortably and nuzzled his face into her neck. "I'll not get sick of hearing that either. Yer food is coming my love." Caitlyn kissed him with a smile on her face, before making her way into the bedroom to get dressed.

Laying her suitcase on the rumpled bed she pulled out a pair of leggings, and a long hunter green cable knit sweater setting them out while she searched for her underwear. Smiling to herself she pulled on the bra and panties she had bought for the sole purpose of Nolan peeling them off of her. Once she was dressed Caitlyn stacked her clothes in the dresser and hung the rest. Walking into the bathroom with her toiletries bag she washed her face and brushed her teeth. Her hair announced to the entire world exactly what she had been doing, there really was no mistaking sex hair. Smiling to herself she left it as it was, wearing it proudly. Sex with Nolan was the toe curling, body quaking, lungs burning, kind. It made her feel powerfully feminine like nothing else ever had in her whole life. Not bothering to put any makeup on, she was just walking back out to him when the knock on the door came announcing their food had arrived.

Caitlyn stood leaning against the bedroom door frame watching a young waiter roll the cart into the room, visibly nervous. Caitlyn guessed he had to be eighteen or nineteen years old, he stuttered and stammered before asking Nolan if he could have his autograph. Nolan's effortless charm put the young man at ease, as he signed the scrap of paper unearthed from somewhere. Watching Nolan humbly thank the young man, telling him that he would be nowhere without his fans Caitlyn found yet another reason to fall in love with him. He might hate the press invading his privacy, the endless paparazzi photos floating around of him, but she could see that he honestly valued his fans. The young man left the room floating on cloud nine, and Nolan turned towards the food without noticing the effect his kindness had.

"You just made his whole week, ya know,"

Caitlyn said pulling away from the door frame and walking over to the cozy table Nolan was setting their meal on.

"I just signed me name is all. It's the least I can do, they pay my bills. Everything I've got is because of them. If nobody bought the albums, I wouldn't be able to do what I love," Nolan said easily and without ego.

"How do you get to be so famous that everyone knows your name, but be completely grounded? That's gotta be a talent," Caitlyn said sitting down at the chair Nolan was politely pulling out for her.

"I know that someday this will all just be a memory. The music industry will move on, I need to still be able to look at meself in the mirror when it does. I don't want to spend the rest of my days living down what a diva I was. Besides, that's just not me. Me Mum would bring me back down to earth right quick," Nolan said sitting down across from her.

He had ordered what appeared to her as half of the menu, seriously there was more food here than Caitlyn thought they would be able to eat in the whole weekend. While they munched Nolan told her about growing up in Galway, where his Mum still lived. He had taken off for Dublin as soon as he was able, renting a small flat with three other guys. He spent his time playing guitar in every bar, party, or street corner that would have him. He picked up shifts waiting tables in Sean's pub to help cover his share of the rent, and it was there playing one night that a record label executive happened across him while the man was on vacation. Nolan chalked it all up to luck, but Caitlyn knew for every spark of luck there were endless hours of hard work. After that, the rest is history as they say. He released an album, it was a smash hit, and he's spent the last five years touring and making music.

After consuming as much of the food as possible they settled on the couch. There was a well-loved acoustic guitar leaning up against the arm of the couch. Without thinking as soon as he sat down Nolan picked it up and began mindlessly strumming as if the instrument was just an extension of himself. "Nol, how did you manage to go an entire week not playing? I mean before, we were together in Ireland?" she asked tucked up against his side, basking in the warmth that always seemed to be radiating off of him.

"I left it at home," he said chuckling quietly. "If I'm near one it's in me hands, can't help meself. Been that way since I first picked one up as a lad. It wasn't that hard, having my hands on ye instead though, love." He looked over at her. "God, but ye had me feelin' some kind of crazed. That first time I didn't know if I could hold it together long enough to take ye there, nothing had ever felt like that before," he confessed.

"For me either. You light me up inside Nolan," she said listening to his fingers move on the strings.

"So where exactly is home for you now?" Caitlyn asked him.

"I've a flat in Dublin, and a house in Los Angeles," he told her.

Caitlyn sat quietly next to him awhile, thinking about what he told her. She hadn't gotten around to saying anything when he spoke up.

"I spend most of me time here in the states. The label is here, so it makes the most sense. I try'n get back to Ireland as much as possible, few times a year at least, but it's not always easy to do." His fingers stopped playing the guitar, and the room somehow felt empty without him filling it with music. "Yer eyes are saying so much love, tell me what yer thinkin'."

"Wondering, logistically speaking, how we're going to manage this," she answered him honestly.

"However we need to Caitlyn. We both have careers that are important to us, that will take us away from each other sometimes. But there is facetime, phone calls, texts, and emails to keep us connected. When the time comes, I've no problem moving. Yer sons need to stay in their school, or near their Da, and I understand that. To be fair though, I'd live in a hut on a deserted island if that's where ye were," he said, his hand gliding to the back of her head, fingers tunneling into her hair.

"I appreciate that Nolan, and it means a lot to

me. But we don't have to make any decisions about that today. When the time comes, I'm sure we will know what to do," Caitlyn said looking into his eyes. Nolan guided her on to his chest with the hand still on the back of her neck and kissed the top of her head.

"I'm a right lucky bastard," he said into her curls. Caitlyn looked up at his smiling face and ran her hands across the muscles of his chest feeling the heat from his skin. Touching him was addictive, and she craved him again.

"Nolan," she said, her voice gone husky with need.

"Aye, love," he answered, pulling her up onto his lap.

"How can I need you so bad again already?" Caitlyn's tongue slid along Nolan's lip hungrily. With a groan he opened his mouth, stroking her tongue with his. While she was all but devouring his mouth, Nolan slid the sweater up her back, pulling away from her lips to pull it up over her head and toss it somewhere in the room. Before Caitlyn could capture his mouth with hers again Nolan caught sight of her bra. The sheer black lace hiding nothing from his eyes. The abbreviated cups stopped just above her nipples, all but presenting the expanse of her creamy skin to him. His hand shaking, he ran a fingertip along the top edge of the bra before taking a deep breath.

Encouraged by his reaction Caitlyn stood up

and pulled the simple black leggings over her hips and down her legs revealing the matching thong. Black lace barely covered her pussy, with lace straps resting snugly along her hips. Nolan's hands clenched into fists; his tongue darted out to wet his bottom lip. Turning slowly around Caitlyn showed him the thin string of lace nestled there. Reaching out Nolan ran his hands over her rounded ass cheeks. He grasped the panties in his hand, but instead of pulling them down her body he snapped the lace, and they floated down, ruined. Gasping Caitlyn looked back at him. The raw edge of hunger clouded his eyes, as he stood slowly, sliding his body sinuously up hers. Nolan licked across her shoulder, moving her hair aside before kissing the nape of her neck, sending shivers shooting through her body. He dragged his fingers around to the front of her sensitized body and gripped the cups of her bra a moment before pulling his hands quickly apart. The lace gave way with a distinct tearing sound before he tossed that away too.

He cupped the weight of her breasts in his palms, squeezing them slightly upwards. His mouth still feasting on her neck Caitlyn reached her hands behind her to push his shorts down. Catching her nipples, he pinched and rolled them as she moaned. His shorts hit the floor, and the heat of his dick scorched her as he rubbed it enticingly between her cheeks. Nolan slid one hand down her stomach, his other still mercilessly working her nipple. He parted the already wet lips with his fingers and rubbed her clit. Caitlyn reached down gripping his hand, needing to hold it to her. "Yer always wet for me, no matter how many times I've had ye," he said against her neck, his voice deep and raspy with desire.

"Because everything you do to me always feels so damn good," Caitlyn moaned breathlessly. His fingers stroking her sped up, and Caitlyn was bucking wildly against his hand, riding the wave. His teeth scraped against the skin of her neck, and Caitlyn shuddered, coming into his hand.

Nolan sat back down on the couch, his hands on her hips he guided her down on top of his waiting erection. Caitlyn took him inside of her devastatingly slow, savoring every inch before she leaned forward and began moving. Nolan wrapped an arm around Caitlyn, holding her as she leaned forward to ride him, his other one gripping her hips. She could hear his breath coming in quick pants next to her ear, and knew he was getting close already. Caitlyn sped up, rocking her hips quickly. The hand on her hip slid down pressing against her still sensitive clit as she moved.

"It's too much," she panted, shaking her head riding that edge between pleasure and pain, her clit screaming.

"Come with me love, I need to feel ye shatter,"

he growled pumping his hips up, meeting hers. Helpless to fight the fire raging through her veins with his fingers moving relentlessly over her, Caitlyn screamed, reaching her hands up in her own hair. Her back arched as the orgasm ripped through her body. Somewhere in the fog of pleasure she heard Nolan's shouted curse as he emptied himself up into her.

Caitlyn collapsed back into Nolan, his chest heaving as they both struggled to breathe. "I take it you liked the black lace?" she asked with a satisfied chuckle.

"I like everything on ye," he said honestly.

"Well, I think they look pretty good in tatters on the floor," Caitlyn said thinking her new goal for buying lingerie was finding pieces that drove him to ripping them off her exactly like that.

# Chapter Twenty-Four

The only sound in the whole hotel room was the metallic zip as Caitlyn closed her suitcase. There was a fog of sadness clouding around them as Nolan sat on the edge of the bed watching her, his brow furrowed, and his jaw tense. This was going to be their life together, stolen weekends, saying goodbye to each other when all they wanted was to hide away together.

"Leaving you is harder than I thought it would be," Caitlyn said standing in the space between his legs. All she wanted to do was climb back into the bed with him and hide out, just the two of them the only ones in the whole world.

"It's different this time though, it's not the end, love," Nolan said holding on to her hands. "No broken hearts, and I'm always just a phone call away."

"I know, I know. This weekend was perfect, I guess I just don't want it to end," Caitlyn admitted with a shrug of her shoulders, the casual gesture at odds with the sadness lurking in her eyes.

"Let's make it a habit then. Hiding away from the world like this, just the two of us. That way I won't have to go too long without seeing ye," Nolan said still holding her hands in between their bodies.

"You want me to meet you wherever you are in the world when you have days off?" Caitlyn asked, thinking it didn't sound like a bad idea.

"Well, I know it's not possible every time I have a day or two free. But yeah, I'd like that. It would mean more time I get to have ye in me arms," Nolan said, his voice sounding thick with emotion.

"It's a plan then. There's nowhere else I'd rather be than next to you," Caitlyn whispered leaning into Nolan until her head was resting on his shoulder.

"I've something for ye love," Nolan said reaching into his pocket, pulling out a small box. He sat it gently on Caitlyn's palm. "You left me with a gift last time, way I figure, its only right I send ye off with something now."

Looking down at the small flat square in her hands Caitlyn took a deep breath and pulled the lid back. Nestled inside was a necklace, a delicate silver chain holding a lovely little shamrock charm. Lifting it from the box Caitlyn held it out to Nolan to put it on her. With a small, pleased smile Nolan reached around her neck and secured the tiny clasp, his eyes never leaving hers. "Thank you Nol, it's really beautiful," Caitlyn said laying a hand where the necklace rested against her skin.

"When yer missing me, remember that it's laying close to yer heart, where I'll always be," Nolan said standing up and pulling Caitlyn in tight against his body.

He really had a way with words. As pretty as the necklace was, the meaning behind his gift meant so much more. Nodding her head Caitlyn pulled his face down to hers. "I love you Nolan," she said against his lips before she kissed him.

"I love ye too Caitlyn," he said pressing a kiss to her forehead, his arms still wrapped tightly around her.

There was a knock on the door, and they both flinched knowing it was Mags. Their time was officially up. Nolan walked them grudgingly out to the door and kissed her softly again. "Wish I could bring ye to the airport at least."

Reaching up and pressing a tiny kiss against his lips Caitlyn said, "I'll call you when I'm back home." Kissing him again.

"I'll." Kiss. "Miss." Kiss. "Ye." Kiss. "Love." Nolan said unable to stop himself from kissing her over and over again.

"Alright you two, for god's sake's, stop acting like this is the last time you'll see each other," Mags' voice rang out from the other side of the door. "The car is waiting to take Caitlyn, and we have to get you to soundcheck, Nolan."

Smiling against his mouth Caitlyn pulled away. "Bye baby, love you," she said pulling the door open, revealing an impatient looking Mags.

"Remind me not to fall in love," Nolan's assistant said with a wink. "Okay, Caitlyn I've emailed you Nolan's schedule, let me know if you have any questions, or if you need anything. Seriously, anything. All of my contact information is in there," she said giving Caitlyn a quick hug.

Caitlyn stepped out of Mags arms, heading away towards the elevator, and Nolan pulled her back for one more kiss. "Keep sleeping in me shirt love, I like knowing it's on ye," he said close to her ear.

Nodding her head, and smiling Caitlyn stepped into the waiting elevator. Nolan stood there a sexy smirk on his face watching her while the doors closed. Caitlyn was still smiling as she strode from the elevator into the lobby. True to her word Mags had a car waiting to take her back to the airport. Sitting in the back-seat Caitlyn watched as Chicago drifted past her window. It was a beautiful city, and she had been there a few times, but this one would always be her favorite. Even though she hadn't done a single thing outside that hotel room all weekend.

The flight crew was the same as before, and Caitlyn pulled out her computer and spent the short trip home working on her latest novel. Walking out to her car parked in the long-term lot at the airport Caitlyn pulled her phone out of her pocket to let Nolan know she made it safely. They only talked for a moment since he was right in the middle of doing his soundcheck. It sounded a little chaotic to her, but he seemed completely at ease. Caitlyn figured it was something a person got used to over time. The drive back home was thankfully a short one, without much traffic to contend with in the middle of the day.

By the time she needed to pick the boys up from school she had already washed and put away the laundry from her weekend and couldn't wait to see them. Wyatt started the second phase of his drivers training, so it was just her and Mason on the way home. He chatted animatedly, filling her in on everything that happened all weekend. Bryan had taken the boys to see some new superhero action movie in the theaters, and Mason thought it was the best one he'd seen yet. That was quite high praise coming from the thirteen-year-old, since he had probably seen every movie in the whole genre.

They were almost home when Mason looked over at her, running a hand through his ginger hair, and mumbled, "So Dad was asking about who your boyfriend is yesterday. I told him that his name was Nolan, but that's it. When Dad asked more, Wyatt told him he should ask you because we haven't even met the guy yet. Dad didn't say anything else about it after that, but I could tell he was in a bad mood the rest of the night."

Mason made it sound like no big deal, but

Caitlyn knew that he was glazing over it. "Mase, it's probably strange for your Dad to think about me moving on." Mason nodded his head at her answer, his fingers fidgeting around in his lap.

"I don't get why though Mom? Dad goes on dates; it shouldn't bother him if you do. I think Wyatt's pissed at Dad about it." Mason said.

"Don't say pissed please," Caitlyn said without even thinking, the habit so ingrained in her. "Jealousy doesn't always make sense, and this is the first time your Dad has been faced with my love life. He'll get over it. Wyatt is at that age where he and your Dad are going to butt heads often, don't worry too much about it. Okay?" Mason shrugged a shoulder up. Feeling like she could easily pummel her ex-husband in that moment she locked it down, and asked as they walked into the house, "What are you in the mood to have for dinner?"

Mason stayed home playing video games two hours later when she drove back to pick Wyatt up from drivers' education. He didn't seem too upset to her, but Wyatt was better at concealing his emotions than his younger brother was. "Wyatt, Mason said that Dad wasn't too happy that I have a man in my life now." Wyatt crossed his arms but didn't say anything. "C'mon Wy, I can't fix it if you don't talk to me," she finally said.

"It shouldn't bother Dad that you have Nolan,

he has loads of women. I don't see you flipping out about that. He can't have it both ways. You're not his wife anymore," Wyatt said, his voice sharp with frustration.

"You're right, I'm not. I'll take care of it," Caitlyn said, then changed the subject, asking him how training was going.

Later that night, after her sons had gone to bed Caitlyn shut her bedroom door and called Bryan. As soon as he answered the phone Caitlyn launched into her tirade. The words came bubbling rapidly up from where she had locked them that afternoon when Mason first told her. "What the ever-loving hell is wrong with you Bryan? Grilling our sons like that? If you have pressing questions about what I'm doing with my life, then by all means pick up the phone and ask me your damn self! All you accomplished was pissing both boys off. Are you honestly trying to push them away?" Bryan tried to say something, but Caitlyn was on a roll, and didn't let him get a word in. "I don't ask them a million questions about the women in your bed when they come home. I trust that when someone is special enough to you that they're going to be in our sons lives then you will tell me! But since you don't seem to be adult enough to afford me the same courtesy, I'll say this; he makes me happy. Really mind-fucking-blowingly happy! Nothing you have to say will change that Bryan. We got a divorce because you didn't see me anymore. It's too late for you to open your eyes and realize what you lost now. Do yourself a favor and get over it." Finally taking a breath Caitlyn's skin felt burning hot. "Did you honestly think that I would never meet anyone ever again?"

"I don't know. I guess I never gave it much thought. Then all weekend it was all I could think about. I'll apologize to the boys. But that doesn't mean I'm happy about the rest," Bryan said stubbornly.

"The beauty of this is that how you feel about it doesn't matter at all. See that you call the boys tomorrow," she said ending the phone call.

Feeling too wound up to sleep she pulled out her computer and wrote until her eyes crossed and she couldn't focus on the letters appearing on the page anymore. Saving her work out of habit she closed her laptop and crawled beyond exhausted into her bed, asleep before her head even touched the pillow.

The days flew past, Caitlyn and Nolan talking on the phone as often as they could, and texting frequently. Wyatt and Mason finished their soccer seasons as the days shortened and autumn painted West Michigan in hues of warmth. Caitlyn was about halfway through writing her book and she felt like her skin was going to wither away and blow off her bones if she didn't see Nolan soon. It had only been a few weeks, but she missed him with a ferocity that made her time spent away from him feel as if it were stretched out endlessly. Pulling up the email from Mags she had already read a dozen times, each time hoping to discover something new. Nolan's schedule was pretty jam packed all of October leading up to Thanksgiving. He was off the last two weeks of November, but that was still a month away. Exiting out of her email and standing up in frustration she started pacing the length of her office in the large, finished basement. She had a view to the back yard that usually relaxed her when she actually worked in there. Seeing the colorful leaves out the window as she prowled around the room, she got an idea.

Sitting back down at her desk she logged back into her email account.

> *Mags,*
> *Hey! I was wondering if you could help me surprise Nolan? My children are supposed to go with their Dad this weekend. I know that he has a show, but I thought, well I've never seen him play live. And I can pack up my laptop and work anywhere really. What do you think? Please tell me that it's doable, I really miss him. I'm going out of my mind here. Thanks a bunch!!*
> *~Caitlyn*

Hitting send she picked up her computer and walked out of her office and up the stairs. Setting her laptop on the counter she fixed herself some lunch. Caitlyn forced herself to stay away from her inbox until after her meal was finished. Rinsing her plate and setting it in the dishwasher she finally pulled up her email account. It had only been about twenty minutes since she wrote Mags, but the suspense was already killing her. There was a reply waiting for her already, and she thanked her lucky stars for that woman's beautiful efficiency.

> *Caitlyn,*
> *That sounds like fun! Nolan has a show in LA on Friday night, and San Francisco on Saturday. He'll be flying up for the show Saturday but staying at his house for the weekend. Let me get you booked on a flight Friday. I'll send you all the details. I like the way your mind works! And FYI, he has been missing you a lot too, moping about and bugging me. So, this is perfect. See you Friday!*
> *Mags*

Jumping up from her stool excitedly Caitlyn

did a happy dance. She was going to get to see Nolan this weekend. Running into her room she pulled out her suitcase, thinking it was getting an awful lot of use these days, and the anticipation racing deliciously through her veins she began packing.

# Chapter Twenty-Five

Determined to put her ex-husband's growing disapproval out of her mind, sitting on the jet Caitlyn focused instead on the fact that she was seeing Nolan in just a few short hours. As expected, Bryan wasn't very pleased that she was, as he had put it, 'running off again.' Well, his immature, and frankly selfish, attitude about Caitlyn's private life was his own problem. All the people important in her life were thrilled she was moving on. Aunt Maura was ready to send her new beau a gift basket, Dad couldn't wait to meet Nolan, and her boys thought the whole thing was cool, as long as she was happy.

Instead of asking Bryan to keep the boys Sunday night this time, Caitlyn asked her Dad to come hang out at her house for the night. She was due back late Sunday, or rather early Monday morning. Which had only seemed to annoy her ex-husband more for some reason. Bryan had been nice and civil about the whole divorce, until she had a man in her life. Now suddenly he was the stereotypical jerk of an ex-husband. Figuring that said more about Bryan, than about the way Caitlyn was living her life she didn't bother letting it upset her anymore. She had given him years of her life, after all, and he hadn't appreciated them. No way was he going to steal these moments of happiness from her now.

Turns out that surprising Nolan was harder than Caitlyn thought it would be. They texted often throughout their day and omitting hopping on a flight to come see him was pretty hard for Caitlyn. Thankfully, Mags kept Nolan extremely busy running around all day Friday, barely giving him the chance to breathe, let alone have in depth conversations with Caitlyn. Thinking ahead, Nolan's assistant had also booked a room for Caitlyn at a hotel near the concert venue. That way she had somewhere to get ready for the show, it also had the added benefit of being somewhere she could stash her bags instead of bringing them along with her. Mags assured her that she would make sure they found their way to Nolan's house sometime during the show, and Caitlyn had no doubt she would make that happen. The woman was a veritable organizational goddess.

Caitlyn had never been to Los Angeles before, so the whole car ride from LAX to her hotel she snapped pictures of everything she passed by. The traffic was as bad as rumored, and Caitlyn was grateful she wasn't trying to navigate the ins and outs of the city. The hotel wasn't anything special, a typically affordable place you expected to see vacationing families eating a continental breakfast in the early hours before heading out to sight see. Her room had a single queen-sized bed, a television on top of a dresser, and a simple bathroom. She set her luggage down on the bed.

Checking the time, she calculated she had a little over two hours before show time. Pulling out her shampoo and conditioner she decided to take a quick shower. Running the razor carefully over her legs, Caitlyn smiled thinking that before the end of the night Nolan would be running his hands over the same spot. This was going to be the first time she got to see Nolan on stage, and it was exciting enough that she was fairly buzzing with adrenaline. She added a generous amount of frizz control cream to her hair, October in Los Angeles is quite a bit warmer than what the temperature back home in Michigan had been.

Walking back out into the small room Caitlyn pulled on the clothes she picked out specifically for this. The moto-style jeans were so dark they were nearly black, with sexy zippered pockets on her hips, and textured knees. The top was a sultry wine color, deep V with a crisscrossing neckline. Carrying her makeup bag into the bathroom she added a little more to her face than she usually wore. Winging out some black eyeliner on her eyes, adding lashings of mascara, and a wine-colored lipstick. It was fall after all, and vampy lips were always in. Bringing everything back out of the bathroom she packed it all back into her bag. Mags had arranged for her stuff to be picked up, but Caitlyn doubted someone was going to wander around making sure she had packed it all. Stacking some bangles on her wrist, and putting hoops in her ears Caitlyn stepped into the black ankle boots. Her phone dinged with a text from Mags letting her know that Nolan was on in ten, and she could head safely over now. It was too warm for the jacket she brought and would only get warmer with all the people packed in for the concert. Caitlyn shoved the jacket back into her suitcase, grabbed her little clutch purse and walked out of the room.

Thinking she would be walking the couple blocks to the venue Caitlyn almost missed the driver from before waiting in the lobby. He laughed at her confusion and let her know that he was told specifically to wait for her. It was probably for the best; she was so amped up that the short walk would have taken far too long. There was a young woman waiting by the front door for her with a VIP pass. Caitlyn put the placard over her head and followed the woman weaving through the crowd. She didn't need the help though, she could hear Nolan singing, the sound of his voice yanking her to him like a moth to the flame. Walking past the adoring fans she stood next to the security guard on the side of the stage. Staring up at all that was Nolan, it took Caitlyn a moment to remember to breathe. He was charming as hell one on one, but up on stage there was a raw magnetism to him that every single person in the room felt, and he owned them all from the second he stepped out onto that stage.

He was wearing dark jeans, scuffed boots, a flannel shirt opened to show the vintage band t-shirt underneath. There was a red electric guitar strapped across his body, and his fingers all but flew across the strings. As he sang into the microphone he winked to a girl in the front and gyrated his hips against his guitar in time to his words. The girl screamed like her ovaries were exploding, and Caitlyn laughed, knowing exactly how she felt right about now. Watching him in his element like this she could see how much he loved being up on that stage. Nothing about him looked nervous, in fact he looked like he lived for this moment. He switched up guitars often, a tech rushing out to hand him the next one and rushing away with the previous. Nolan sang two more songs before he finally spotted Caitlyn. He was next to his bass player jamming out when he looked up and his eyes met hers and she watched his face go absolutely blank for a heartbeat before the biggest grin she had ever seen in her entire life took over his face. It lit him right up, and she could actually feel the waves of joy pouring off of him. Strutting back to his microphone stand he sang the rest of the song directly to her.

Caitlyn was so lost in his eyes that it wasn't until he finished the song that she realized it was the one describing the way her eyes looked while she came beneath him in the dark. He wagged his eyebrows at her, telling her he had been well aware of what he was singing to her, before turning his attention back to the rest of his audience. Caitlyn spent the next hour and a half jumping and dancing excitedly with the rest of the crowd until the young woman from earlier came and tapped on her shoulder. She had to lean in really close, all but yelling into Caitlyn's ear telling her that Mag's said it was time to bring her backstage. Caitlyn sent Nolan a little wave, which had him smirking as he bobbed his head to the beat. That was a sight she clicked away to memory right then and there as she walked away.

They made their way through the security, and followed the corridors around, until the woman left her next to Mags just off stage.

"Looks like you had a good time," Mags said hugging Caitlyn.

"Oh, yeah! He's just incredible!" Caitlyn gushed proudly.

Mags laughed at her, then explained how he would come off stage for a minute giving the audience plenty of chance to scream, before running back out to do his two-song encore. Nodding her head Caitlyn stood off to the side unable to keep her eyes off Nolan.

The song ended, and he thanked the audience before exiting the stage. He walked right over to Caitlyn, slinging the guitar still strapped to him around so that it hung from his back. Not stopping his momentum, he grabbed her, his body colliding with hers. Shoving both of his hands into her hair he kissed her like he hadn't seen her in years. She felt the heat pouring off his skin, the energy zinging through him as he feasted from her mouth. Pulling his mouth away from hers he leaned down and rested his forehead against hers.

"Missed ye so much, love. Best surprise ever!" he said, his voice low and husky.

There was a flurry of activity around him as he stepped away from her wiping the smudge of her lipstick off his mouth with his thumb. His eyes never leaving hers, he lifted the guitar, handing it off and accepting the new one, adjusting the strap on his shoulder. Caitlyn could hear the crowd chanting his name now "NOL-AN! NOL-AN! NOL-AN!" He sent her a cocky wink and strutted back on stage to the roar of a deafening scream. He played his first song, then thanked the crowd for coming, told them to get home safely that he wanted to see them all the next time. The last song seemed to go on forever, dragging out the guitar solos, and adding in another round of the chorus before it ended with Nolan and the drummer dueling it out while the lights pulsed. Nolan walked briskly off stage as the last note rang out.

Stopping a hairsbreadth in front of Caitlyn his breath tickling her face, he handed his guitar off, pulled the in-ear monitors out, and all the wires and battery packs out of his back pockets.

His eyes were blazing blue fire at her, the muscle in his tense jaw standing out. Caught up in the desire she read clearly in his eyes, Caitlyn's tongue flicked out licking her top lip, and she felt Nolan's control snap. Grabbing her hand, he stormed away. Caitlyn almost had to jog to keep from being dragged behind Nolan through the corridors. He pulled her into a room and kicked the door shut. Reaching a hand back he turned the lock on the knob with an audible click. "Ye look so fucking sexy, Caitlyn," he said his hands roaming all over her body.

The slow burn that had been simmering while she watched him play suddenly ignited inside of her, and she yanked the flannel off his shoulders. He kissed her while he pulled the top over her head, pausing to look down at the burgundy bra she had on. He growled appreciatively in the back of his throat. His hands came up cupping her breasts, thumbs rubbing against the satin against her nipples. Caitlyn pulled his belt buckle, and opened his pants reaching her hand into his boxers to find his dick. The feel of him beneath her fingertips was like velvet warmth covering steel. She worked her hand up and down his shaft, kissing him as his hands undid her pants, pushing them down her hips. Nolan turned her around and opening her eyes she saw the table in front of her. It was shoved against the wall, which had a large mirror hanging on it. Looking up into his eyes Caitlyn planted her hands on the wooden surface and pushed her ass invitingly into him. Nolan gripped his dick, and she watched his face as he rubbed it across her slit, teasing her. Moaning, she begged, "Please, Nol, I want you so bad right now."

Biting his bottom lip, he thrust his hips forward, his dick finally sliding into her pussy. It always felt right, like they were made to fit together. Nolan pumped into her hard and fast, still flying high from all the energy from being on stage. "Shit," he said as his breath came in hard pants. He reached down and stroked his finger across her clit in time to his dick moving inside of her. "C'mon baby, hurry."

Seeing him take her this way, his fingers working her, his own pleasure written on his face as his hips slammed into her was the hottest thing Caitlyn had ever seen. "Yes, yes, yes!" she chanted as she raced to catch up with him. Just as she felt him swelling impossibly bigger inside of her, she broke apart. Bucking her hips back into him she rode the wave crashing through her. She heard his groan as he twitched deep inside of her, coming in a warm rush. He moved in and out lazily a moment, savoring every second of her pussy shuddering around him before he finally pulled out.

"Can ye stay standing?" Nolan leaned over and asked against her ear.

Nodding her head, "I think so."

He walked over to the bathroom in the corner of the room and disappeared inside. A few moments later he came back out, his pants back in place, with a wet washcloth. Caitlyn turned around, facing him, her back against the table. Nolan leaned down and cleaned up all of their fluids from her thighs. Once he had wiped all the traces away, he walked back into the bathroom, presumably to take care of it. Caitlyn leaned down to grab her own pants, but Nolan beat her to it, and pulled them gently up her legs. His t-shirt had never even made it off, and she spotted hers across the room. Walking over to it on legs still shaky she shook it out and put it back on.

He walked over to her and wrapped his arms around her. "God it was so hard to watch ye all night." He buried his head in her neck.

"I kind of liked it. You look really good up on that stage Nol. And if this is what waiting to touch me does to you, I've got zero complaints." Caitlyn ran her hands up and down his back, feeling at home in his arms.

"I didn't get too rough?" She shook her head in answer. "How long are ye here with me for?"

"I fly back on Sunday. I'm coming with you to

the show tomorrow too," she told him. He smelled warm and spicy like usual, but there was an unapologetic raw new dimension with the sweat from playing so hard on stage. If they could find a way to bottle it, insatiable women would buy it by the gallons.

"Fuck yeah!" he said excitedly, lifting his head up. "Where's yer bags?"

"Mags was having them sent to your house, so I'm thinking there," she said laughing. "Don't ever let her get away, she is scary good at her job."

"Oh, I've no intention of that," he said raising his brows in agreement.

"How long after a show do you usually stay?" Caitlyn asked.

"Since I'm just going home from here, I can leave any time I want. Wanna come see me house love?" he said, his fingers stroking the sides of her rib cage where he held her tenderly.

"Aren't you hungry after working so hard?" Caitlyn asked him, tilting her head to the side.

"I'll order us a takeaway pizza." He said unlocking the door and walking out of his dressing room hand in hand with Caitlyn.

People were rushing around everywhere, busy taking care of the stage, instruments and every other little thing that goes into putting a show together. Nolan waved or said goodbyes to everyone as they passed. Mags had a clip board in her hand when they found her, and she was talking into her phone. Holding a hand over the receiver she said, "Your car is waiting right outside the stage door Nolan, be at the airport by eleven. See you later guys," before turning back to her conversation.

Nolan held the passenger door open on the black Mercedes coupe while Caitlyn climbed inside, then walked around the hood and climbed in the driver's side. They pulled out and were on the road before anyone had a chance to notice him. In a city brimming with wealth a Mercedes blended right in. Caitlyn lounged in the supple leather seat holding his hand thinking about how different this was than her life. If his car rolled through her small town, you could bet that everyone would take note. Nolan drove them high into the hills away from the bustling city. Most of the houses up here were hidden by hedges, foliage, or walls. People who lived here clearly valued their privacy, and Caitlyn figured at home was probably the only time they got it.

He pulled up to a gate, sent his window gliding down, and reached out to punch in a code. The horizontal slats of wood slipped into the rest of the fence and he drove past, sliding back in place a moment later. Driving the short distance to the house, he pushed a button on his visor, the garage door whizzed up, and he pulled smoothly inside. His house was big, but nothing she would call an opulent mansion, and that make her happy. Caitlyn had been a little worried on the drive up what she would find. He had to have more money that he could ever spend but seeing his house she was grateful she was right about the kind of person he was.

Her suitcase was sitting in front of the door leading inside, and Nolan grabbed it as he unlocked the door with another keypad before motioning for her to walk inside. He hit the light switch on the wall and Caitlyn saw they were standing in a mudroom, with a laundry room leading off to one side. Nolan kicked his shoes off, so Caitlyn stepped out of her ankle boots. He smiled at her, and led her the rest of the way into his house.

Nolan's taste ran to modern. There were a lot of clean lines, white walls, sandy colored wooden floors. But it all looked comfortable, the couch was a large gray sectional, with a low-slung coffee table in front of it begging you to relax. The kitchen was spacious, with more of the same color scheme, but it all looked well loved, like it was actually used. "You cook?" she asked turning to look at Nolan.

"Of course. I like to eat, don' I? Although I doubt I've got much to throw together right now," he answered back. "I'm the same man, love. I can see ye were wondering if I live in a palace like some egotistical king as we pulled in." He pulled her close against him. "That's no' me."

"I don't really know what I expected, but driving past some of the houses, I'll admit I started to get a little worried," she confessed sheepishly.

"I thought the same thing when I first came up here to look at this place. Truth be told, I think I've got the smallest house in the whole of the area," he said laughing.

He asked what she liked on her pizza, she told him everything but pineapples, to which he whole heartedly agreed. While he ordered their food, Caitlyn roamed his house. There was a patio area just off the living room, standing at the French doors she looked out and saw a pool in the yard. She found an office slash music room with guitars hanging up on the walls on the first floor, there were awards sitting on the shelves, mixed in with pictures of him and his band on stage. There was also a guest room, and bathroom down the hall. Taking a moment, she appreciated the stairs with their cool suspended cable railings before walking up them. Upstairs on one side there were two more bedrooms that looked meant for friends and family to stay in when they visited. Walking back past the stairs again she went to the other side of the hall.

There was only one door on this side of the stairs. Nolan's room was large and with a decidedly masculine air. A king size bed sat against one wall, with its massive black headboard as tall as she was.

There was a television hanging above a small fireplace on the opposite wall. There was a pair of comfortable chairs in front of the window, walking over to it she guessed he had a nice view of the yard from here. There were two doors on the other side, in one she found a large walk-in closet that was well organized. Closing the closet, she walked to the other door guessing it was his bathroom. Opening it she felt along the wall for the lights. Finding them she flipped them on and blinked while her eyes adjusted. The room was gorgeous. Directly across from the door was a large granite countertop vanity with double sinks, and a huge mirror. Stepping in and turning she saw a jetted tub made for relaxing after a long day, and the frosted glass walls of his shower. He favored light gray marble, and although it was stunning, nothing looked elaborate. This was only the third bathroom in the whole house. There was one on the first floor, another up here by the guest rooms, and this one. She had two bathrooms at home, but it wasn't unheard of to have three. It wasn't as if he had twenty-three bedrooms and fifteen bathrooms that all had a different theme.

Smiling she wandered back downstairs. Nolan was sitting on the couch and had turned the television on low. She could see the ESPN logo in the corner of the screen. But his eyes were all for Caitlyn as she walked down to him. She could easily read the questions in his gaze and sitting down next to him she laid her head on his chest. His arm immediately came around her, and she sighed, "I love your home Nol, its beautiful." He let the air out of his lungs slowly, and she felt his body relax. "How long until the pizza gets here?"

"Twenty minutes or so. Mind if I grab a quick shower? I feel a might ripe. Pizza's already paid for, but I'll be out before they get here with it," he said, his fingers drawing circles on her shoulder.

"You don't have to ask, go ahead." He kissed her quick on the lips, then headed upstairs.

# Chapter Twenty-Six

Sitting on the couch eating their dinner of pizza they laughed and talked while the television droned softly on in the background, ignored. Nolan had put on a pair of navy sweat pants, slung low on his hips after his shower, but hadn't bothered with a shirt. The pizza delivery guy earlier had seemed to really appreciate the view, getting all flustered and tongue-tied while handing Nolan their pizza. Caitlyn enjoyed watching other people react to him knowing that she was the one who got to run her hands over all that tantalizingly inviting skin. Adoring fans came with the territory, but even before she knew he was famous she had noticed everyone checking him out. He was just the type of man that people noticed. Nolan would have to be rather dense not to realize his appeal at this point, but he didn't seem to let that guide him. He wasn't shirtless right now to show off his chest to its best advantage, he was just comfortable, relaxing at home. She all but forgot about his fame when he was like this with her, just Nolan and Caitlyn.

A little while after their food was gone her phone on the coffee table started buzzing, over and over. Thinking that someone must be texting her repeatedly she picked it up, a little worried. There were so many notifications coming through that her eyes couldn't keep up as she tried to read them all. They were rolling over her screen in an endless loop. Looking questioningly over at Nolan, she turned the phone towards him, showing him the screen. She watched him as the confusion in his gaze cleared quickly.

"Looks like me fans figured it the hell out," he said standing up and jogging briskly up the stairs. Calling out, "Turn yer phone off love."

Since the notifications were still flooding in, turning it off didn't seem like a bad idea. She was powering it down when Nolan came back down the stairs, holding his own phone in his hand.

"Yer trending. It might be time to adjust yer settings on Twitter, probably Instagram too, or it will keep overloading yer phone," he said shrugging his shoulders, knowing what he was talking about all too well.

"What do you mean I'm trending?" She asked walking over to the suitcase they hadn't brought upstairs yet Caitlyn pulled her laptop out.

"Well, technically **#NolanLovesCaitlyn** is trending, but they're taggin' ye too," Nolan said scrolling through twitter on his phone. "I gotta keep me notifications off because I get tagged in so much, absolutely all a da time," Nolan explained.

Siting back down on the couch Caitlyn turned her computer on and logging into Nolan's WiFi pulled up her twitter. "Holy shit! Nolan, I have over twenty thousand notifications, and three hundred direct messages."

Wiping a hand down his face he said, "Yeah, I'm not surprised. I'm sorry love, this kind of comes with me job. I was hoping we had more time just for us."

Caitlyn adjusted her settings, but she couldn't make her profile private because she used it to market her books, which was why she was so easy for the fans to find in the first place. Sighing she logged into her Instagram and found thousands of new followers there too. Someone had taken a picture of Nolan kissing her on the side of the stage, and from the angle it couldn't have come from the crowd, and it looked like every single fan he had posted it and shared it, tagging them both.

"How did they figure out who I was so fast?" Caitlyn wondered out loud.

"Ye would be surprised at how fuckin' thorough they can be sometimes. Looks like someone hangin' round backstage posted that." He motioned his head at her computer and sighed, slumping wearily back into the couch. "Changing yer settings only stops yer phone from buzzing all day, but long as yer with me this is gonna keep happening."

Setting her laptop down in front of her on the coffee table, Caitlyn curled herself into him. "Nolan, you're worth it. This might end up being a real pain in the ass, but it's a small price to pay to have you in my life. I meant what I said before. I'm yours, nothing is going to change that." The clouds of doubt and worry were written clearly in his eyes.

"And when ye get papped doin' something so normal like loading groceries into yer car?" He said, but he pulled her closer wrapping his arm tight around her.

"Then I'll remember Belfast, Nolan. Crying on the floor of my hotel room because getting up just wasn't possible. I'll remember the nice stranger, Gloria, from Oklahoma who held me as I sobbed my heart out at The Giants Causeway. I'll remember that consuming pain and know that nothing the paparazzi will ever do to me can come close to matching how that felt," Caitlyn whispered into the comforting warmth of Nolan's chest. Her voice shaking as she remembered the crushing weight of pain as her heart bled out its love. "If I never feel like that again, it will still be too soon."

"Shit, Caitlyn." Nolan tipped her face back, his eyes searching hers. "I'll no' ever, in me whole life lose the image of that now. God help me, I believe ye really mean it about the paps. They can be a proper pain in the arse though."

Staring up at Nolan, Caitlyn nodded her head. His rich brown hair had dried waving every which way, made worse by his own hand cruising through it often. The stubble growing on his chin telling her he didn't bother to shave this morning. The swirling blue and green pools of his eyes, that saw her for exactly who she was, and loved her for it. Touching his face reverently she whispered, "Nolan, I do mean it."

Caitlyn watched his face smooth out, the strain finally melting away. One side of his mouth tipped up in a small smirk. "Baby, I fuckin' love ye." His face inched slowly down to hers.

"Good," she said against his lips, before he kissed her softly. He told her with his lips and tongue everything he was feeling, and Caitlyn was blinded by how bright the feelings he poured into her soul were. This man of hers had an endless well of love inside, and she knew that she was the luckiest woman to have ever existed that it was all for her. Nolan laid her back on his couch and linking her arms behind his neck she gloried in his weight pressing her into the plush cushions. Pressing her thighs to his hips, everything else in the world floated away.

Nolan took his time, kissing her long and deep. He leaned back and watched her, his lids heavy, as Caitlyn sat up enough to pull her shirt off while his hands roamed softly down her sides. His hands gliding around her back he unsnapped her satin bra, pulling it slowly off her. Leaning back down Nolan kissed her again, his fingers barely grazing the sides of her breasts, sending delicious chills cascading through her body. His lips rained kisses down her chin, and along her jaw before finding the spot just under her ear that drove Caitlyn crazy. Scooting down her body Nolan's lips blazed a trail across her collar bone before stopping to worship each of her nipples until she was gasping, her body filling with need. Just when she was about to beg him Nolan licked down the center of her stomach, stopping to swirl his tongue teasingly around her navel. Looking up at her, he undid her pants and sitting up he pulled them off while Caitlyn lifted her hips to assist him.

His hands gripping her leg, he kissed and nibbled slowly inside of her leg from the knee up. Still wearing the matching burgundy satin panties, Caitlyn shivered with need as he stroked a finger across the material, right down the front of her. Finding her clit through the silky material he rubbed it softly. Laying down Nolan watched her eyes as he touched the tip of his tongue exactly where his finger had been. Flicking slowly back and forth he teased her. Caitlyn reached her hands into his hair, needing to hold on to something. He sucked her clit into his mouth, and she arched her neck back groaning. He worked her like that, through her panties, until they had soaked through the satin. Moving the barrier aside she finally felt his tongue sliding along her skin. He licked her so, so slowly while she gulped in huge gasping breaths of air, her body blazing with need. Her legs shaking against his shoulders she begged, the orgasm frustratingly, just out of her reach. "More, please baby, more please."

"Don't ye worry, I'll take care of ye," he said, his mouth pressed to her as he slowly pushed a finger into her achingly empty pussy. Stroking her so slowly that his finger was barely moving, Caitlyn bucked her hips in desperation. She heard his low laugh, felt the rumble of it tickle along her clit as he closed his teeth around it, nibbling gently. Finally feeling the delicious pressure inside of her building Caitlyn dug her fingers into his hair. Nolan added a second finger to the one inside of her and swirled his tongue determinedly. Her body finally breaking apart, Caitlyn screamed out in relief as she came.

Nolan licked her slowly while her aftershocks pulsed. "God, that's the most beautiful thing in the whole of this world," he said, his accent thick and voice full of the awe he was feeling.

Unable to form words, her brain so fuzzy with pleasure, she reached down pulling him up her body. Nolan laughed and she felt him pushing the sweatpants he still had on down his hips. His dick lay heavy between them, and not giving him the chance to tease her more Caitlyn lifted her hips up into him, taking him quickly inside her pussy. She heard his sharp hiss of breath above her and opened her eyes slowly. Watching his face, she moved under him, sliding his dick in and out of her exactly as she needed. He reached down and stroked the side of her face as she worked her body underneath his. The trembling quakes started slowly, but they built quick, like ripples on the water. Crying out she came a second time, as he watched her break apart underneath him.

Finally, Nolan's hips started moving, finding a slow, patient rhythm, Caitlyn lost count of how many times she came, one orgasm seeming to flow endlessly into the next. Each time Nolan gritted his teeth, and held still, locked deep inside of her absorbing the pulsing all around him. She could see he was barely holding on by a thread each time, battling back his own orgasm. Lost in the torrent of sensations burning through her veins she slid her hands up his neck and pulled him down to her waiting mouth. Caitlyn kissed him as he made relentlessly slow love to her. Her body trembling again, she bit her teeth down into his bottom lip. His arms slid behind her back pulling her impossibly closer, and she felt his muscles shaking as he finally let go. Pressing her deep into the couch he swiveled his hips against her, making her gasp into his mouth as he pulsed inside of her. The heat as he came was nearly enough to melt her insides, as he finally emptied into her.

As they lay there completely spent on the couch, their hearts thundered in their chests. Caitlyn ran her fingers through his hair, watching the way the shades of brown changed in the light. Sometime later he lifted himself up off her and stood up. Reaching a hand down he helped her to her feet, but her legs wobbled unsteadily underneath her. Not missing a beat Nolan swooped her up and carried her up the stairs to his bed. Neither of them noticing that all the lights were still blazing downstairs.

# Chapter Twenty-Seven

Turning her phone back on the next morning Caitlyn saw that Wyatt had texted her a few minutes prior. Putting the phone up to her ear she decided to call him instead of just texting back.

"Mom! Holy crap. You're all that everyone is talking about," Wyatt blurted out as soon as he answered the call.

"Good morning to you too." She laughed. "What do you mean?"

"The pictures of you and Nolan! C'mon Mom!" he explained, his tone clearly stating that she should have already known.

"Oh, those," Caitlyn said. She had completely forgotten about her twitter blowing up, Nolan had quite a talent for eclipsing everything else.

"Everyone at school's been texting me. They want autographs, concert tickets, and to meet him. Its way crazy," Wyatt said.

"Seriously? I'm sorry Wyatt. What are you telling them?" Caitlyn asked watching Nolan as he carried her suitcase up the stairs.

"To chill out basically." She could almost hear the shrug of his shoulders. "Mase is pretty geeked you're famous now too."

"Oh, geez. I'm not famous," Caitlyn said plopping down onto the soft gray couch.

"Do you have any idea how many followers you have now?" Wyatt asked sounding exasperated with her.

"No, I haven't looked this morning," Caitlyn said grabbing her laptop. Logging into her twitter she was shocked. "I have over a half of a million followers. OK, other than this how is everything back home?"

"Fine, like anything would be as exciting as that. Dad is taking us to a hockey game tonight though, should be pretty sick," Wyatt added.

"Have fun, bundle up, it's gonna be cold at the rink," Caitlyn reminded him.

"I know, I'm not a baby Mom," he sighed.

"You're my baby," she joked just to hear the annoyed grunt she knew he would make.

"I'm flying up to San Francisco for the day, so if I don't text immediately back don't worry," Caitlyn said tucking her legs up under her on the couch.

"I won't. Have fun, tell Nolan to kick ass tonight. Love ya."

"Wyatt, language." She heard him laughing. "Love you too. Send Mase my love too. Bye honey," she said hearing the click signaling he had hung up.

Setting her phone down she turned her computer off. She could check out her newfound social media popularity just as easily from her cell phone as she got ready for the day. Walking up the stairs she headed straight into Nolan's bathroom and into the shower. Caitlyn got lost in the simple tasks of washing her hair, shaving, and cleaning her body. Turning the water off she stepped out, she was reaching for her towel when she saw Nolan leaning against the door frame, his arms crossed.

"How's it back home?" he asked her.

"Wyatt is now even more popular than he was yesterday, which is saying something. Half his classmates end up at my house on any given weekend. Everyone is asking him for your autograph, or to get them all tickets. But my boys seem to be taking it all in stride. Mason thinks I'm famous now I guess," Caitlyn said as she toweled off her body.

"Ye are, love," Nolan said, his voice tight.

"No, you're famous. I'm just a curiosity right now. But hey, if they all want to buy some of my books I wouldn't mind that," she added wrapping the towel around her hair, and walking to him.

"Honestly, Nol, I meant what I said last night." She tipped her head up and laid a kiss on his scruffy jaw. Walking over to her suitcase she pulled out some clothes.

"San Francisco is colder than LA right?" she called over her shoulder.

"Yeah," he said, finally stepping away from the

door frame into the bathroom. A moment later she heard the water start up again.

Deciding on dark skinny jeans, and a snug black three-quarter sleeve top she got dressed. Her favorite cognac colored riding boots, and the olive-green jacket would look good with it, and hopefully keep her warm enough. Nolan was just stepping out of the shower as she walked up to the mirror to get her hair and face all set for the day. Watching him run the towel over his skin collecting all of the drops of water had her mouth going dry. He wasn't paying any attention to her, just drying himself off, and it still made her feel weak in the knees.

"Nol?" she said.

"Mmmm?" he said rubbing the towel over his hair.

"I love you," she said turning around to face him, her voice gone soft and dreamy. The smile that spread across his face was worth more to Caitlyn than just about anything else in this world.

"Love ye too baby," he said walking over. He laid a kiss on her lips, still smiling, and walked out of the bathroom to get himself dressed. Smiling at herself in the mirror she shook her head and finished putting on her makeup.

They arrived at LAX right on time, as instructed, and Mags met them with security. "How many?" Nolan asked his assistant. Then nodding at the man with Mags, said for Caitlyn's benefit, "This is Rob."

"Only a few hundred thankfully. This is LA though, and they're used to it. They already have areas cordoned off, trust me man, its handled," Rob replied decisively.

"A few hundred what? People? He means people? There are a few hundred people here for you?" Caitlyn asked repeating herself, turning from person to person. Rob looked kind of familiar to her, but he also had one of those indistinct faces you really weren't meant to notice.

"For the both of you. Your romance is creating quite the buzz," Mags replied. "Alright, game faces on people," she said looking over at Rob. At his nod she turned to lead the way.

Nolan took Caitlyn's hand, walking a half step in front of her. His protective gesture was not lost on her, after all people watching was something she excelled at being a novelist. There was a sense of excitement in the air, and the crowd, although not screaming, weren't quiet either. Questions were called out, most of which asking for details about their relationship. Papers were stuck out, arms waving them around desperately. Nolan stopped randomly here and there and scrawled his name, thanking people for coming to see him off safely. Caitlyn noticed a few copies of her paperbacks sticking out, and walking along feeling shell shocked she signed them. One girl told her excitedly that her mother had read Caitlyn's work for a while, so she didn't have to run out and buy a book this morning like everyone else. Caitlyn just nodded her head, and let Nolan tug her away.

Rob shepherded everyone past the crowd, and out to the private jet ready and waiting for them. He was somewhere between forty and fifty years old, with a short buzz cut that didn't actually disguise his growing bald spot. He wasn't bulky with bulging muscles, but he looked like he could hold his own should the need arise. He had murky hazel eyes, that were constantly moving, Caitlyn could tell he didn't miss much that went on around him. Everything about him said, don't mess with me, but once they were all seated safely on the plane his demeanor visibly relaxed.

Nolan wrapped his arm around her and murmured softly against her ear, "Ye with me, love?" Gauging how she was feeling faced with the scope of his celebrity. Nodding her head she turned to him and laid her palm on his cheek.

"Always. That was pretty crazy though, if I'm being honest. How do you get used to it?" she asked him.

"I dunno, I'll let ye know when I have," he said with a shrug.

"So Rob is your personal security?" Nolan nodded his head. "How come he wasn't with you in Ireland then?" Caitlyn questioned.

"He was in Ireland, just not with us. He wasn't too happy about that truth be told. But, they tend to leave me alone there, for the most part," Nolan replied as the plane took off.

"And if something had happened? That probably wasn't very smart of you, Nol," Caitlyn chided him, the mother in her going through all of the worst-case scenarios.

"That's what I told him too, but he wasn't about hearing it," Rob said from next to Mags. Caitlyn could see from the look on his face that her worry over Nolan's safety sat well with him.

"Nothin' happened. Besides how would I have explained that? No, that wouldn't do. I'da looked as mad as a box of frogs." Nolan shook his head.

Thinking about it Caitlyn realized he was probably right. If Rob had been tagging along things would have gone very differently between them. The risk still didn't sit well with her though, even if she was grateful for their time together. "Do you slip your security detail often?" she asked Nolan, then before he could answer she added, "After all, why pay them to protect you if you're not going to help them do their job."

Mags laughed outright, and Rob disguised a

chuckle with a completely unbelievable cough. Nolan just stared at her. "No, I don't, that was the first time love. I'll not be doing it again, that's for damn sure. Ye'd have me ass for it, I'm thinkin'."

"I sure would. I'd like you around for a while, not ripped apart or trampled as you get mobbed." Caitlyn kissed his cheek.

"Me Mum is gonna love ye," Nolan chuckled. "She never lets me get away with anything either."

It was decided by all that tonight Caitlyn would watch the whole show from backstage, for safety reasons since she was now probably recognizable to everyone in that crowd. Caitlyn was a little disappointed, but she also completely understood. It just made the night before even more special to her. They went straight from the plane to a waiting car bypassing any crowd waiting, and that took them straight to the venue. As expected, there was a line of fans around the block waiting to get into the show. They managed to sneak in unnoticed through the back of the venue. She hung out in the dressing room with Nolan while the crew got everything set up for the afternoon sound check.

Nolan sent out the tweet, "Can't wait to see everyone tonight, let's do this Bay Area! Saw what you trended, thanks for all the love! **#BestFans.**"

Caitlyn opened the Twitter app on her phone, and turned on notifications for Nolan's tweets. Then while she was there she retweeted what he said, figuring it couldn't hurt. They headed out to the soundcheck, which Caitlyn found so much fun. His band members were all pretty cool guys, and they joked around having a laugh, while randomly jamming out. After they got everything for the show sounding exactly right, they let in a small group of fans. Mags explained they had bought special tickets and would get to take a picture with Nolan after. Sitting off to the side Caitlyn watched as Nolan answered questions and played one of the lesser known songs from his first album. Apparently one that didn't make it to the set list for the show this time around, but the fans loved. It took well over an hour to shuffle the fans through, but Nolan was kind to each and every one of them. His smile in the last picture was just as bright as the first shot had been. A few fans waved to her, still standing out of the way, and she smiled and waved back.

There was catering waiting for them in his dressing room when they made their way back there. Caitlyn noticed Nolan only had a bite here and there, but she figured going on stage with a full stomach wasn't ideal. His phone rang, and he spent twenty minutes on facetime with his mother, before handing the phone off to Caitlyn. She was introduced to his Mum, Cora, and they chatted for a bit getting to know each other. Cora clearly passed down her hair and eyes to Nolan. Her soft brown hair hung in a flattering bob style, with a few subtle highlights to frame her lovely face. Cora invited Caitlyn, and her sons, to come over to Ireland as soon as they could. Cora was a little disappointed that she couldn't make it for Christmas, but the kids went over to Bryan's house that night for the rest of Christmas break.

While she got to know his mother, Nolan got up and restlessly prowled the room. She could feel his energy building, when he muttered something about wardrobe. He walked out of the room, and Caitlyn sat there a little confused.

"Don't worry darling, he gets wound tight before a show. It's like he is storing everything up," Cora said noticing. Caitlyn thanked her for the advice, rattled off her phone number when Cora asked, and they ended the conversation. Caitlyn liked Cora and was happy when she had asked it it would be alright to ring her from time to time.

She was setting Nolan's phone down next to her on the couch when he walked back in. He was now in a pair of nice jeans, that just happened showcase his ass to perfection. A short-sleeved olive-green button-down shirt, sleeves rolled just so on his biceps, top two buttons left undone so his chest hair peeked out. The look was casual, but very masculine, and carefully put together for maximum impact on stage. His hair was messed to perfection, and Caitlyn figured if she touched it that she would feel paste, or wax keeping it together that way. His in-ear monitors hung loosely around his neck. He saw her watching him, walked over, pulled her to standing and kissed her devastatingly thoroughly. Caitlyn could taste the excitement on Nolan's tongue, and it swept her away with him. "C'mon love, it's show time," he said pulling his mouth away from her finally, and led her out of the room and down the corridor to towards the stage.

Caitlyn watched the flurry of activity as people ran around every which way. There were a dozen people, at least, but everyone knew their job, and it looked like a well-choreographed dance as they darted here and there. Someone strapped something around his waist, and tucked a battery pack in his back pocket. Another person handed Nolan an electric guitar, and he lifted it over his head taking a moment to adjust the strap. His band members walked out one by one, and the crowd screamed. The first drawn out notes of a song flowed through the venue, and Nolan pushed the buds into his ears. Bopping up and down on his toes he shook his body out, winked at Caitlyn and sauntered out onto the stage as the audience erupted in adulation.

# Chapter Twenty-Eight

After her weekend away surprising Nolan life back home was very different than before. She was the talk of the town, and everywhere she went people came up asking her questions about Nolan. It was quite strange to have women approach you in the produce section at the grocery store, to ask you what your boyfriend was like, or how big his penis was over the tomatoes. If she had been the one to ask that it would be a whole different story, but nobody seemed to grasp that concept. For some reason his well-known status seemed to make people forget he was still just a man. The first time it happened Caitlyn just stood there baffled, blinking at the person until it filtered through her brain. It took some audacity to approach someone you didn't even know and ask them intensely private questions like that.

Her dentist had even asked her at her teeth cleaning if she could get him backstage passes. His hands were knuckle deep inside of her mouth at the time, checking on her teeth, and all Caitlyn could do was shrug her shoulders. The man had never once been anything but completely professional, but start dating a rock star and he hits you up for tickets and passes. It nearly boggled her mind, and it had to be so much worse for Nolan than it was for her. At least there weren't any paparazzi hanging around her small town to contend with. She knew they were hounding Nolan quite a lot recently, shouting questions about his relationship with her at him whenever they got close enough. Caitlyn had actually been talking on the phone with him the other day and heard it herself. Nolan just kept right on talking to her without missing a beat, telling her later that if you gave them an opening they stormed right in. They could sense weakness and exploit it the same way a shark could smell blood in the water.

The short tour to promote his new album was winding down, his last gig for a while, the Monday before Thanksgiving. It had been nearly a month since they saw each other, and Caitlyn had been counting down the days until she could see him again. Her sons couldn't wait to meet Nolan either, but she had all but sworn them to secrecy, the last thing they all needed was that little tidbit getting out. The only people who knew Nolan was going to be at her house for Thanksgiving were her boys, her Dad, Mags and Rob. Caitlyn had invited the both of them along to dinner, but since they were both American they were celebrating with their own families. Nolan would be on his own this time, with strict instructions to lay low.

The temperature was hovering somewhere below frigid as Caitlyn drove down to the airport to pick Nolan up Tuesday afternoon. She had been so nervous all morning that she had walked around her house straightening up what she had already cleaned the day before. She ran the vacuum so many times that the carpet probably hadn't even been this clean when it was first installed on the floors. Getting annoyed with herself for freaking out only made her more nervous. After all, a person's home said an awful lot about them.

Remembering the look on Nolan's face when he brought her to his place Caitlyn smiled as she pulled into the airport. After parking her car she jogged into the waiting warmth of the building. She was hoping to be early, but everyone must have been on their lunch because traffic had thrown a wrench in her schedule. She was waiting less than ten minutes when Nolan walked out. She spotted him first and stood there absorbing the feeling of the butterflies taking flight in her stomach. He had on a pair of comfortably worn jeans, a brown jacket, with a charcoal gray thermal underneath. The navy flat cap was covering his hair, and his jaw was darkened with the brown stubble that always made her fingertips all but ache to touch it. He was clenching the same brown leather bag he had brought to her hotel room so many months ago in Ireland in one hand, his other tucked into the front pocket of his jeans. Smiling Caitlyn waited for him to see her as he scanned the room. She felt the impact of his eyes landing on her as she watched a devastatingly handsome smile spread across his face.

She met Nolan halfway, and wrapped her arms around his waist, tucking her head into the crook between his shoulder and his neck. He held her tightly to him with his free arm, and said with a chuckle, "Nice welcome, love. Ye look right adorable in yer coat."

Pulling away she kissed his lips, "its freezing cold out Nol." Her black puffy coat kept her warm, which was high on her priority list this time of the year. The cream-colored ribbed turtleneck sweater, and jeans with fuzzy winter boots completed the rest of her cold weather chic. "Do you have a heavier coat?" She asked him thinking the brown jacket looked great, but wouldn't be much help against elements here in Michigan.

"Yeah, it's in me suitcase," he said slinging an arm comfortably around her shoulder as they went to collect his luggage from the baggage claim.

She filled him in on everything she could think about her hometown on the drive back, answering a question he asked here and there. As they rolled through she pointed out the boys schools, but tried to let him make his own impressions. When they left town he turned to her with a confused look. "I live just outside of town, most people do around here." As she pulled into her neighborhood and slowed to the speed limit her nerves started growing again. Reaching up to hit the garage door button clipped to her visor Caitlyn's hands were trembling slightly. Climbing out of her car in the garage she hit the button closing the door behind them. She met him at the back of her car, and opening the hatch for him he reached in and grabbed his suitcase and leather bag.

"Show me yer home, love," Nolan said softly.

"You've seen some of it already, in the background while we face-timed," she muttered leading him to the door.

"True enough, I have," he said as she unlocked the door and stepped inside. Much like his house they entered a mudroom, except hers also doubled as the laundry room. Nolan set his bags down, and they hung their coats on the pegs inside the built in wooden open style lockers on the wall before stepping out of their boots.

Caitlyn walked with Nolan through the whole house. The kitchen with its big island that she often sat writing at. The dining room just off the kitchen with the large wooden table, and industrial style chandelier. Nolan walked ahead of her into the living room with its comfortable white slip covered sofa and love seat gathered around the low coffee table. He took his time looking at all the pictures scattered around the bookshelves, and atop the mantle. She watched him touch the framed picture of the Cliffs of Moher before he turned to her with a smile. "One of the best days of me life so far."

Caitlyn nodded, the memories floating through her head. "Me too."

He walked to the French doors leading out to the balcony looking out. Her house backed on to a small patch of woods, but with the spindly trees naked of leaves you could see the houses off in the distance. She led him down the open staircase to the finished basement. At the bottom of the stairs was a large family room, with a large mocha colored sectional. A large television hung from the wall with all of the boy's video game systems on shelves beneath it. Turning into one of the doors along the wall she showed him her office. Her shelves held her own books alongside all her favorites, the desk directly in front of the window.

"I can picture ye sitting here watching yer sons out that window while writing," he said smiling and taking her hand in his rubbing his thumb across her knuckles like he often did.

"I do that a lot in the summer, but I get sick of being cooped up. I'll take my computer and sit on the couch, or at the island in the kitchen quite often too," she said as they walked back out. Pointing out the door a little ways down the wall she said, "That's my guest room. I, with the boys, I wasn't really sure it would be a good idea, especially the first time they meet you. I mean..."

Nolan leaned down silencing her rambles with a kiss. "Caitlyn, I wasn't thinking I'd be sleeping in yer bed. I'm sure the lads would not appreciate that much, and in all fairness, I'd not blame them." He held her face tenderly in his hands. "I plan on makin' a good impression, and them thinking of me spending time in yer bed won't do that."

"Thank you for understanding Nolan." She leaned in and laid a gentle kiss on his neck, just to the side of his Adams apple. Turning out of his arms she opened the door to the guest room. The simple room was done in shades of blue. A queen-sized bed sat against one wall, with a dresser under the window. There was a large photograph of sunflowers a friend of hers had taken on the wall, and an alarm clock sat on the dresser. There was a closet, but that was basically it. Most of the time family members stayed here, and they really only slept in there. Looking at it now she laughed. "I hope you don't need to come down here to escape us."

"I'd sleep happily on yer couch love." He winked at her, then added, "I didn't come here to be spending time on me own." He walked back out of the room, heading past the large couch in the family room to the slider on the wall. The pool was covered now, the lounge chairs put away, but he stood there a moment looking out. "Can I see yer rooms now?"

Back upstairs they peeked into each of the boy's rooms, first Wyatt's, and then Mason's. Typical teen boy rooms, filled with sports odds and ends, pictures of their friends, and the random treasures they'd collected over the years. Caitlyn had given up on their rooms being clean ages ago, but thankfully for once they didn't look too crazy.

Following the hallway back she walked into her bedroom and watched struggling to stay silent as he wandered around. She had two windows, one looking out front, the other to the side yard. Her king-sized sleigh bed dominated one wall, with its green comforter, flanked by nightstands, a reading lamp atop each. A matching dresser topped with her television stood opposite. A completely feminine chair sat in front of the front facing window. Caitlyn liked to sit there and read in it from time to time. Nolan ignored her closet but looked into the master bathroom. Her bathroom was one of the reasons she bought the house in the first place. The large bathtub, and separate shower appealed to her.

"How long until yer lads get back home?" Nolan asked her standing in the doorway.

"I have about an hour before I have to leave to go pick them up from school," Caitlyn answered immediately. "Would you like to ride with or stay here?" she asked as Nolan walked towards her with slow determined steps.

"That's not why I asked, love. But it might be less uncomfortable for them if I wait here." Nolan wrapped his arms around her waist, his hands reaching into the hem of her sweater to touch her warm skin. He leaned down and whispered into her ear, "I've missed the feel of yer skin so damn much," he said before licking the outer shell of her ear.

The hands Caitlyn had put up on his chest gripped his shirt as she leaned her head to the side giving him better access and made a satisfied sound in the back of her throat. Nolan stepped back and pulled off his shirt. It took Caitlyn longer to get out of her sweater with the turtleneck, and by the time it was off her Nolan was working on her jeans. Caitlyn reached to unhook his pants. His dick bobbed out of his boxers as she pushed them down his hips and reaching out a hand she gripped him. Nolan groaned and his head fell back a moment absorbing the feel of her hand stroking him. His mouth came hungrily down on hers, and she realized that he must have been keeping a tight lid on his hunger. She could taste his need flooding through her system and pushed Nolan backwards. He pulled her panties down as they walked towards the bed. Nolan sat down on the bed, grabbed Caitlyn to him, and pulled her on top of him as he fell back across the comforter. Caitlyn leaned down kissing him, rubbing herself back and forth over him, teasing them both. His dick slid over her clit, and across the entrance of her pussy. Smiling against his mouth Caitlyn sat upright, and finally took him inside. The feel of him had her sighing in relief.

"It's been too long," she said huskily, reaching behind her back to unhook her bra. As she pulled it off her arms Nolan's hands reached up to caress her nipples.

"Way too fuckin' long," Nolan groaned in agreement.

Caitlyn started moving up and down slowly, but it didn't take long for the delicious feelings to build. She moved against his dick, finding exactly the right spot. Laying her hands against his chest she sped up. Nolan reached between them pressing his thumb up against her clit. Caitlyn cried out at the new layer of pleasure and felt the first shudders deep within her pussy. Lost to the way her body felt, she closed her eyes and chased the sensations.

"Look at me love, fuck, I need to see yer eyes," Nolan said beneath her, through clenched teeth.

Caitlyn opened her eyes and looked down at him watching his face as her body worked his. "Oh god, oh god, oh god," she chanted pulling his hand away from her clit before crying out and stilling on top of him. The orgasm tore through her body, the walls of her pussy clenching his dick violently. Caitlyn watched Nolan bite his lip as he felt her orgasm, before he groaned and pushed his hips desperately up, his dick twitching erratically inside of her.

"Oh yeah, quite the welcome my love," Nolan sighed.

Caitlyn smiled down at him and replied with a wink, "Definitely memorable."

# Chapter Twenty-Nine

Wyatt was quiet on the ride home from school, and as the miles passed Caitlyn grew more nervous about her elder son's silence. Mason's excitement was palpable, but she couldn't get a read on Wyatt. As soon as they came to a stop inside of the garage Mason was shooting out of the car and sprinting into the house. Wyatt shook his head, reached into the backseat, grabbed Mason's forgotten backpack, and ambled unhurriedly into the house. Caitlyn took a deep breath, squared her shoulders and followed along inside. Nolan was standing in her kitchen, near the island with Mason. His face was lit up in a smile, listening intently to what Mason was saying. Wyatt stood leaning against the wall halfway into the room, watching but hesitant to join in the fray.

From where she was standing, she saw the deep breath Wyatt took before walking over, hand outstretched and introduced himself to Nolan. "I'm Wyatt, it's, ah, nice to meet you." Caitlyn realized his silence the whole way home must have been nerves, he wasn't mad to be meeting her new boyfriend, he was feeling a little anxious about it. He wanted this to go well just as much as she did. Thinking that was incredibly sweet, she smiled.

Nolan shook her son's hand, giving him a manly tip of his chin. "Ye as well, although yer Mum talks about ye so much I already feel like I've known ye lads for ages."

Caitlyn could see Wyatt's body visibly relax, and the three of them started talking about soccer. Standing there seeing something she never thought she would Caitlyn had to blink her eyes rapidly to fight back the tears shimmering there, threatening to fall. Nolan looked up, catching her eyes, and completely understanding what she was feeling he sent her a wink. As Caitlyn walked further into the house Nolan reached out and snagged her wrist before she could pass. He held it only a fraction of a heartbeat, giving her hand the barest squeeze before releasing it. Her eyes met his, and the relief written in them was plain for her to see.

Caitlyn spent an hour in her office attempting to write, while they got to know each other. She could hear their voices floating down to her, the easy camaraderie among them already clear. Instead, she found herself leaning back in her chair smiling out the window, her head resting on her palm, with a dopey smile plastered on her face. The sky was a sunless light gray outside but filled to overflowing with happiness Caitlyn thought it was just beautiful.

"Mom! We're gonna go outside and kick the ball around," Mason shouted down the stairs, loud enough that the neighbors probably heard. That child was just not built with volume control.

"Yeah, gonna kick Nolan's butt," Wyatt said laughing.

"We'll see about that boyo, this arse mightn't not be so easy to kick as yer thinking," Nolan said, and she could all but see his face lit up as he joked with her sons.

Caitlyn heard the door shut as her guys headed outside. Standing up on impulse she grabbed her camera off the top of her desk and ran up the stairs to the mudroom. Shoving her feet into boots and pulling on her coat she rushed across the living room and out on the balcony. From her spot she could see the three of them kicking a soccer ball around in the yard below. She took picture after picture in the watery late afternoon light. Some shots of all three of them, some of each individually.

Leaves were crunching underneath their thundering feet as they moved, and she could hear their grunts of effort as they pivoted and kicked. They were all trash talking each other but laughing the whole time they did it. Shoving her camera in her pocket she rested her hands on the railing and just absorbed the wonder of the scene below her. The man she had fallen helplessly in love with while seated on a stool in a little pub three thousand miles away, was kicking a ball around the yard before dinner with her teen sons. This was going to be okay, she thought, it really was going to work. It was everything she was too afraid to allow herself to hope for, and here it was happening anyway. Wiping away the happy tears slipping down her cheeks she walked back inside to fix her guys dinner.

Caitlyn was just setting everything out on the table when they walked in. All their faces were pink from the cold, but she could see a bond was forming, linking them together now. Without thinking she walked over grabbed Wyatt's face in her hands she gave him a loud smacking kiss. She saw the happy confusion on his face as she turned to Mason repeating the same kiss. Mason laughed outright and gave her a hug. Then laying a hand on Nolan's cheek she gave him a quiet soft kiss, the barest pressure of her lips against his. He held her face, fingers tunneled into her hair, and rested his forehead against hers a moment.

When he released her face, she turned to her sons, saw Wyatt with smiling eyes, and Mason blushing to the tips of his ears. "Go on now, and get your hands washed for dinner guys," she said. They headed off down the hall to the bathroom, and Nolan walked over to the kitchen sink.

"Its goin' well, I'm thinkin' they like me," Nolan

said as he rubbed his soapy hands together under the water rushing from the faucet.

Walking up behind him, Caitlyn wrapped her hands around his waist, and laid her head between his shoulder blades. "What's not to like?" she whispered against the soft material of his shirt.

"Hmm?" Nolan asked, unable to hear her soft-spoken words over the water.

"I think it's safe to say you're a hit Nol," Caitlyn answered while Nolan dried his hands off. He turned around in her embrace and hugged her back.

"Good. I'll not be losing ye then," he said into her hair.

Caitlyn had thrown together stir fry and served it over rice. Her sons devoured it with the intent focus teen boys typically had towards food. Conversation flowed easily between the four of them, bouncing around from subject to subject. Mason took some time as the meal wound down filling Nolan in on what he considered the pertinent details about the guests coming over for Thanksgiving.

Wyatt picked up his glass shoring up his nerves, looking at Caitlyn while he drank, then asked, "Hey, Mom, I was wondering if I could go over to Alex's house for dessert? Her parents invited me, and well, I mean, if you don't mind, I'd kind of like to."

The table had gone quiet, everyone looking at Caitlyn, waiting for her answer. She could see this meant a lot to Wyatt, from the way he fidgeted uneasily in his seat, and the careful way he watched her face. "Yeah, Wy, you can go," she said, knowing she was watching another small piece of the little boy he had been fall away.

Wyatt grinned a blindingly happy smile before he ducked his head, and said, "Thanks Mom, mind if I go call and tell her? She is gonna be so happy," he asked standing up to clear his empty plate.

"Go ahead, just make sure you get your homework done too please, honey," she said. Wyatt walked into the kitchen rinsing his plate and stopped by to kiss her on the cheek before he headed down the hallway to his bedroom.

"More pie for us," Mason said happily still shoveling food into his mouth.

Nolan was standing up to clear his plate, and chuckled. "I can see if'n I want any I'll have to get to it before ye do." He patted Mason on the shoulder before walking into the kitchen.

"Don't worry, I'll make sure ya get at least one piece," Mason tossed back easily at him while laughing.

Caitlyn stood up and cleared the rest of the table, aside from Mason's plate. As usual, there wasn't any leftovers to pack up and put in the refrigerator for another day. Nolan was helping Caitlyn load the dishwasher, like they spent every evening side by side in the kitchen. Mason's plate was the last to go in. Then he too headed off to his room to get his homework finished.

"Want to drink, and cuddle on the couch with me in celebration for how well today went?" Caitlyn asked holding up a bottle of wine and waving it invitingly.

"Love, yer couches are white. That's red wine yer holding up there," Nolan said dubiously, crossing his arms.

"I'll trust you not to spill. Besides, those are slipcovers. I pull them off and wash them every so often. And if you really make a mess of it, I can always buy another cover from the store, they were smart enough to sell replacements," she said over her shoulder as she reached up into the cabinet and pulled out two wine glasses.

"Then, I'd love nothing more than to sit on yer couch and drink wine with my arm around ye. That's smart, that, slip covers. Bet me Mum would've liked those while I was coming up." Nolan laughed shaking his head.

Caitlyn pictured a young Nolan sitting on the couch snacking on something when he knew he shouldn't be. "What'd ya spill?"

"Which time?" he answered laughing.

Caitlyn poured wine and handing him his glass they walked out of the kitchen into the living room.

Nolan sat in the corner, against the arm, and Caitlyn settled into his side. They talked for hours, and her sons had each come out and said goodnight already. All that was left of the bottle of red was in their glasses, sitting all but forgotten on the table. Caitlyn was laying stretched out on top of Nolan, as they made out. At first the knocking didn't filter through the haze of lust blanketing them. But Nolan sat up, taking Caitlyn with him, saying "Love, I think someone's at the door."

She blinked at him, confused when the banging came again. Standing up looking over at the clock on the wall she walked to the door, leaving Nolan still seated on the couch. Looking out the window aside the door she swung it open, finding Bryan standing underneath the porch light.

"It's after midnight Bryan, what are you doing here?" Caitlyn said annoyed, crossing her arms in front of herself.

"Called Mason on the phone earlier, he was out playing soccer with your boy-toy, said he couldn't talk," Bryan said clearly agitated as he took a step into the house. "Got to thinking, he's still here isn't he?" Bryan tried to look around her, but from this angle he couldn't see into the living room.

"He flew in from out of town, of course he's still here. The closest hotel is like twenty minutes away, you know that. And keep your voice down, the boys are sleeping for Chrissakes!" Caitlyn said.

"He's UN-fucking-escapable Cait, that song of his is all over the god-damn place laughing at me. I can't believe you're giving it to some young Irish punk like that now. How old is he, twenty? Not too worried about the noise though when you're fucking him, with my sons in the house," Bryan swore loudly.

Nolan walked over next to Caitlyn and put a supportive hand on the small of her back. "His age isn't the problem, and I can have whoever I want in my home, for whatever reason I want to. I bought it my damn self." Caitlyn watched as Bryan's face mottled red with anger at Nolan beside her. "I think it's time for you to leave Bryan."

"C'mon mate, the lady asked ye to leave," Nolan said calmly.

Bryan didn't spare Nolan a look, just raised an eyebrow at Caitlyn and said, "Seriously Caitlyn. Exactly how long did you know him before you let him crawl all the fuck over you like some desperate groupie?"

"I don't think that's any of yer business, and ye shouldn't be talking about her that way. Caitlyn is the woman I love, she's no groupie," Nolan replied.

Bryan finally turned his head to the younger man. "Love! You fucking love her? She's my wife, I'd say that makes it my business."

"*Was* yer wife, and ye broke something deep

inside of her when she was, instead of treating her like the fucking treasure she is. But Caitlyn's not been yers for a while, long before I found her in Ireland. Now I'm the lucky one who got to light a fire inside her soul, mate, and I made her forget ye ever existed," Nolan told him.

Bryan's arm swung out, his fist clenched, aiming for Nolan's face. Seeming to have been expecting it Nolan ducked down, simultaneously shoving Caitlyn out of the way. Bryan missed, his fist connecting with nothing but air. While he stood there his chest heaving with the effort of his breathing Nolan pushed him, sending him back a foot even though Bryan had a few inches on him.

"I'll give ye the one try. I'd be right cross if I lost a woman like her too. But ye swing at me face again, I'm gonna swing back at yers. And I've been in my share of fights, I'm an Irishman after all," Nolan said rolling his shoulders gamely one at a time.

"I can't believe you did that Bryan. I'm calling the police!" Caitlyn said, her phone in her hand.

"Dad?" Wyatt said from where he was standing in his flannel pajama pants in the opening to the hallway. His blond hair standing up everywhere like he regularly combed it with a weed whacker.

Caitlyn stared at her son, her heart shattering into a million fragments at the disappointed look on his face. Nolan ran his hand through his hair, glancing over at Wyatt, but keeping his focus on Bryan in case another fist came for his face. Bryan froze, all the anger leeching out of his face, leaving him looking lost. "Wy. Shit Wy, I didn't mean to wake you up," he said.

"Really Dad? What did you think storming over in the middle of the night to yell at Mom, and punch her boyfriend in the face would accomplish?" Wyatt asked, sounding much older than his fifteen years.

"I didn't actually punch him in the face," Bryan said sounding embarrassed at being called on it by his son.

"Only because he moved faster than you did." Wyatt shook his head. "You didn't want Mom, Dad. That night she asked you for a divorce, I heard. You said *so, when are you moving out*." Wyatt held his hands up, making air quotes with his fingers. "You didn't ask her to stay, tell her you loved her, nothing." Wyatt shook his head. "If Mom having Nolan here bothers you so bad then why do you have women over after you think we're asleep at night? Nolan is cool, Dad. Mason and I like him, he actually makes Mom happy too. He isn't the problem here, you are." Wyatt walked forward standing next to Caitlyn, she put her arm around him, and felt his body trembling slightly betraying his emotions even though his voice held steady.

"Wyatt," Bryan started.

"Mom asked you to leave, Nolan did too. You shouldn't be here," Wyatt interrupted. "I don't wanna hear anything you have to say tonight," he said staring at his father. Whatever Bryan saw in his son's face had him walking back to his truck in the driveway.

"I'm so sorry Wyatt," Caitlyn said as Nolan closed the door turning the lock.

Wyatt wrapped his arms around her in a hug, whispering, "Not your fault Mom." He pulled away then looked over to Nolan, "Would you have punched him if he tried it again?" Nolan stared at Wyatt a second then nodded his head yes. Wyatt turned back to Caitlyn saying, "I'm going back to bed." He made it as far as the hallway when he paused, glancing back over his shoulder. "I would have too Nolan." Then Wyatt walked into his bedroom closing the door behind him.

# Chapter Thirty

The drama with Bryan had cemented Wyatt's bond with Nolan. The two of them were linked now through a mutual respect. Nobody had told Mason about what happened, mainly because they didn't want him to feel responsible since Bryan had used the phone call with Mason as an excuse to come looking for a fight. Caitlyn's younger son wore his heart on his sleeve, and it was easily crushed. She had lain awake the rest of the night, alone in her room staring at the dark ceiling, thinking. Wyatt had never mentioned before that he'd heard that conversation, she had years ago, and it ripped her open. He shouldn't have had to know how little his father had cared for his mother in the end, shouldn't have that weight resting on his soul. Here she had always thought her boys handled their parents split so well, patted herself on the back even for working so hard at being civil for them. Feeling like a damn fool she tossed and turned.

It was painfully clear to her now that Bryan saw her as a possession, one he had no problem packing away in storage, but that didn't mean he thought she wasn't still his. That was why Bryan hadn't fought the divorce, he got free reign to go out and sleep with whoever he wanted guilt free, and to his thinking he kept Caitlyn tucked safely in his back pocket. It was easy for him to say he was minding his own business when there was nothing going on to worry him. His selfishness was suffocating to Caitlyn, like tripping into quicksand, the more she fought against it the more power it had to drag her down. That is not love, no matter what Bryan told himself to justify his actions.

After barely sleeping for the second night in a row Caitlyn was up at the crack of dawn on Thursday getting the turkey prepared to cook. She was in the kitchen in her robe, her hair giving its best impression of an auburn Medusa. Wrestling with the massive bird, when Nolan walked up the stairs barely awake. All his burnished brown hair was disheveled, eyelids still heavy, there was even a crease from the pillowcase on his cheek. Chest bare, sweatpants slung low on his hips, he looked magnificent. Caitlyn watched fascinated as he walked over to her coffee maker, turning it on, putting a single serve pod in, and pulling her favorite mug down from the cabinet. While the mug filled, he grabbed the jug of French vanilla creamer out of the refrigerator. Nolan added the perfect amount of sugar and creamer, swirling it with a spoon before walking over to Caitlyn.

"He might cooperate better with ye once yer

caffeinated my love." Nolan kissed her nose as he set the mug of coffee down next to her. He walked back over to the coffee maker and got a second mug down for himself.

"What did I do to deserve you?" Caitlyn asked bringing the mug up to her mouth and taking that first sip of the beautiful life-giving elixir.

"Loads of things." Nolan turned and sent her a cheeky wink. "Right now, yer barely awake, fighting with that there bird so we can all eat him later today. As ye may know, I have great appreciation for eating. By the by, I love seeing ye all grumpy in the mornings." Nolan walked over with his coffee to sit on one of the stools at the island.

"You love seeing me grumpy?" Caitlyn asked in disbelief.

"So much. Because that means I'm still with ye in the morning," Nolan said taking a sip of his coffee.

"I bought breakfast tea for you if you would rather," Caitlyn said knowing he preferred it over coffee.

"Didn't feel like messing with the kettle in all fairness," he admitted with a shrug. "So, coffee it is. Do ye need any help?"

"Not right at the minute, no. But thank you, I'll put you to use later on today. I shouldn't have tried to mess with getting this thing in the oven without coffee first," Caitlyn said as she smeared the herb and butter mixture all over the bird. "Do you celebrate Thanksgiving living in LA?"

"Nope, this will be me first. I was invited to a friends-giving last year but couldn't make it." Nolan smiled at her. "Now I'm glad I couldn't."

Caitlyn tented the aluminum foil over the turkey and loaded it into the preheated oven. "I'm going to grab a shower before I lose the chance to," she said to Nolan as she walked out of the kitchen. "Ya coming?"

Nolan jumped off his stool, almost sending it crashing with his momentum. He had to reach a hand out and steady it a second before he could follow after Caitlyn into her bedroom. He closed the bedroom door quietly behind him, turning the lock. "What about the lads?" He asked.

"Nol, it's not even seven yet, they're teenagers, they won't roll out of bed until at least ten," Caitlyn said tossing the robe on her bed and walking into the bathroom. She reached in to turn on the water in the shower. "It's not as big as in the hotel in Dublin, but I'm sure we can make do," she said pulling the tank top and boy-short panties she had slept in off.

Nolan stared at her body appreciatively, and Caitlyn watched the swirling vortex of his blue green eyes heating up. Running her hands over his chest, the hair tickling her fingertips, she lifted her face up expectantly. He didn't leave her waiting very long, leaning down to press his lips against hers. She felt him shove the sweatpants down his hips, and then his hands were roaming all over her skin, touching her everywhere. Caitlyn stepped back into the shower, pulling Nolan with her. The water streamed down over them, and he smoothed her hair back from her face as they kissed.

Caitlyn reached down and gripped Nolan's dick in her hand. She felt the graze of his teeth on her lip, telling her exactly how much he liked what she was doing to him. Returning the favor Nolan reached down, stroking her clit in time to her hand pumping him. Caitlyn gasped into his mouth, swirling her thumb against his sensitive tip. He grunted into her mouth and pushed her back up against the wall. Caitlyn lifted her leg up and ground her pussy against his dick. Nolan's teeth bit down on her bottom lip and grabbed her leg. Knowing what he wanted, Caitlyn trusted Nolan to support her weight, and lifted her other leg up. Nolan caught her thigh, and holding her legs open for him, slid his dick quickly inside of her waiting pussy.

Caitlyn dug her fingers into Nolan's hair, holding on as he set a devastating rhythm. He pumped into her hard and fast, and within minutes Caitlyn was whimpering, her body clenching greedily as she came. Nolan's hips didn't slow down though, and instead of the quaking in her pussy slowing to aftershocks it built again, a second orgasm crashing into her moments after the first one ended. He kept his mouth on hers, kissing her deep, swallowing her cries of pleasure. He stilled as her body trembled around him, and Caitlyn thought he was getting off too, but after a few seconds he started moving in and out of her again. The heavy pressure deep inside of her was growing fast again. She could barely breathe, her whole body felt so tight, balancing on the edge of that tightrope. Caitlyn dug her legs into Nolan's sides, as she came hard a third time. This one bigger, like it was stepping up on top of the previous two and growing in magnitude. Nolan pounded into Caitlyn as she shattered into a million beautiful pieces around him. He grunted into her mouth with each thrust of his dick, and finally he stilled, locked deep inside of her, and she felt him come, violently, like his body had barely been able to contain all of it.

Nolan finally pulled his mouth from hers and looked down into Caitlyn's eyes as he slipped out of her body and set her down on her feet. Her legs felt a little shaky, but mostly she felt invigorated. He reached down and touched the shamrock charm hanging around her neck, that she hadn't taken off once since he had put it on her. "I really like seeing ye in nothing but that, love."

Caitlyn stood leaning against the shower wall while Nolan washed his hair and his body. With a wink he stepped out to dry off. By the time Caitlyn was ready to get out of the shower herself Nolan was already gone, and so were the pair of sweatpants he had been wearing. She got dressed for the holiday with a giant smile on her face. Comfortable jeans, a simple white t-shirt, mustard colored cardigan left open, and a leopard print infinity scarf looped around her neck. Clothes she could move easily around the kitchen in. Taking the towel off her head she squirted a generous dollop of anti-frizz cream in her palm, rubbed them together and tipping her head upside down, scrunched her hair. After brushing her teeth, she swiped on mascara, and a deep berry colored lip balm. It was the same brand as her favorite pink one, and the pleasantly lemon sugar taste reminded her of her vacation in Ireland.

Nolan was standing at the French door looking out into her back yard, but he turned to face her as she walked out. His hair was completely dry, the benefits of having shorter hair, Caitlyn figured. He had on jeans as well, with a navy thermal Henley. Like usual he left the top button undone, and Caitlyn smiled. He looked so right standing in her living room, that Caitlyn had to pause for a moment while she remembered how to breathe. He watched as she stood there staring at him, and a slow knowing smile spread across his face as he waited for her to walk the rest of the way to him.

"In Los Angeles I thought your house was perfect for you, and I didn't want to make you leave it. But then you come here and look so damn right in my house too Nol, that I want to see you here always," she said, her voice shaking slightly with the emotions surging through her.

"I know what ye mean love. I'm thinking we're after splitting time between them both." Nolan said cupping her cheek.

"And your flat in Dublin? What about that?" Caitlyn asked.

"I'm not there much, only when I make it home. Think of it more like where I go on holiday, or as ye American's are fond of saying, vacation." He smiled. "We can stay there when we go to Ireland, love. Or we can buy something bigger if it doesn't suit ye."

Mason woke up first just after ten and scarfed a quick breakfast of pop tarts. Mason was just stepping out of the bathroom after his shower when Wyatt trudged in looking like a zombie. Meanwhile Nolan helped Caitlyn in the kitchen, he happily chopped or mixed whatever she set in front of him. As usual the first guest to arrive was her father, his arms loaded down with bags. Nolan rushed over to help as soon as he stepped into the door, "Here let me help ye with that."

Handing off half of it her Dad said, "Thanks, I

was going to bring in half and make a second trip, but it's cold as hell out there today."

The two men set the bags on the kitchen island and Nolan held out his hand to her Dad. "Nolan Hayes, it's nice to meet ye."

Her Dad smiled shaking Nolan's hand. "Jack Sullivan, same, same." He walked over to give Caitlyn a big hug, and a kiss on her cheek. "Mind if I steal your fella?"

"Hey Dad. No, go on ahead. Aunt Maura and her girls will be along any time now. From the sound of it the boys already have the TV on down there," Caitlyn said handing her Dad a tray of the sliced cheese and meat with crackers. Nolan kissed Caitlyn's cheek and followed her Dad out of the kitchen heading down to the family room presumably to watch the football game.

Caitlyn had barely taken care of the items her Dad brought when Aunt Maura burst through the door, with all her usual flair. She was already hugging Caitlyn when the rest of her crew made it inside. Caitlyn's cousin's Allison, and Melanie followed by Melanie's fiancé Nate who was loaded down with bags. Allison, the younger of the two, had long straight honey blonde hair, currently back in two Dutch braids. Melanie had the same honey colored blonde, but hers was wavy, and fell only to her collar bones in purposeful disarray. Aunt Maura's honey blonde had long since been streaked generously with white, and she wore it in a sassy angled bob that flipped a finger at aging. Nate was tall and lanky with dark brown hair and a kind face full of freckles.

After unloading all the bags carefully on the counter Nate took off down the stairs for the other men. Aunt Maura laughed and looking around asked, "So where is your mystery beau Cait, dear?"

"He's downstairs, let me go grab him a minute." Caitlyn smiled at the women and walked down the stairs.

In the basement the men were all lounging in various positions around the large sectional, Nate seeming to not know, or care who Nolan was. Caitlyn's heart melted seeing her sons on either side of Nolan and pulling out her cell phone she snapped a picture before anyone noticed she was there.

"Yer always sneaking pictures of me, love." Nolan smiled at her.

"Get used to it, she can be a real creeper sometimes," Wyatt joked and they all laughed.

"Shall I post that one baby picture of you, with your cute little butt hanging out Wy? Oh, and tag you in it of course? I'm sure Alex would like to see it," Caitlyn asked quirking her eyebrow deviously at her son.

"On second thought, its sweet that you want to take our pictures. Nolan, you're on your own man,"

Wyatt added shaking his head.

"Nol, come meet my aunt?" She asked.

"Love to, leave me some snacks lads," he said to the guys and stood up following Caitlyn up the stairs.

They made it almost to the kitchen when Allison let out a strangled sounding squeak. Aunt Maura turned to look at Allison who was now covering her mouth with her hand, attempting to stop another squeak most likely. Melanie was staring wide eyed, slowly shaking her head in blatant disbelief.

"Aunt Maura, Allison, and Melanie," Caitlyn said pointing out who was who. "This is my..."

Allison interrupted Caitlyn blurting out, "Nolan Hayes! Your boyfriend is Nolan frigging Hayes?"

"That I am, although me middle name is Michael." Nolan laughed. "It's nice to meet ye."

"I think I'm missing something very important," Aunt Maura said still confused.

"Can I hug you? I'm going to dance to your song at my wedding in February, I'm gonna hug you," Melanie said finding her voice.

"Ye absolutely can darlin, and I'm honored ye chose me song," Nolan said as Melanie walked slowly over to Nolan so he could wrap his arms around her in a hug. "I'd like to see that, Caitlyn love, am I yer date?"

"You're always my date Nol. I'll ask Mags what your schedule looks like though." Caitlyn laughed at

Nolan.

"Song? Caitlyn, you better fill me in right now!" Aunt Maura demanded clearly getting frustrated to be the only one out of the loop.

"I met Nolan while I was in Ireland, and we fell madly in love. I left him, thinking it was for the best, and came home with a broken heart, as you noticed. Turns out that Nolan isn't just some guy in Dublin like I had assumed." Caitlyn shrugged. "He's a pretty famous singer Aunt Maura, but I didn't know that until I saw him on TV in September. He forgave me for breaking his heart, and we figured out the only way to be happy is to be together."

"Stupidly happy, love," Nolan said, after Melanie had hugged him Allison came over for one too.

"Stupidly happy," Caitlyn corrected with a smile for Aunt Maura.

"Wait, wait, wait," Allison said looking at Caitlyn, "You just happened to meet one of the biggest musicians on the planet right now while on vacation, and didn't know?"

"She had no idea, it was absolutely grand," Nolan said grinning from ear to ear. "Her eyes can't hide a damn thing."

"No, they can't, been that way since she was a little girl," Aunt Maura said, giving Nolan a hug. "Welcome to the family Nolan."

# Chapter Thirty-One

Caitlyn found it easier to write with Nolan around the house than she expected to. He genuinely enjoyed the early morning chaos, getting up and drinking his tea, or coffee if he was lazy, while the three of them rushed around. When Caitlyn got back from bringing her sons to school, they ate breakfast together, a few times Nolan even had it ready and waiting for her when she got back. Then he would wander off in the living room, with a book, his guitar, or just the television and Caitlyn would head down to her office. She found herself leaving the door open so she could listen to him strumming absentmindedly on his guitar while she wrote. Nolan never made Caitlyn feel bad for spending the mornings writing, he never asked her to focus on him instead. Laying in his arms one night while the boys were at their Dad's she asked him about it. He told her that his soul craved music to exist, so he understood hers needed words.

Nolan was right, Caitlyn needed to get out the words that were constantly floating around inside of her. Writing came as naturally to her as breathing did, it wasn't something she did, a way to make a living, it was who she was, part of her DNA. She thought about that long into the night, after Nolan had fallen asleep. Nolan understood, and accepted her exactly as she was, and loved her for all of it. He wasn't shy about expressing his love, but more important to her he showed her in a million little ways every day without ever having to use words. The more time she spent with him the deeper that love grew. It was bright and exciting sometimes, and quietly consuming at others. This was what she had always written about, the happy ever after she always gave her characters. Except it was infinitely better because it was real.

Nolan had to leave just as the holiday craziness was beginning though. He had a few Christmas shows to do, before he was done for the year. Caitlyn dropped her sons off at school and spent the mornings finishing up her shopping, then writing in the afternoon. She was so close to the end and needed to push it to completion so it wasn't weighing on her mind at Christmas. When she was in the middle of a book it always felt like she was living her life on pause, just waiting to be able to sit back down and finish it.

Bryan didn't try to say anything else to Caitlyn about Nolan. Whether it was because of what Nolan said, or Wyatt seeing his father make a fool of himself she didn't know. Worrying about the workings of Bryan's mind wasn't something she had the energy to waste on anymore. She was happy in love, and his blessing wasn't required. That was the beauty of being divorced.

Caitlyn was having the hardest time trying to find a Christmas gift for Nolan though. What did you buy a man who had everything? What he didn't have, he could certainly buy if he wanted to. It was the day before Christmas Eve, and Nolan was flying in tomorrow. She was talking to Cora on the phone, something she did a few times a week now, when she knew what she needed to get him. Letting Cora go she ended the call and yelled down to the boys that she would be back in a little while. They were playing video games in the basement, Mason told her to pick up snacks, and Wyatt just yelled up "Yeah." Caitlyn brought back pizza instead of snacks, and as the boys were tearing into a box to pile their plates high with slices, she set the small present under the tree with a smile.

This time Wyatt and Mason rode with her to the airport, as they were almost as excited for Nolan's return as she was. Mason was the first to spot him as he came walking out of the terminal. He jogged excitedly over to Nolan, giving him a friendly hug. Caitlyn could see them talking, and Nolan slung his arm comfortably over Mason's shoulder, and they walked exactly like that. Needing to capture that moment forever, Caitlyn snapped a quick picture as they approached while Wyatt laughed at her. Nolan gave Wyatt a back slapping manly hug, and Wyatt offered to carry the leather bag for him. Nolan tipped his chin at Wyatt and handed the bag over. Caitlyn figured she was missing some top-secret man communication happening between the two of them.

His arms now empty Nolan wrapped them around her and pulled her in tight against his body. He smiled down at her, his eyes sparkling like the sun hitting Caribbean waters. Nolan leaned slowly down and kissed Caitlyn so tenderly it had goosebumps raising all over her skin. "Missed ye love," he whispered against her lips.

"Missed you too Nol," Caitlyn softly replied. Nolan held her a moment longer before they headed to pick up the rest of his luggage.

"Mags said that ye got the box of presents I sent?" Nolan asked later in the car as they drove back home.

"Yeah, it came yesterday. She told me to leave the box exactly as it was, and you would handle it, so that's what I did," Caitlyn assured him.

"Good, I wanted to set everything under the tree meself." Nolan smiled, all but beaming.

As soon as Caitlyn parked the car in the garage Wyatt and Mason hopped out to bring Nolan's luggage in the house. She watched them work in tandem, wondering what they were up to. Shrugging shoulders at Nolan whose face said he was wondering the same thing they climbed out of the car. Inside the house Caitlyn spotted the boys walking out of her room.

"So Wyatt and I were talking about it, and we don't think you should have to stay down in the guest room this time, Nolan," Mason said shuffling his foot on the floor.

Nolan looked over at Wyatt. "Ye don't have to do this for me."

"We know," Wyatt said back. They stared at each other a few beats. Then Nolan nodded his head, and Wyatt turned to Caitlyn. "Mom, Mase and I are old enough to understand that you would rather have Nolan sleep next to you, than on a whole other floor of the house."

"Yeah, you sleep in his bed at his house," Mason said, always good at stating the obvious.

Caitlyn smiled at her sons, asking, "Is this my present?"

"No. This is us telling you we know where Nolan belongs," Wyatt said, his cheeks turning pink.

Tears shimmering in her eyes Caitlyn reached out and grabbed both boys, one with each arm dragging them to her for a hug. "Love you guys, I'm the luckiest Mom in the whole world."

"Geez Mom," Wyatt muttered.

"Does the luckiest Mom feel like Chinese takeout for dinner?" Mason asked, then pulled out of

Caitlyn's arms to explain to Nolan, "Every year for Christmas Eve we get takeout, you know like pizza, Chinese, burgers whatever, as long as Mom doesn't have to cook it."

"She says she cooks enough on Christmas Day," Wyatt added.

"Seems fair to me," Nolan said. "How's about I get all me stuff settled, and set those gifts under yer tree then we all go pick it up for her too?"

"Cool!" Mason said then took off downstairs to play some video games until it was time to leave. Wyatt nodded and followed his brother, his phone up to his ear before he even hit the stairs.

"Can I borrow yer car love?" Nolan asked as they walked into her room.

"Sure." Caitlyn laughed thinking they were going to come home with everything on the entire menu.

"I'm thinking next time I'm here I'll need to get that handled," Nolan said.

"What?" Caitlyn asked.

"A car of me own, so I don't have to borrow yers," Nolan said carrying his bag of toiletries into the bathroom.

"Makes sense," Caitlyn said, and it did. It wasn't even strange to her anymore how easily he talked about things like that.

"No point doing it now, be leaving day after

tomorrow," Nolan said leaning in to kiss her head as he walked back out to the living room.

"Is everything wrapped, or should I stay hidden in here?" Caitlyn called.

"Ye can come out, I already wrapped them all," came Nolan's laughing reply.

"You wrapped them yourself?" Caitlyn asked dubiously.

"Of course I did it meself," Nolan said grabbing the scissors out of the drawer in the kitchen and walking over to the large box.

Caitlyn sat on the couch and watched Nolan pull presents out of the abundance of packing Styrofoam peanuts. Each present had different paper, and he did a decent job wrapping them. It made her heart stutter at the thought of him sitting there meticulously wrapping all of their gifts himself instead of getting someone else to do it like he easily could have. Once the box was empty, he carried it into the garage. Nolan walked back in and leaned down to kiss her.

"What do ye want from the Chinese place in town?"

Caitlyn rattled off her favorites, and he smiled at her then walked over to the stairs. "C'mon lads, lets grab some dinner," he called down.

The boys came jogging up the stairs. Mason waved to her as he went to grab his shoes and get his coat on. "Don't worry I won't let him get lost. Remember we drive on the right side of the road here." Wyatt jokingly bumped his shoulder with Nolan.

"Is that so? Thank the saints I'll have ye with me to keep us on the road." Nolan winked at Caitlyn and followed Wyatt out, both of them laughing. Nolan was used to driving around the Los Angeles traffic, so navigating this small town was going to be easy.

All three of them came in a little later their arms loaded with bags. Just as Caitlyn suspected they ordered enough food to feed a family of fifteen. "Mom, I invited Alex for dinner, hope you don't mind," Wyatt said setting bags on the kitchen island.

"Of course not honey. But she can't stay late, or Santa won't come," Caitlyn joked.

"You mean, she can't stay late, or Santa *AKA Mom* will fall asleep instead of doing her Santa duties." Mason laughed.

"Do I get to help be Santa? I've never been Santa before," Nolan asked joining in the fun.

After they ate Alex and Wyatt went downstairs to watch a movie, and Mason making kiss kiss faces behind his brothers back went into his room to play on his phone instead. Putting some Christmas music on, Nolan sat on the love seat. Caitlyn laid her head in his lap, stretched out with her feet up on the arm. His fingers sifted lazily through her hair as they cuddled.

Sometimes talking, sometimes he was singing quietly along with the music. Caitlyn's heart felt brilliantly full. No matter what they were doing it was such a natural fit with Nolan.

Wyatt and Alex came upstairs later when their movie ended. She didn't live very far, but it was after nine at night, and dark. Caitlyn sat up to drive her son's girlfriend home when Nolan said, "Let's get yer girl home Wyatt. Be back in a minute love."

Caitlyn sat there on the couch grinning from ear to ear and watched Nolan follow the young couple out to the garage. Nolan and Wyatt walked in the door less than ten minutes later. Wyatt walked over to give her a kiss goodnight on the cheek and headed to his room.

Caitlyn got up from the couch and checked on Mason, who had fallen asleep in his room, still holding his phone in his hand. Putting it on the charger for him, she brushed his hair back and kissed his forehead. She covered him up and shut the light off backing out of the room and closing the door quietly.

Gathering all the rest of the presents and stocking stuffers out from her closet she carried them out to the living room. She arranged the gifts under the tree, while Nolan watched. Then sat on the floor and dumped out everything in the bag dividing it into piles. Nolan got down and sat across from her.

Working together it didn't take long before the stockings were done. Caitlyn hung them from the hooks waiting on the mantle.

That night they made love as quietly as they could in her bed and fell asleep happily exhausted in each other's arms. Mason woke them up banging loudly on the door and shouting, "Wyatt is starting coffee Mom, does Nolan want tea instead though?"

"Coffee's fine, thanks lad. We'll be out in a minute," Nolan answered, his voice slightly groggy still. Caitlyn buried her face in the pillow and giggled. Nolan pulled on some pajama pants, while Caitlyn pulled on some pajamas and a robe.

By the time they made it out to the kitchen there were two cups of coffee sitting on the counter waiting for cream and sugar. They both doctored their coffee the way they liked and made their way out to sit on the couch. The boys were munching on the candy from their stockings as they sat down. Caitlyn picked up the camera she had remembered to set on the coffee table the night before. The boys opened their presents from her, posing impatiently for pictures. Mason handed a box to Nolan. "This one's from Wy and I for you."

Nolan set his coffee down and carefully peeled the wrapping paper off the gift. Pulling the lid off the white garment box he lifted out the hooded sweatshirt. It said their school name across the front, with their mascot and a soccer ball. "We thought you might wanna wear it when you come watch us play," Mason explained.

"I'd like that," Nolan said nodding his head still looking at the shirt in his hands like it was a priceless treasure. "I'd really like that. Thank ye lads." He held a hand out and shook their hands one at a time. Wyatt and Mason looked so happy that he liked their gift. Nolan set it gently down on the couch and walked over to the tree. Picking up the right boxes he handed one to Wyatt, and one to Mason.

The boys ripped into their presents, tearing the paper. Inside there was a jersey for each boy from Nolan's favorite football club in Ireland. Wyatt pulled it out to hold up, and something fluttered down into his lap. He looked down and picked up the paper. "Really?" he asked Nolan, his eyes alight.

Mason was looking in his box to see what it was that Wyatt had found.

"Yeah, just us fellas," Nolan said.

"What?" Caitlyn asked the room at large. Mason had found his by then and figured it out.

"Nolan wants to take us to watch his favorite team. In Ireland," Wyatt said grinning.

"You're not coming with us to Ireland, you have to go to your Dads," Caitlyn said confused.

"There isn't a date on the ticket, it's a season pass Mom. We can go whenever we want with him, as much as we want," Wyatt told her.

"Thanks Nolan! We're gonna have an awesome time!" Mason smiled.

"That we will lad. I've already got me jersey, so we'll even match." Nolan beamed at Mason.

Nolan patted the boys on the back and reached under the tree pulling out his present for Caitlyn. He sat back down next to her on the couch and handed her the heavy flat box. Caitlyn smiled at him and carefully unwrapped it. There was a very recognizable robin's egg blue box under the paper.

Caitlyn looked up at Nolan, who was smiling at her. "Go on love," he said with a soft smile.

Taking a deep breath, she pulled the lid off the box and pulled back the tissue paper. She touched trembling fingertips to the picture inside the lovely sterling silver frame. It was the one that sweet older couple had taken of them at the Cliffs of Moher, and the date was engraved at the bottom of the frame. Reading the words etched on the top of the frame had tears shining in her eyes she hugged the gift to her chest.

"What's it say love?" Nolan asked her.

"Definitely Memorable," Caitlyn whispered.

"It was one of the best days of me life. I've looked at that picture of us every single day since, Caitlyn," Nolan said wrapping his arms around her, the frame in her arms pressed between them.

"Thank you Nolan, its perfect." Caitlyn smiled and set it gently down on the coffee table. Standing up she walked over to the tree and picked up the small box. "This is for you." She handed it to him and sat back down.

Nolan sent her a lopsided smile, looking at the tiny box in his hands. Peeling the paper off he opened the small box and Caitlyn watched the smile on his face grow to blindingly bright. Looking up from the box, the tears visible in his eyes he asked, "Are ye serious?"

Caitlyn nodded her head, tears slipping down her cheeks. Nolan lunged at her wrapping his arms around her. "This is the best present I've ever gotten in me whole life love!" he said into her shoulder.

"What is it?" Mason asked from where he still sat sprawled on the floor.

Nolan lifted his arm up, showing them what was in the box, his head still buried in Caitlyn's neck.

"A key? I don't get it," Mason said confused.

"It says *home*, on the key Mase. She made him a key to our house telling him it's his house now too," Wyatt explained.

"Ohhhhh! Romantic stuff," Mason said with a mock shudder.

"I'll remind ye of that in a few years lad." Nolan laughed finally lifting his head, but keeping Caitlyn pressed into his side.

Nolan and the boys picked up the wrapping paper debris from the living room as Caitlyn got up and got the ham ready to go in the oven for Christmas dinner. Her Dad was the only one coming for dinner today, and he showed up a few hours later loaded down with gifts. Nolan walked out to the car helping him carry it all in. There were lots of video games and movies for Wyatt and Mason. A beautiful silk scarf for Caitlyn, that she immediately put on. He got Nolan a vintage t-shirt with a 1970s band logo emblazoned across the front.

Nolan hugged her Dad, and said, "So, I picked this Jack, and talked Caitlyn into it." He handed over an envelope with a big bow on the front.

Her Dad took the envelope and opened it peeking inside. His eyes went as round as saucers. "Oh, shit."

Caitlyn smiled over at Nolan. "He likes it." Nolan nodded his head in agreement.

"There is only one ticket in here," her Dad said in disbelief. "Are you not coming with me?"

"Oh, we're all going with ye Jack." Nolan laughed giving her Dad a hug.

"Even the boys?" Caitlyn's dad asked.

"Where are we going?" Wyatt asked leaning over to look. "Those are Super Bowl tickets! Nolan, you got everyone Super Bowl tickets?" Wyatt yelled excitedly.

"Might be fun." Nolan laughed as Wyatt and Mason both attacked him with hugs.

Caitlyn sent everyone downstairs to get out of her hair while she cooked. She kept smiling over at the picture frame from Nolan where it now sat on the bookshelf reflecting the twinkling lights on the tree. Setting the table, she called them all up to come eat. Wyatt came up the stairs first, then Mason, her Dad, and finally Nolan. They were all strangely quiet, and her Dad came right over to her giving her a big hug. Caitlyn hugged him back thinking he was still touched by his gift.

Caitlyn brought the boys over to their Dad's house just after the sun went down promising to call and email from Ireland. She kissed their faces and watched them carry their bags into Bryan's house. Waving to them once more before pulling out of his driveway.

# Chapter Thirty-Two

Smiling out at the puffy white clouds she could see out the window of the private jet, Caitlyn thought about how different her life was this time as she made her way to Dublin. She was very excited to finally meet Cora in person. Nolan's Mom was a wonderful woman, and they were already growing quite close. They were going to split time between Cora's house in Galway, and Nolan's flat in Dublin. It was going to be so good to be back in Ireland. Especially since when she left the last time, she didn't think she could ever face coming back again. Nolan sat beside her softly strumming his guitar, humming melodies occasionally. Relaxed, listening to his music Caitlyn dozed off.

Nolan shook Caitlyn gently awake to tell her that they were about to land. Caitlyn sat up still groggy. "How long was I out?"

"About four hours love," Nolan laughed at her.

"I'll be up all night now," Caitlyn said.

"Mmmm," Nolan said kissing her. "I think I could probably find some way to wear ye out if I put my mind to it."

"You're insatiable," she said when his mouth left hers.

"You've no problem keeping up with my appetite, love." Nolan winked at her.

Caitlyn just smiled back at him because he was right. She was always just as hungry for him as he was for her. It was just past ten at night local time when they walked out of the airport. Caitlyn helped Nolan load their luggage into one of the taxis waiting at the curb before climbing in. Nolan told the driver his address as he pulled away from the airport. A few minutes later the driver asked, "What's the craic Nolan? Showin' yer bird the home country?"

"We actually met here in Ireland mate. How's it?" Nolan asked back.

"Alright. Didn't expect ye in me taxi tonight," the driver answered.

"I try not to announce when I'll be comin' home," Nolan laughed.

"Bloody brilliant of ye, otherwise we'd be overrun with fuckin paps over here from London snapping pictures all the day long."

"Ye ain't lying." Nolan shook his head.

"We do right be ye though, a man's got da right to come home in fuckin peace."

"Thanks, I really appreciate that."

They pulled up in front of a trendy modern looking apartment building. Lots of steel and glass. The driver got out to help them unload their luggage. Nolan paid him, they shook hands, and he drove away.

"He didn't ask for your autograph, or a picture at all. And he knew who you were," Caitlyn said confused as they made their way to the front door.

Punching in a code on the pad next to the door he pulled it open. "It's usually like that here. They all know me, but not many people ask for me autograph. We just have a little chat, and that's that. It's part of the reason I knew I'd be fine without Rob last time."

"Are we on our own this time too?" Caitlyn asked following Nolan into the elevator.

"Tonight, yes. Rob will be here tomorrow, and with us the rest of the time. Lots of tourists come to Ireland this time of year, and its usually pretty crazy." Nolan pushed the button for the penthouse, punching in a code on the keypad.

The elevator carried them smoothly up to the top floor. When the doors opened with a ding, they exited into a small classy entryway. There was only one door, and Nolan walked to it, pushing the buttons on yet another keypad. "Are the codes all the same?" Caitlyn asked.

"No, they're all different, and they get changed each time I'm home for safety reasons. I memorized them while ye were sleeping on the plane." He shrugged. "I've got yer copy of the paper in me wallet, I'll give it to ye after we're inside."

Nolan held the door open for her to walk in

ahead of him. It was ultra-modern inside, the word swanky came to Caitlyn's mind, but the further she walked in she realized it managed to look fun and comfortable too. One big open space with floor to ceiling windows, a massive island separated the kitchen from the living room. There was a balcony just off the living room big enough for a dozen people to hang out comfortably on. It had a tinted glass overhang, and looked out over Stephens Green.

"Three bedrooms, two baths. Me Ranger is parked in the garage, there is a gym on site, and I've clocked Grafton Street at a three-minute walk," Nolan summed it up for her.

"Which is why you were on foot the night I met you," Caitlyn said considering. "It makes sense this place was so close; I just didn't think about it at all."

Nolan laughed heading across the wide room. "I usually walk when I'm gonna have some pints. But then I saw ye sitting there, yer wild red hair curling everywhere. My fingers all but burning to touch it and see if it felt as good as it looked. I sat down next to ye thinking of spending a few hours passing the time, then ye turned and looked at me. Those big blue eyes with their tiny flecks of gray looked into mine and I was lost. Ye were the only person left in the whole room, and I knew that a few hours would never be enough for me."

Caitlyn followed him into his room as he talked

about the day they first met. "Back when you were just some hot guy in a pub."

"Oh, and what am I now?" Nolan asked turning around in the middle of the room to face her.

"Everything. You're my everything," Caitlyn said breathlessly.

Nolan's finger caught a curl, and he twisted, winding it around and around. "I feel so damn much for ye it scares me sometimes."

"Me too," Caitlyn admitted tipping her head up and kissed him, barely pressing her lips to his.

Nolan used his hand already in her hair to tip her head further back so he could plunder her mouth greedily. His lips left hers to trail hotly down the side of her neck as his hands reached down and pulled her top up and over her head. His tongue slid wetly across her collar bone before dipping down. Nolan licked down the valley between her breasts as he reached around and undid her bra. He slid it slowly down her arms, before tossing it. He peeled her leggings and panties down her legs, helping her step out of each leg one at a time.

Nolan smiled at her, and picking her up tossed Caitlyn onto her back in the middle of the bed. Laying there watching him, her body already on fire as he pulled the shirt up and over his head. He left his pants on though, climbing onto the bed. Nolan grabbed her ankle and kissed the side of her leg slowly until she was squirming. His mouth passed just over her pussy, so close she could feel his breath before he licked down the side of her other leg. Caitlyn moaned in delicious frustration each time Nolan's mouth came close to where she needed it the most. But he always moved on to somewhere else, barely grazing her center.

He had kissed every single inch of her skin when he finally leaned in close and blew over her sensitive clit. She reached up to grab his head, but he caught both of her wrists and pinned them to the bed. "Not yet love," he said, sliding his tongue teasingly up her lips. Caitlyn bucked her hips whimpering in desperation.

"Nolan," Caitlyn said her voice husky with need.

"I've got ye, there's no rush," he chuckled. "Let me enjoy ye. I want ye all but boneless when I'm finally inside of ye."

Caitlyn had no argument to that, especially since Nolan's tongue was now circling slowly around her clit. The first orgasm took ages, brought on by his teasing, it was a slow, trembling wave rolling over her system when it finally came. His tongue kept licking her as she shuddered, taking her there a second and third time in rapid succession. Caitlyn was gasping for breath as her body broke apart over and over again. Nolan stood up, and Caitlyn watched him, fingers fumbling on his belt buckle, before he unsnapped his jeans and pushed them down his hips. His dick was straining against the white fabric of his boxers as he carefully eased them down and stepped out. Caitlyn smiled knowing he had been teasing himself the whole time too.

Nolan crawled up her body as Caitlyn opened her legs for him. He threaded his fingers through her hair and leaned down kissing her. She could taste herself still lingering on his lips. He moved his hips, his dick finally pushing inside of her waiting pussy. Caitlyn planted the heels of her feet in Nolan's lower back, holding him to her. Nolan growled low in his throat as he moved slowly inside her. Nolan lifted his head and looked down at her, his breath mingling with hers. Caitlyn watched his eyes seeing everything he was feeling written clearly in them.

She felt her body tightening, and knew she was close again. "Nol..." Caitlyn gasped as she came again.

"So fuckin beautiful," Nolan said as she broke apart around him, her muscles milking him. "I love watching ye come."

He kept his hips moving slow and deep, through her trembling aftershocks. There was sweat glistening on his brow from the effort it was taking to hold himself back. Running her hands through his hair Caitlyn begged, "Please, Nolan, please."

"I'm right here baby, always right here," he said

through clenched teeth.

"Come... with... me... please," Caitlyn chanted out with each panting breath. Moving against him, she met each thrust of his hips with her own.

Nolan nodded his head stroking his fingertips across the skin on her temple. Caitlyn struggled to keep her eyes open and on his as the first shudders started. Nolan moaned struggling to keep his hips moving steady. Caitlyn cried out as another endless orgasm tore mercilessly through her. Nolan gasped and stilled inside of her, and she finally felt the warmth of his orgasm.

They lay there limbs intertwined breathing heavily while their heart beats slowed back to normal. "Welcome back to Dublin, love. Ye should be able to sleep now," Nolan said smiling tiredly at her.

"Mmmmmhhhhmmmmmm," Caitlyn said her eyes drifting closed. She felt him rolling them over and settling her comfortably on his chest. "So much love Nol," she mumbled falling asleep while he lay there playing softly with her hair.

# Chapter Thirty-Three

The phone's incessant ringing woke Nolan up the next morning. He stumbled out of bed and picked his jeans up off the floor, trying to figure out which pocket he had left his phone in.

"Lo," Nolan answered, his voice gravelly from sleep still. "Yer here? What time is it? Shite. Give me a minute."

He walked over and touched her shoulder giving it a gentle shake. "Love, love. C'mon baby, we overslept. Rob's here already."

Caitlyn rolled over trying to peel her eyes open. "Here?"

"Remember he's coming to me Mum's house with us?" Nolan asked pulling clothes on.

"Yeah, oh shit. How late are we Nol?" Caitlyn jumped out of bed frantic.

"We were supposed to leave thirty minutes ago," he said rushing out of the room.

Caitlyn ran to her suitcase and pulled out the gauzy white button-down shirt with the black windowpane pattern, a black tank top, and a pair of jeans. She hopped into the bathroom still zipping up her jeans. Splashing water on her face she gathered her hair up in a big bun on top of her head. Realizing that her toiletries hadn't made it in there last night she ran back into his room and found her toothbrush. Less than five minutes since Nolan walked out of the room Caitlyn emerged, looking far more put together than she should have considering how fast she got ready.

"Good to see you again Caitlyn." Rob smiled at her.

"You too Rob. Sorry we overslept, it's pretty unusual for me to do that."

"Jet lag will kick anyone's ass," he said with a straight face.

Caitlyn smiled a thanks at him that he was giving her an out when they both knew that jet lag probably wasn't the reason for the late start.

"I'll get yer bag love," Nolan said walking back into the bedroom.

"That's right, we are staying at Cora's for a few days. I was rushing around to get ready and forgot." Caitlyn shook her head at herself.

"Not a problem, ye didn't unpack anything did ye?" Nolan asked.

"Thankfully no, I just reached in and pulled clothing out at random. I'll put some makeup on in the car," Caitlyn said slipping her feet into the black flats with sassy pointed toes. Winter in Ireland was much milder than what they had just left back home in Michigan, so Caitlyn could wear the pretty shoes without having to worry about trudging through piles of snow in them. She was pulling on the navy woolen pea coat as Nolan held the door open for her.

"Mum won't mind. I'll call her from the car once we're on the road," Nolan whispered reassuringly in her ear as they stepped into the elevator.

Once the back of the Range Rover was loaded with their luggage, including Rob's, they headed to Galway. Nolan called his mother after navigating through the Dublin traffic, and he was right, she didn't mind they were late, so long as they were still coming. Sitting in the front seat Caitlyn pulled the visor mirror down. She put a pair of pearl studs in her ears. Her face looked a bit washed out and pale thanks to the lack of sun in Michigan recently, so she dabbed a little cream blush on her cheeks, swiped on a generous coat of mascara, and a pretty berry lipstick. Checking her reflection, she decided the overall look was classy, but still not overdone.

Flipping the visor back up she saw Rob had his hand out between the seats. "I'll put it back in your bag, so you don't have to hold it up there the whole ride, if you'd like."

Caitlyn handed her makeup bag back to him with a grateful thanks. Glancing over she saw Nolan was grinning as he drove. "What?" she asked leaning into him.

"Just waiting for yer hand love," he said linking his fingers through hers.

"It's yours any time you want it Nol. You just gotta ask," Caitlyn said running her thumb affectionately along the side of his pointer finger.

"Is that so? Did ye hear that Rob? All I've to do is ask for her hand and its mine," Nolan said winking at Rob in the rear-view mirror.

"Sure did Nolan." Rob smiled back. "You're a lucky man."

"Am I missing something?" Caitlyn asked glancing at Nolan. He just picked up their linked hands and kissed her knuckles. Glancing back at Rob he just shook his head at her. He wasn't going to tell her anything either. Caitlyn didn't worry over it very long though; she was too excited to finally be meeting Nolan's mom.

They pulled into the looping turn-around driveway of what could only be described as a mansion. Caitlyn sat up in her seat gaping at the house. "You grew up here?"

Nolan laughed, the sound bouncing around the interior of the car. "No, love. I'll show ye the house I grew up in while we're here." He got out of the car, and she watched him rounding the hood.

"You bought this place for your mom, didn't you?" Caitlyn said once he had opened her door, realizing what he wasn't saying.

Nolan nodded his head. "Seemed the least I could do for the woman who brought me into this world."

Touched beyond words at the sweet gesture Caitlyn laid her head on Nolan's chest and wrapped her arms around his waist. "I really love you Nol."

His arms automatically came around Caitlyn, holding her to him. She felt his shaky intake of breath, and knew he was battling deep feelings. Caitlyn was still holding on to Nolan when Cora all but floated out the front door.

"Leave her be for a moment Nolan Michael, I've a mind to finally hug the woman," Cora laughed. She was even more lovely in person, her eyes smiling in the exact same way Nolan's could. This was where he had gotten his warmth and natural charm.

Caitlyn stepped away from Nolan, and into Cora's open arms. "It's so good to finally see you in person," Caitlyn said while they embraced.

"So it is, so it is," Cora said giving her a squeeze. "Any time ye want to bring those lads of yers over I'm well up for it."

"Well, Nolan got them season passes to watch football here, so I'm thinking you'll see more of them than you'd like soon enough." Caitlyn let go of Cora so she could hug Nolan. She watched the look on her face as his arms wrapped around her and knew exactly how Cora felt. It didn't matter that Nolan was twenty-five years old, he was still the baby she had rocked to sleep at night, and she missed him terribly while he was away from her.

"Good to see ye again Rob," Cora said smiling at her son's security guard.

"Always a pleasure Cora," he said pulling their luggage out of the back of the Rover.

"Come on, I'll show ye to yer room while the men grab the bags, it makes them feel so strong after all." Cora laughed linking arms with Caitlyn and leading her in the house.

"You have a lovely home Cora." Caitlyn said looking around.

"That I do. Nolan's a good boy." Cora smiled proudly.

As soon as Cora opened the bedroom door Caitlyn knew it was Nolan's room. There was a guitar on a stand in the corner, and a signed football jersey, the same team he gifted to the boys framed and hanging on the wall. He was everywhere, little things like the guitar picks sitting on the dresser, a leather notebook on the bedside table. The room itself was spacious, with a big bed, an oversized chair in the corner, and a French door leading out to the balcony. Caitlyn could see that it had its own bathroom too. Turning she looked at Cora, "This room is Nol's."

Cora's blue green eyes twinkled, and she said,

"And now it's the both of yers." With a laugh. "Yer both adults, if yer not having sex it would be a shameful waste of all the chemistry even I can see. Nobody knows how long they are for this world, and ye have to enjoy every day while ye can after all."

Caitlyn blushed until even the top of her ears were pink. "We're not wasting it," Caitlyn managed to squeak out.

Cora hugged her laughing. "I don't need to put ye in separate rooms darling, being together makes the two of ye happy, and that's all I want. It's so good to see my boy so in love."

Nolan walked into the room while the two women were embracing. "That's a lovely shade of pink yer wearin' love."

Cora let Caitlyn go, patting her back and walked out. "I'll get the tea around while ye unpack yer bags."

Caitlyn whispered to Nolan, "She said that I get to sleep in here with you because she didn't want us wasting the chemistry, she could see we have. I'm serious Nol!" she said when he laughed at her.

"Me Mum's not daft love." Nolan shrugged.

"Have all your girlfriends gotten to share your room like this?" Caitlyn asked unzipping her suitcase and digging out her toiletries bag, carrying it into the bathroom.

"Yer the first one." His voice carried into the

bathroom.

"Maybe you weren't old enough for her to be comfortable with it before now," Caitlyn said pulling more items out of her bags and putting them away.

"Caitlyn, love, look at me," Nolan said. She turned to face him before he spoke again. "I've not brought a woman home with me to visit like this ever. Yer the first one," he repeated.

Caitlyn stood there staring into the bottomless ocean depths of Nolan's eyes. "Nol."

Nolan closed the distance between them. He caressed her cheek. "Nobody else was important enough before." He leaned down and pressed the barest kiss to her forehead. Caitlyn held on to his waist, until all the butterflies dancing in her stomach settled.

The next few days were filled with laughter and flew too quickly by. Cora took Caitlyn out for a girl's lunch and some shopping on the second afternoon just the two of them. Cora was an absolute treasure, and Caitlyn was blessed beyond words at everything Nolan had brought into her life. The next day he showed her the little house right in town he had grown up in, stuck in a row of identical ones attached on either side. The four of them went out for a couple of pints at Cora's favorite pub, and they convinced Nolan to get up and play a song. He surprised Caitlyn with his versatility by playing a traditional Irish song for them instead of one of his own. While he sang the whole pub got up and danced, and Caitlyn took picture after picture. On the very last day before heading back to Dublin Nolan took her to the Salthill Promenade. Caitlyn could tell it was a special place for him, as they walked hand in hand. Rob was there with them, but he stayed unobtrusively a few yards back. Standing there next to Nolan staring out across the Atlantic Ocean as the cool wind danced through her hair, nobody else in the world existed but the two of them. The sun sinking towards the horizon, its last rays shimmering on the water.

"It's lovely here. I want to come back here every year and stand in this exact spot." Caitlyn sighed leaning her head against his shoulder. "Counting all of my blessings from the last year and collecting hope for the upcoming one. Tell me you'll bring me here each year, Nolan. To watch the sunset just like this."

"I'll bring ye here each and every year if it's what makes ye happiest, love," Nolan said resting his head atop hers.

# Chapter Thirty-Four

Sitting at home watching the ball drop on television was usually as exciting as it got for her. In fact, she couldn't even remember the last time she had gone out to ring in the New Year with a bang. Standing in the bathroom looking at her reflection in the mirror Caitlyn figured like so much else in her life these days that tradition was changing too. She had on a blush-colored top, the sheer gauzy fabric almost see-through, but not quite. The short cap sleeves were adorned with hundreds of rose gold sequins, and the back dipped halfway down her back. A pair of badass faux leather leggings and rose gold strappy heels on her feet completed the outfit. When Nolan said he was taking her out for New Year's she had gone and bought the whole outfit especially for the occasion. Her curly auburn hair was pinned to drape artfully over one shoulder showcasing her back. Doing her makeup differently, she added bronzer, golden shimmering highlighter, a sexy cat-eye flick, and pink nude lipstick, with a few coats of mascara.

"Almost ready love?" Nolan called from out in the bedroom.

Adding a spritz of perfume at her neck and on

both wrists, Caitlyn opened the door. "Ready."

"Sweet Jesus," Nolan said exhaling. His eyes boggling out of his head, as he tucked a hand into his pocket. "Ye look fuckin fantastic love."

Caitlyn turned around slowly to show him the back. In the heels she was almost his height, and took advantage pressing the lightest kiss to his lips, careful not to smear her lipstick on his mouth. He had on a navy-blue button-down top that fit him exactly as it should, accentuating his broad shoulders, and narrow waist to perfection. He was wearing dark jeans instead of dress pants though, and Caitlyn loved the combination on him. His hair was styled back from his face in sexy disarray. He hadn't shaved in a few days again, and the dark stubble riding along his jaw had always been her weakness. Running her hand across it she licked her lips.

"Ye keep that up we won't me making it to the pub tonight, and I've a mind to show ye off," Nolan said grabbing her hand and leading them out of the bedroom, and all its delicious temptations. He helped her into her black boyfriend style blazer and put on his own black suede bomber jacket.

"You'll look great on my arm tonight Nol, I like your hair like that." Caitlyn smiled at them as they headed out of the flat towards the elevator. "No Rob?" she asked as the doors closed behind them.

"He's waiting with the car," Nolan answered

tucking a hand deep into his pocket again.

Rob was indeed waiting with the car, in the driver's seat, as the Rover idled by the curb. Nolan held the door open for Caitlyn and slid in the back seat after her. Nolan usually drove himself, but Caitlyn figured that Rob was playing double duty as the designated driver along with security guard tonight. They didn't drive very far though, pulling up in front of Sean's pub less than five minutes later. Caitlyn turned to Nolan grinning from ear to ear. "Perfect place."

"I'm glad ye agree, love," he said with a small smile.

Nolan waited until Rob got out and opened the door to the back seat. He climbed out first, then held a hand out for Caitlyn. Rob followed directly behind them into the pub. Glancing around Caitlyn didn't recognize most of the people in tonight. With the holiday the pub was completely packed, and there was a band playing music over in the corner. As Nolan led them through the crowd and up to the bar Sean spotted them. He let out an excited whoop and came around the bar to meet them.

"Caitlyn! So good to see ye back in here girl!" he said wrapping her up in a warm hug.

"I'm so glad to be back Sean!" she said as he gave her a squeeze.

"And look, yer stools are empty," Sean said

tipping his head to indicate the stools in front of them. Caitlyn gave him a strange look, but he quickly added "I'll get ye some pints."

They handed their jackets to Rob when asked and settled on their stools. Keely stuck her head out of the kitchen and gave a big wave. She had a lovely green silk top on under her apron. Caitlyn waved back before she disappeared back into the kitchen. The band was quite good, playing a mix of what Caitlyn thought of as traditional Irish drinking songs, and classic rock songs everyone and their brother were sure to know. They started playing one of her all-time favorite songs, *Now and Forever* by Richard Marx. Caitlyn smiled swaying to the music on her stool.

"Will ye dance with me love?" Nolan asked holding a hand out in invitation, a knowing smile on his face.

Caitlyn nodded and tucked her palm in his, wondering if he had asked the band to play the song for her. They walked to a space in the crowd, and Caitlyn wrapped her arms around Nolan, linking her fingers behind his neck. His hands rested lightly at the small of her back. She gazed into his eyes, as they swayed to the music thinking that nothing could make this night any better. As the last notes of the song ended, he laid his forehead against hers and pulled her in tighter to his body for a moment. She felt him take a deep breath in, like he was going to say something before he let her go and walked them back to the stools that were still empty. She realized that Sean must be stopping anyone else from sitting in them and wondered if Nolan asked him to do that too.

As midnight neared the pints of Guinness turned to glasses of golden bubbling champagne. Nolan was strangely quiet beside her as she talked with Sean across the expanse of the bar. Keely walked out from the back, her apron off. Sean wrapped his arm around his lovely wife, and Caitlyn figured the count down to the new year was about to begin. Keely had a strange smile on her face, and Sean gave a nod. Caitlyn turned over to Nolan to ask why everyone was acting so strange. But the stool next to hers was empty. Caitlyn turned all the way around and saw that everyone was staring at her. Nolan stood a few feet away, and he lifted a hand out to her in invitation, beckoning her to come join him. Caitlyn slid off her stool and walked over to him, setting her hand into his palm. She could feel that his hand was trembling, but as she opened her mouth to ask him what was wrong, he dropped down to one knee in front of her. Every single thought flew right out the top of her head, and she let out a shaky breath. "Oh, god, Nol," Caitlyn blurted out, and covered her mouth with the hand he wasn't holding.

"Yer heart is the most important thing that I own in this whole world Caitlyn. I've known this was what I wanted from the first moment that yer eyes met mine, on that stool right over there. I want to be the last man ye ever kiss. Ye told me the other day that yer hand was mine anytime that I wanted, all I had to do was ask. This is me asking, love. *Ta' gra' agam duit*. Will you do me the incredible honor of becoming my wife?" Nolan asked stumbling slightly over his words, all his usual charm clouded with nerves. As soon as the last words left his mouth Nolan held his breath waiting for the answer, his eyes pleading with her just like that first night in June when she kissed him on the sidewalk.

Caitlyn exclaimed, "Yes, yes, a thousand times yes!" Nodding her head. Nolan jumped up grabbing her in a hug and spinning her around to the cheers and applause of the crowded pub. Setting her back down on her feet he pulled a small box out of his pocket, the same one he kept putting his hand in all night. Opening it up he took out the precious treasure tucked safely inside, and holding her hand slid the stunning ring on the third finger of her left hand. Glancing down Caitlyn saw the single round stone set in a classic platinum band. It was just perfect. The facets of the diamond winking in the lights. Pulling his face to hers in a kiss Caitlyn heard the countdown to midnight echoing around them. Pressed against him she could feel Nolan's heart racing in his chest. Everyone was cheering and shouting but the only thing that mattered to her was the man in her arms.

His forehead resting on hers he said, "I asked the lads, and yer Dad for their blessing on Christmas."

"You've been sitting on this for a week?" Caitlyn asked surprised. Realizing that was why they had all been quiet when they came up for dinner Christmas day.

"I bought that ring after our weekend in Chicago love. But it had to be here, in this pub," Nolan said grinning from ear to ear.

Rob handed Nolan back his phone, and Caitlyn realized he had been recording the proposal.

"Wait, we need a picture!" Caitlyn said. Nolan handed the phone back to Rob and wrapped his arm around her. Caitlyn held up her hand showing off the ring, and they both grinned.

Nolan showed Caitlyn the picture, and she watched as he posted it to his Instagram account, tagging her, with the caption, *"She said yes! #HappyNewYear."* Then Nolan leaned in and whispered into her ear, "Lets get home, I wanna see ye in nothing but that ring."

# Epilogue

As the June sunshine sparkled off the sea Caitlyn looked across the grass towards where Nolan waited beside O'Brien's Tower. He looked so handsome in his tuxedo, the tie the same oceanic color as his eyes. Wyatt and Mason stood beside him looking dapper and so very grown up in their own tuxes.

"Are you ready honey?" her Dad asked, his voice shaking slightly. "I can safely say that I think you got it right this time around. I've never seen a man more in love with a woman than your Nolan."

Words failed her with all the emotions swirling around inside, so she just nodded her head up at him. He patted her hand in the crook of his arm and started the slow walk towards the man waiting at the end of the isle for her.

The harp started playing softly at their approach and Nolan turned around, the eyes she loved so much locking on hers. She watched as tears swam in their depths and knew in that moment, she had picked the right gown. A scalloped A-line style with delicate straps, and lace detailing. As soon as she saw the ethereal dress, she knew that it was perfect for her. His shamrock necklace hung proudly from her neck, and a pair of Cora's lovely sapphire studs adorned her ears. Her hair was down and curling wildly in the sea breeze.

They said their vows to each other surrounded by everyone that they loved. Standing atop the Cliffs of Moher exactly one year to the day after they first met. The happiness emanating from the both of them tangible.

The man finally pronounced them man and wife. "Ye may kiss yer bride boyo."

Nolan cupped his hands-on Caitlyn's cheeks and kissed her deeply, with everything he held for her in his soul. A loud cheer went up behind them, and Nolan wrapped his arms around her waist and spun her happily around, while Caitlyn's laugh rang out joyfully.

"I'm the luckiest fuckin' man alive, love. Welcome to the rest of yer life Mrs. Hayes," Nolan said beaming down at Caitlyn.

"Nobody has ever loved someone as much as I love you Nol." Caitlyn said running her fingertips across his jaw, feeling the stubble there scratching her fingertips. "Going to finally tell me where you're taking me on our honeymoon?"

"All ye need to pack is a bikini, love," Nolan answered with a cheeky grin.

"And sun-cream?" Caitlyn asked as Nolan

winked down at her.

Thank you so much for choosing Caitlyn and Nolan's love story.

This couple has meant so much to me over these last few months,

and I'm happy to finally be able to share them with you.

I hope you enjoyed reading it as much as I loved writing it for you.

If you're interested in reading more, please check out my other

works.

Keep a look out for more titles coming soon!

~Cara

## About the Author

Hi, thanks for reading my book!

Hi, I'm Cara, which is my pen name, but I think of Cara as the most intimate and genuine part of who I am. I live in Michigan with my family, and our fabulously sassy dog. I drink far too much coffee, read all the books I can, hoard makeup, swear more than my mother would like, and dance around my kitchen -poorly- while I cook.

Find me on social media @CaraRomanAuthor! I have zero chill, and LOVE to connect with my readers. It's kind of the best thing ever.

# Other books by Cara Roman

## Still Yours

High school sweethearts, Ridge left Leigha shortly after graduation to follow his dreams of a career in the music business. Finding his success, but missing home, he is back twelve years later trying to earn a second chance with Leigha. Ridge isn't some eighteen-year-old teenager anymore, a lot has changed. Can Leigha open up and trust her heart to the man who broke it all those years ago?

## Without A Wolf (Big Woods Pack Book One)

New in town, Emma Lowe was hiding a big secret. Wolf shifter Kian Decker needed to find out who she was, and why she was so very appealing to him. Turns out Emma wasn't the only one in town with secrets. Now their lives have been turned upside down, and they need to figure where they stand.

# Running From The Wolf (Big Woods Pack Book Two)

The second book in the Big Woods Pack series, Kayla Decker spent years being mad at Lex Kolter. Using her anger as a shield to keep Lex at bay isn't working so well since the shake ups in the pack. Just when they stop fighting each other new information comes to light threatening the pack once again.

## Other Books From Baying Hound Media

## Tell-Tale Hearts
### by H.A. Blackwood

Darcy Ford is coming off an ill-advised relationship that ended in disaster. When she's at her lowest point, she meets a woman who takes her back ten years to a night of wild passion. A night when she met-and lost-someone who opened new worlds to her. A night where her heart was stolen. A night which was the beginning of this most recent disastrous affair. Only by re-telling these tales can she find her way back to her lost love and the return of her heart.

# Candid Camera
## by H.A. Blackwood

A new relationship. A secret from the past. Will their love survive?

Darcy Ford and Gemma Amante are contemplating the next big move in their relationship when Ashleigh, a lover from Gemma's past, shows up unexpectedly. She brings news that has Darcy and Gemma on a trip to Los Angeles.

Gemma's friends from her old life as a sex worker are in trouble and need help. Going undercover as sex cam workers in the city of sin may seem like a literal pleasure trip, but when they go up against a new type of criminal, they're going to need all of their sexy savvy. Between steamy escapades, clues begin to emerge. If they're going to solve this mystery, they'll have to risk their way of life, their relationship, and their very lives.

Adored: A Collection Of Poetry
Volume One
by H.A. Blackwood

Whimsical. Fantastical. Celestial.

The poems in this book reflect a lot of different things, but they all have one thing in common: you'll wish they were written about you. You'll wish this was a permanent tribute to you, the reader, on display for the world to see.

Such is the magic of the written word. It can bring out many emotions, but the one you'll be left with after reading this book is simply this: adored.